KOSTAS KROMMYDAS

ATHORA*

Something wicked this way comes
William Shakespeare, Macbeth

With the kind support of
REALIZE
Via Donizetti 3, 22060 Figino Serenza (Como), Italy
Phone: +39 0315481104

*Athora ***

To my sisters Calliope, Agoritsa, and Fotini
To Marina and Vaia,
for the boundless inspiration they provide, every day.

Contents

Athora *

Prologue

The group of tourists that had just entered the courtyard of the Blue Mosque in Istanbul was attentively listening to the young guide's tour of the impressive monument.

She spoke expressively, passionately, as if performing on stage, and her voice, rolling through the arches, echoed as it bounced back from the enormous stone walls. Her vivid narration and orchestral hand movements had piqued the curiosity of other visitors strolling through the building and they hovered on the outskirts of the group to listen.

"...Sultan Ahmed I, who was a very religious man, wanted to build an impressive mosque that would bear his name, in the way that all notable monuments and mosques bore the names of his predecessors. Moreover, he wanted a building that would surpass the majestic splendor of the Hagia Sophia, which stands opposite the mosque," she said pointing in the direction of Justinian's glorious church, which could not be seen from that spot.

"The first stumbling block presented itself even before construction began and it was none other than the enormous construction cost of the project. He decided to use state funds and that's when the troubles started..."

The soft breeze cooled down the tourists and carried the footsteps of a young man walking toward the group. He wore a blue baseball cap pulled low over his eyebrows and walked with his chin tucked down to his chest so that his face was barely visible. Glimpses of a black mustache which half-covered his upper lip could be caught whenever he raised his head ever so slightly to see his way through the crowd. Every few seconds he would mechanically stroke his mustache with his right hand.

He came to a stop beside an elderly man and adjusted the straps of his heavy-looking backpack.

Sensing the presence of the young man standing beside him, the old man gave him a quick, appraising look, smiled, and turned his attention back to the young guide, who was still talking tirelessly, with undiminished enthusiasm.

"The mosque combines two exceptional architectural styles. It is a blend of traditional Islamic and Byzantine architecture, having been modeled on the Hagia Sofia, whose beauty it rivals, although any comparison between the two is uncalled for. Its domes and minarets dominate the Istanbul skyline, glistening like a precious jewel in the setting sun.

"The Sultan himself struck the first blow with a pickaxe when the foundations were laid—you can see the pickaxe at the Topkapi Palace Museum. He carried the first bushel of soil in his cloak when the foundations were dug, praying to Allah that the work proceed smoothly. The mosque was completed seven years, five months and six days later, on June 9, 1617. Upon completion, thousands of lambs were slaughtered and given to the poor.

"The interior walls are decorated with twenty thousand handmade Iznik ceramic tiles depicting fifty different tulip designs, and their blue color gives the mosque its popular name."

In the brief pause that followed, the young man asked the old man standing beside him whether he knew how long the tour would take. In response, his elderly neighbor rubbed his index finger and his thumb together to show that it would not take that long. They looked at each other intently during that brief exchange and then both turned, almost in tandem, toward the guide and her final words.

"More than two hundred windows with intricate vitro designs disperse the natural light, which is augmented by huge chandeliers. Ostrich eggs are placed in the chandeliers to keep spiders away."

A few visitors took her last sentence as a joke and laughed, but her serious expression turned their laughter into exclamations of surprise.

"The floor is covered with luxurious, handmade carpets, donated by the faithful," she added.

Concluding her tour, she pointed at the towering minarets. "The Sultan Ahmed Mosque, the only mosque in Istanbul to boast six minarets and such luxurious construction, sparked vehement enmity toward the Sultan. Up until then, the Great Mosque of Mecca was the most splendid mosque and the Sultan was heavily criticized for his arrogant act. Wishing to appease the critics, he paid for the construction of a seventh minaret at the Great Mosque, thus restoring the peace he yearned for."

The group of tourists enthusiastically applauded, as did the other bystanders. Some started taking photos, while others sought refuge under the arches from the hot afternoon sun.

The man in the blue cap turned to the elderly man who remained standing beside him and pointed to his camera, asking him if he would take his photo. The elderly man readily accepted and, taking a few steps back to frame the young man against the mosque, he found the right angle and took the picture.

The young man thanked him and offered to return the favor. The elderly tourist nodded with a smile and posed, staring fixedly at the camera.

It did not take the young man long to take a few shots from various angles. He walked up to his subject and showed him the screen.

"Excellent! These photos are really excellent," exclaimed the elderly man, brushing up against the young photographer as he leaned forward to look at the camera screen.

"Yes, I'm a professional photographer," the man in the blue cap replied somewhat coldly, pointing to the camera bag strapped over his shoulder.

"I want them...," the old man declared in a voice loaded with meaning, gently stroking the other's hand.

The young man glanced inscrutably at the back of his hand where the old man had touched him and then let his eyes wander over the crowd crossing the courtyard. "That won't be difficult. I could print them for you right now. My studio is close by."

The elderly man squeezed his hand and asked in a shaky voice, "How much would that cost?"

"Not so much that it's not worth paying for." He slowly released his hand from the old man's grasp, casting furtive glances all around him.

The old man could barely contain his excitement. "That's great. How do we do this? Would you like to come to my hotel? It's at Taksim Square."

"There is no reason for you to wait that long. We can head straight to my studio. As I said, it's not far."

Just then, the voice of the imam delivering the *ezan* and calling the faithful to prayer rang over the courtyard. The high-pitched, melodic tenor of his voice made everyone fall silent and many of those milling in the courtyard hurried inside the mosque to perform their religious duty.

The two men, indifferent to everything that was happening around them, came to an agreement with a nod and moved toward the exit. The imam's plangent voice praising Allah and asking for His mercy followed them even when the courtyard was some distance behind them.

They walked for a while and found themselves on a street with a view of the Bosporus. Dozens of ships dotted the horizon, anchored at large or slowly crossing the straits. They paused before the enchanting spectacle and took some more pictures. The elderly man seemed to be enjoying the young man's company and his laughter resonated down the narrow alleys.

The man in the baseball cap took a sharp turn down a narrow lane, forcing him to hurry to keep up. The back streets they were now crossing stank of mold and decay, although the sound of children's voices and blaring televisions sets bore testament to life going on behind the crumbling walls.

Men sat outside some of the houses on white plastic chairs. They smoked their hookahs, indifferent to the two men walking past. The aromatic smoke filled the air around them, an oasis of pleasant scents in those dank streets.

The young man scurried ahead, constantly switching direction through the labyrinthine lanes, until he came to a small street where most of the buildings seemed abandoned.

The elderly man stopped and looked around him with curiosity. Somewhere nearby, the speakers of a minaret filled the air with the sounds of prayer. "Listen..." he said, cupping his ear. "Listen how imploringly the imam begs for Allah's mercy," he added once he was certain he had his companion's undivided attention.

The other man stood still, fixing him with his gaze. He slowly removed a key from his pocket and walked to one of the doors, padlocked with a heavy chain, beckoning the old man to follow him. The door opened, revealing a mound of mud and dust at the entrance.

"What is this place?" the old man asked, narrowing his eyes.

"It's my studio. Don't judge it by its cover. It might not be the cleanest neighborhood around, but rents are very low. Come in. We'll have a good time, just the two of us..."

The old man, hesitating but unable to resist the urge, slipped through the narrow passage resting his hand on the young man's chest as if to emphasize his anticipation for what was to follow.

The young man pulled his hand away gently and signaled that he should be patient, nodding toward the interior. He cast a quick look up and down the street to make sure no one had seen them enter the house. Once certain that the street was deserted, he pulled the heavy rusty door behind him as quietly as possible and bolted it shut, not without some effort.

The light that crept through the newspaper-covered, broken windows was so low that the two silhouettes moved like shadows through the gloomy front room. The next room they entered was much brighter, however, as nearly half of the roof was missing. Water trickled down from broken pipes all around them and dark patches of mold crept up the peeling walls.

"I don't think this is a studio," the old man said, anxiously looking around him. He turned sharply and tried to dash back to the entrance.

He was too slow. The young man sprang on him like a wild cat, pulling him in a headlock. He grabbed a syringe from a long steel table standing in the center of a room and swiftly stabbed his neck. The old man tried to resist, but the drug worked instantly. He slumped heavily in the young man's arms.

Dragging him by the armpits, he stretched out the limp body of the man on the table. The shreds of light creeping through the collapsed roof hit the man's chest like razors as he lay completely still, but not entirely unconscious.

"I know you can hear me, so you must be wondering who I am. Certainly not one of the men you usually pick up on your travels." The young man spat the words through gritted teeth as he pulled on a pair of white latex gloves and began to strip the old man's clothes away.

Shaking them over the table, he emptied out all the pockets and placed their contents in a neat row, carefully examining them one by one, as if looking for something specific. The old man's cell phone and hotel card caught his attention. He examined them briefly and stuck them in the back pocket of his jeans, a satisfied smile spreading across his face. "Maybe you know you are not the only one; then again, maybe not. It doesn't really matter anymore, not to you."

His victim struggled to speak, his eyes bulging with agony and fear. When he saw his assailant approach holding an open laptop, he summoned all his strength in an effort to raise himself, but to no avail. The man in the cap shoved the laptop under the old man's nose, the veins in his arms and neck throbbing. "Do you recognize anyone in this picture?" he fiercely asked, removing his cap and sharply pulling off the fake mustache. The old man's eyes flitted between the screen and the revealed face of the man standing before him. "Maybe you are having trouble remembering. The time has come for you to pay for what you did. I'm sure I can find a way to jog your memory."

He carefully placed the laptop on the floor and ran his fingers along the edge of the table. He pulled out a doctor's bag that had been strapped to its underside and placed it on the shiny surface. Releasing the magnetic latch, he removed a long scalpel. He brought it close to the old man, who could only stare helplessly.

He raised his victim's right arm and held it up, examining his armpit, as if searching for something there. The faded traces of a tattoo that had been laser-removed caught his eye. He leaned close to the old man's face, his features twisted in a terrifying smirk. "You tried to erase it, didn't you? Did you think you could get away with it? You won't. None of you will. Let's get started then..."

He pulled a dirty rag from the bag and violently stuffed it in the old man's mouth, then made the first incision. A choked, muffled cry came as the sharp blade separated the thumb from the palm. Blood began to flow over the edge of the table, dripping onto the grimy floor.

* * *

An hour later the door to the abandoned building creaked half-open. The man in the blue cap stuck his head around the doorway and surveyed the alley in both directions. The fake mustache was once again theatrically perched on his upper lip.

Having made sure he was all alone, he flung the door open and pulled out a heavy black rubbish bag. He took out a handkerchief and wiped down the parts of the door he had touched. Once he was done, he heaved the heavy bag over his shoulder, hunching under its weight.

He pulled his cap low over his forehead and headed in the opposite direction to the one they had come from. The sound of the *ezan*, calling the faithful to their salvation, could no longer be heard.

* * *

At Ataturk Airport, a man holding his passport and boarding pass was waiting in line to go through security checks before boarding the plane for Milan. No cap or mustache covered his features.

Athora *

Chapter I

The Island, August 14

We were nearing the chapel of the Virgin Mary *Pyroessa*, when the priest heading the procession asked us to stop for a moment, turning his gaze to the east.

Petros, walking fast behind me, almost slammed into me. It was not the safest way to move when walking on a narrow path along a steep cliff dotted with large, sharp boulders. "Sorry," he mumbled and looked at the priest, puzzled at the unscheduled stop.

There were about twenty of us and I was the only woman present. Up until the previous year, women were not allowed to join the procession. When Father George took over the parish of the Chora, the island's small town, he put an end to that old custom, declaring that everyone was welcome. I pounced on the chance. My ancestors were founders of the chapel and its main caretakers to this day. One of their responsibilities was organizing the festivities for the Dormition of the Virgin Mary.

In the early days of the previous century, my paternal great-grandfather had funded the chapel's construction. In a feat of hard work and dedication, a monk had carried all the building material on his back, using this very same narrow path. Single-handedly, he built the chapel, laying stone upon stone with his bare hands.

We had set off from the Chora at dawn and were nearing our destination after a long, hard trek up the mountain. I felt proud to be a part of the procession. I looked forward to the evening's festivities, when we would all gather in the chapel's small courtyard and sit around a bonfire, watching the fiery tongues grow stronger in a bid to reach the dark heavens above. This custom had given the chapel its name, *Pyroessa*—literally translated into, "of the flames."

"What's he doing, Fotini? Why have we stopped?" Petros wheezed, trying to catch his breath.

Silently, I raised my hand and pointed to the east. Far into the distance, a waterspout was forming, pulling the seawater up toward the sky. We all stared open-mouthed as it spun for about a minute, then slowly faded away and the sea resumed its usual glassy surface. None of us had ever seen anything like it in these waters before.

A sudden, sharp gust of wind interrupted the stunned silence that followed. Like a trumpet call, it spurred Father George on. Without a word, he resumed his march to the chapel.

I glanced at Petros, but he seemed unperturbed. I fell in line with the people walking before me, like a column of ants climbing up to the chapel. We would spend the night at the chapel and return the following morning, after the church service. I loved this feast day and all the happy memories it held for me.

The skies ahead, however, did not bode well. Heavy grey clouds were gathering at all four corners of the horizon, threatening to spoil the evening festivities. My parents had told me it had rained heavily at the beginning of August, a two-day downpour like no one had ever seen before.

Lost in the Aegean Sea, the small island of Athora enjoyed mild winters and long, dry summers, which usually led to drought problems. The sudden, unexpected rain had fallen like manna from heaven on its parched soil, which greedily gobbled it up and burst into green patches, breaking the monotony of the barren, craggy landscape. They were not the only reminders of that unexpected cloudburst; in places, the torrential water had furrowed the slopes with deep gullies in its race down to the sea, which now gaped like open wounds.

The chapel came into view and, if my estimations were correct, we would reach it in fifteen minutes at most, in time to help the locals who had already gathered there, piling food on the trestle tables and stringing up festive banners.

The gentle breeze stirred the thyme and oregano bushes, filling the air with a heady scent. Our island was famous for its cornucopia of rare herbs, some of which, according to herbalists, had powerful medicinal properties.

I reached out and pulled a few leaves from a bush that had taken root between the rocks to my right and, without breaking step, handed it to Petros to smell.

"Wild oregano," he said condescendingly, as if I did not know what it was, and then flung the leaves over the side of the cliff. He did not look happy to be here and I suspected he had only joined the procession for my sake.

As we got closer, the sound of instruments being tuned floated on the breeze and came to greet us, washing over us and spurring us on. I grinned in anticipation. The musicians were old friends and classmates; locals who had never left this place. Sometimes, I felt a tinge of envy toward those who had chosen to stay.

Just before we reached the chapel, Father George unzipped his backpack, took out his stole, and draped it over his robe. He had only been on the island for a few months and was meticulously formal, cautious not to give rise to any gossip or disapproval from the locals. His guarded stance was offset by his graceful, polite manner toward his parishioners. Well-traveled and educated, the fifty-year-old priest had asked to be sent to Athora after spending many years in Africa as a missionary.

I watched him rummage through his backpack and was once again struck by his appearance. I had never seen an Orthodox priest with such a short, well-trimmed beard before. One could say that there was a certain, well, cosmopolitan air about him and I wondered why such a man would choose to exile himself on our secluded island.

A few minutes later, he was cradling the old icon of the Virgin Mary against his chest, encased in its carved wooden frame, and we covered the last stretch of the path to the whitewashed steps of the tiny church. At its doorstep, Father George's voice burst into a sweet hymn accompanied by the festive tinkle of the church bell, which echoed over the rocks announcing the arrival of the icon.

The pilgrims who had accompanied the icon on foot quickly merged with the waiting crowd that packed the courtyard, standing around the tall pile of dry branches that stood ready for the evening's bonfire. Most of them had driven for about an hour on a winding, bumpy dirt track, then parked at a nearby plateau and covered the last stretch, an easier five-minute walk, on foot. Almost all of them would be spending the night in the courtyard.

I spotted my parents among them and, dropping my backpack to the floor, I skipped happily toward them. My mother gave me a tight hug, visibly moved. *"Panta axia,"* she said in my ear, "may you always be worthy."

My father cupped my face in his palms, cleared his throat and whispered shyly, "You make me very proud, Fotini, every single day."

I felt my eyes well up and my cheeks burn. I pulled him into a hug, trying to hide my emotions. Looking over his shoulder, I spotted Petros sidle up to one of the trestle tables covered with a long white sheet, furtively sampling the food that had been laid on it.

Mortified, I pulled away from my father and walked up to him, pausing along the way to greet various acquaintances and exchange pleasantries. "Shouldn't you wait for everyone else? At least wait for the priest to say the meal prayer," I scolded when I finally stood beside him.

He hastily swallowed and had the decency to look slightly embarrassed at his greediness, then took my hand and pulled me toward the band. They had set up their instruments on the low, wide wall that divided the courtyard from the cliff below. The band had started playing island tunes with gusto and Lukas, playing his lute, sang louder when he saw me, as if dedicating the song to me:

> I'll meet you on the sea shore
> I'll meet you among the waves
> I'll build an azure boat for us
> So we can sail away

I loved that song. The lyrics awoke deep buried feelings inside me; a longing for adventure shared with a special someone, although I was reluctant to acknowledge it. Of their own accord, my feet carried me to the circle of dancers who opened up to let me join them.

Athora *

Petros stuck close to me and, putting his arm around my shoulders, tried to follow the rhythm of the tune the four-man band was playing. It was no use. All he managed to do was get his feet tangled up in mine and we both nearly tumbled over, pulling the other dancers in the circle down with us. I could feel his sweat drench my already humid top and I twirled out of the circle, discreetly pulling him away.

We stood to face each other. He took my hands and, still attempting to dance, pulled me close to him. I could feel his hot breath on my face. "Fotini, I don't think there will be a better moment to ask you to..."

It was easy to guess by the look on his face what he was planning to say. I couldn't believe he was going to do it so mundanely, in such a big crowd, as if he was asking me whether I wanted to go for a walk.

Petros had often mentioned that, as far as he was concerned, marriage was just the natural conclusion of any long-term relationship. I was in no mood to have that conversation there and then and desperately tried to think of a way out.

A strong gust of wind came to my rescue from the east. It whipped up the tablecloths of the makeshift buffet, catching everyone's attention. It died out as suddenly as it had arrived and the band resumed playing, unperturbed.

I had breathed my sigh of relief, albeit too soon. Undeterred, Petros took my hand and squeezed it tightly, signaling that he was about to deliver the words many women anticipate as one of the most beautiful moments in their life and which I now dreaded.

Nature once again came to my rescue, commanding everyone's attention and putting a stop to Petros' imminent proposal. Before I could come up with a polite way to decline his offer, startled cries rang out as a huge, spinning cloud of dust descended upon us, forming a fearsome dust devil.

It swirled through the crowd with ferocious speed, blurring our vision with dust and spreading panic. Such was the force of the wind, I clumsily grabbed Petros to steady myself, as did the others around me, who grabbed onto the nearest person to avoid getting knocked over.

The musicians hastily abandoned their instruments and jumped down from the low, exposed wall they had been standing on. Lukas did not manage to get down in time. He struggled to keep his balance on the wall, leaning into the wind that fought to push him over the cliff. His body, like a marionette whose strings had snapped, was at the mercy of its blasts, swiveling in this and that direction, and his shirt billowed like a sail, getting battered and torn to shreds.

The wind suddenly dropped with deafening silence. A defiant smile of triumph lit Lukas' face as he raised his leg to jump down from the wall. As abruptly as it had died down, the gale returned, stronger, and lifted Lukas off the wall, suspending him in midair for a split second before flinging him into the void, hurling the scattered branches of the bonfire after him.

There had been no time for anyone to react. The frightened cries of those close to the wall rang out like a bad omen. We ran through the dust and the leaves still swirling around us and carefully crept toward the spot where Lukas had stood. His fall had ended fifteen feet down and he seemed to be conscious. Getting to him was going to be difficult, though. It could only be done by abseiling down the steep edge of the cliff.

The force of the wind had started to abate. The air was filled with agitated voices, as people wildly gesticulated and shouted, at a loss as to what to do. I asked them to be quiet and an anxious hush fell over the courtyard. I could hear Lukas groaning softly as he lay on the sharp stones.

Realizing that every passing minute could prove costly, I ran to where I had dropped my backpack, hoping to find it still there. Unexpectedly, it was very near that spot, probably due to its weight—I had stuffed my mountain climbing gear in it before we set off, just in case. "In case" was right now.

I hurriedly removed the rope and pulled on my gloves. I returned to the edge of the wall and asked Petros and a few of the stronger men to hold the rope as I abseiled.

No one objected; they were all aware I knew what I was doing. Her hand clasped over her mouth, my mother gaped at me anxiously, supported by my father who tried to appear calm.

Making sure the ropes could hold my weight, I leaned backward bringing my body parallel to the bottom of the cliff and placed one rubber shoe sole on the vertical rock. I slowly released the rope and started to climb down, feeling everyone's eyes on me, holding their breath.

A couple of minutes later, I placed both feet firmly on the ground where Lukas lay and crouched beside him to check his injuries. A deep gash stretched from behind his left ear to the top of his crown and blood was flowing everywhere. His right foot jutted out at an odd angle. He was groaning in pain and in his delirium spoke of a demon pushing him over the wall. There was no doubt he was badly concussed.

I looked up toward the wall and shouted that they should fling down anything I could use as a bandage. Seconds later, a large shirt landed by my feet. I promptly tore it into strips and started bandaging Lukas' head. It was one of those moments when I felt grateful for my studies in medicine, which had time and again proven useful in unexpected circumstances.

I nonetheless knew that this time my efforts would not suffice. My old friend was seriously injured and urgently needed to get to a hospital, but the nearest island with a hospital was many miles away. Carrying up Lukas and transferring him there would take hours. More importantly, I knew that if we, rather than suitably equipped paramedics, tried to move him, we risked causing him further injury—or worse. I quickly considered the few options we had.

Petros was already holding on to the rope and descending slowly. I shouted at him to be careful. One terrible accident was more than enough for one day. Everybody else crowded by the small wall, silently looking down.

The wind had calmed but still sounded ominous, whistling through the cracks in the rocks.

As soon as Petros reached us, I turned to him and said, "Call for help, now. We need a helicopter. I don't think we can move him ourselves. He's badly injured, we're running out of time."

He seemed taken aback and stared at me frightened, as I tried to stop the bleeding from Lukas' head wound. He snapped out of it, though, and dialed the ambulance service on his cell phone. I heard him anxiously explain what had happened and how critical the situation was. Then he fell silent, obviously listening to the voice at the other end of the line.

He hung up and looked at me, disappointed. "It's going to be difficult to get a helicopter straight away," he said. "They have put in a request and they'll let us know. In any case, it's going to take a few hours until the request is processed and a helicopter gets here from Athens. They said a doctor should give him first aid and that we should move him to the Health Center if we can..."

There was no way the young medicine graduate doing her obligatory year of service in a rural health center was equipped to cope with such a severe incident. Outraged, I interrupted Petros. "We mustn't move him! We'll make it even worse. Did you explain the situation to them? Do something! You have so many contacts!"

Petros opened and closed his mouth, at a loss. He seemed startled by my outburst. I don't think I had ever spoken to him so sharply. He stared at his phone for a few seconds and then said decisively, "Give me a minute."

He moved farther away and I realized he was calling the Secretary of Defense, who was a regular guest at his hotel. While Petros waited for an answer, I tried to comfort Lukas, whose pain seemed to be worsening. After a few minutes of interspersed conversation and waiting, Petros hung up and announced with evident satisfaction, "He reassured me that a military helicopter is on its way from the island of Chios. It should be here within the hour, with a doctor and paramedics on board..."

I didn't have the means necessary to make an accurate diagnosis, but anyone could see that Lukas' condition was critical. It was doubtful whether he could last that long. His pulse was becoming weaker by the minute and his incoherent speech showed that he was severely concussed.

I doubled my efforts to keep him awake, talking to him or shouting out his name. If he lost consciousness, he might never regain it. Focused as I was on Lukas and still reeling from the shock and upset, I did not see Kimon, Petros' business partner, come down. He was carrying a backpack, from which he promptly removed a bottle of water and a first aid kit someone had hurriedly brought to the church from one of the cars parked farther down the hill.

"There isn't a doctor up there, is there?" I asked, knowing it was unlikely, but hoping that someone better trained than me might be present. Kimon's expression killed whatever faint hope I had been nursing.

The sun broke through the thick clouds overhead and shone down on Lukas' face, burning hot and causing him further discomfort. I looked around and noticed a spot where the surface of the rocks was smoother. I beckoned the two men closer and, telling them how to lift the injured man with extreme care, we shifted him there, placing the backpack under his head as a pillow.

His leg hung off his body like a splintered log. I tried to align it, but a piercing scream from Lukas forced me to stop. I wet his lips and talked to him incessantly trying to keep him alert, but he was growing weaker by the minute and appeared to slip in and out of consciousness.

The bandage seemed to stem the flow of blood from his head injury, but it still soaked through the strips I pressed against it. A red spot appeared above his right ribcage, indicating yet another injury.

My mind was on fire, filled with rapidly switching thoughts on what we should do. Barely would one thought form before another would come along and contradict it. Attempting to lift him up using my rope would be pointless, as the risk of slipping on the rocks and precipitating another fall for poor Lukas was too great. Our only hope was the timely arrival of the helicopter, which would airlift him and carry him to the hospital. Until that time, it was imperative that we keep him awake any way we could and protect him from the searing sun.

I wet one of the strips and dabbed his lips and his forehead. Petros asked the people up at the church to throw down one of the sheets that served as tablecloths. With Kimon's help, he haphazardly secured it onto an overhanging rock, giving Lukas some shade.

The droning hum of the crowd's anxious murmurs wafted down the cliff. I raised my head and shouted at them to keep calm, explaining that our only option was to wait. My parents leaned over the wall and I could sense the silent encouragement in their eyes.

Every moment spent waiting went by with agonizing slowness and, after what felt like an eternity, the sudden quiet made me look up again. I quickly scanned the sky to see whether the sight of a helicopter in the distance had made the crowd fall silent. No, something else was happening.

The rope swung wide and I saw an elderly woman rappel down toward us. She seemed to know what she was doing; she placed her feet at the right spots and knew which protrusions on the face of the rock could carry her weight. I wondered who she was. She descended with impressive speed toward us and turned to face us. I recognized her as soon as I saw her face.

She rarely appeared in public, and I had heard rumors upon my arrival that she had passed away, because no one had seen her for ages. She was so rarely seen that the locals called her by the name of the island: Athora—that which is invisible, which cannot be seen. Her real name was Sophie.

Nobody knew anything about her, who she was or where she had come from. Her age was also a mystery. Some guessed she was nearing sixty, others claimed she was past one hundred.

There was something otherworldly about her presence. Rumors, suppositions and scary stories about her abounded, but in reality she had never bothered anyone. She lived off the land and many islanders would leave food parcels for her at various locations, in exchange for herbs she gathered and used as medicine for all sorts of physical or mental ailments. Whoever had a health problem would leave a note describing it in big capital letters inside the parcel. The following day he would return and find the cure for his ailment wrapped in that same note. According to local lore, she had a concoction for every single illness, but I had never believed it. As a scientist, I was aware of the therapeutic properties of certain herbs, but was seriously skeptical regarding the cure of diseases in such a simplistic manner.

On my rambling mountain walks, I had seen her wander along the most treacherous mountain paths with impressive ease, but had never actually met her. I was told that she avoided any human interaction.

Her house was on a hill near the chapel, burrowed inside the mountain, indistinguishable from the boulders surrounding it. Only once you knew where it was could you spot the wooden door, framed by lanterns on either side, which were there to help its occupant find her way home in the dark.

I had passed by that spot once, years ago, on a group trek across her hill. One of the locals, who believed there was something supernatural about her, had insisted we pass by the small rocky cluster. We paused outside the wooden door to have a rest. Stupidly, some of the mountain climbers starting calling her by her nickname, mockingly. Even though she was evidently inside the house, Sophie pulled the curtains of the tiny windows shut and did not step out to see who it was or to protest.

This was the first time I was close enough to her to make out her features. Her long, white hair billowed majestically behind her, making her appear like a fairy tale witch. Her face, baked and lined by the sun, looked like a map crossed by a thousand rivers. Her eyes were an indefinite color, a mix of brown and green, a reflection of the landscape surrounding her. She was extremely thin, almost skeletal. She wore faded black linen trousers and a dark t-shirt, which emphasized her strong, wiry arms and explained how she could have climbed down so quickly.

She approached us and met my eyes with a look so intense and penetrating I felt that she could read my thoughts. She turned her back to us and placed her palms on the rocks as if divining an answer to whatever she was muttering under her breath. Then she knelt beside Lukas. A hand-woven, misshapen bag was slung diagonally across her torso. She pulled it over her head and let it drop to the ground.

"He won't last very long," she said in a calm voice that sounded eerily thin from disuse. She raised both hands over Lukas' chest and made a circular motion, then placed them gently on his heart.

Lukas' body jerked as if a current passed through him. He then moaned softly and opened his eyes. "Fotini..." he whispered gripping my hand. "I don't want to die."

"You won't die. At least, not today," Sophie replied, stroking his forehead.

Her slight, foreign accent sounded French, I thought and then felt angry with myself for paying attention to irrelevant details.

Sophie reached inside her bag and extracted a small glass bottle containing a murky liquid. I turned to Petros and Kimon in alarm, but they were staring mesmerized at the scene before them. I grabbed her hand, intending to question what she was about to administer.

"We don't have much time, if he falls asleep he will never wake up," she replied without looking at me and gently pried my fingers loose. She placed the bottle against Lukas' lips and administered its contents in small sips, with all the solemnity of communion. With every sip, she murmured words I could not make out and only stopped when the very last drop of the cloudy mixture was gone.

Lukas slowly closed his eyes. His head dropped to his chin and he lay absolutely still. I felt a chill run down my spine; he had lost all consciousness. I felt for his pulse and realized with creeping horror that I couldn't feel it. I grabbed her hand more forcefully this time and anxiously asked, "What's happened to him?"

Our eyes met in a standoff. Without replying, she turned her attention back to Lukas, who looked like he had suddenly returned from the dead. "Fotini, it hurts...," he whispered. He tried to push himself up, but fell back with a loud groan and just squeezed my hand.

The strange woman gathered her bag and stood up, never saying a word. She silently walked back to the dangling rope, gripped it and swung up as easily as she had descended. When she was a couple of feet up, she secured her feet against an indentation in the face of the rock and stretched her arm out, pointing to the east. "The Harpies," she said, and then scurried up the cliff.

It was impossible to see what she was pointing to from our lower height. I scanned the sky overhead but couldn't see anything particularly unusual. The weather was unseasonably overcast. Dense, silver-grey clouds had blotted out the sun that had been burning down on us minutes ago, scudding to the west. I wondered what her peculiar words could possibly mean. The last time I had heard anything about the Harpies was in history class when I was in junior school and I could not recollect who or what they were.

I watched Sophie disappear over the wall, turning to look at Lukas and me just before she clambered over, ignoring the hands that stretched out to help pull her up. Less than five minutes later, the chopping sound of an approaching helicopter filled the air.

Chapter 2

Seated in the front row of the large amphitheater at UC Berkeley, I was attending the lecture of one of the most renowned paleontologists in the world. The discoveries, as well as the writings, of Professor Jose Marcus, distinguished, award-winning scientist, were awe-inspiring. Someday, I hoped to achieve if only a fraction of what he had accomplished.

His views, almost heretic, had often divided the international scientific community, especially when he claimed that humans were simply the outcome of the evolution of bacteria that had landed on a meteorite, an event he dated at the aftermath of the dinosaur extinction. He claimed humans had evolved on the planet solely to destroy it someday if they themselves did not become extinct by their own technology in the meantime.

I was listening attentively to the concluding remarks of his lecture. A few days earlier, he had announced that it was to be his last; he wished to spend his remaining days in peace.

Professor Marcus paused and wistfully scanned the overflowing amphitheater. He then delivered the words that would conclude his scientific career. "As I stand before you, looking at you, my mind is filled with this one word: *the end*; the end of my career; the end of my life in some months or years; the end of life in general. Those of you who have followed my work know that I believe the curtain raised by humanity thousands of centuries ago is about to drop. We are nearing the point of no return when the world will end, *not with a bang but a whimper*, as T. S. Eliot wrote in one of his poems. We do not know if and how it will be reborn. What I am about to say may sound selfish, but I sincerely hope that I will not be around to witness the grand finale of this otherwise singular and amazing show..."

A fleeting pause, lasting for a few seconds, and his eyes drifted in my direction. Addressing everyone once again, he continued, "I am convinced, though, that some of you or your children or your grandchildren at best, will be the last of our species. When that final moment comes, when the curtain drops, I am afraid no one will be around to applaud. Moving to other planets is a wonderful vision, but I don't think it can become a reality in the next two hundred years, so humanity is moving with mathematical precision to its extinction." His mouth twisted into a sarcastic smile and, wagging his finger, he delivered his final warning. "A word of advice: don't invest in seaside property..."

Very few laughed at his joke about rising sea levels. Unperturbed, he concluded his speech. "*Fiat lux.*" *Let there be light.*

The crowd was numb, and I was the first to applaud the final words of this idiosyncratic yet gifted man timidly. He never accepted questions and now I watched him descend from the podium aided by two assistants and slowly walk past the front row. I stood up in respect as he approached and he looked at me again and smiled. To my astonishment, he stopped and shook my hand, addressing me by my name. "Miss Fotini Meliou, I heard you will be joining us here to teach Paleontology?"

I was so stunned I kept shaking his hand like a robot. I muttered "yes" so softly I doubted it reached his ears.

"That was my first teaching post, almost forty years ago," he said stroking my hand before letting it drop.

My eyes widened in surprise, as I had had no idea. He leaned toward me and gave me a friendly wink. "Of course, that only lasted for a couple of months. I never taught again after that." He nodded goodbye and followed his companions, who had stopped a few steps ahead.

I felt like an awkward undergraduate. One of the men I admired most in the world had been standing before me and all I had managed to say when I had his attention for a few moments was "yes." Not even a complimentary remark about his enormous achievements.

The Dean interrupted my angry self-remonstrations. "I imagine that whatever he said surprised you," he said with a smile.

"Indeed. I didn't expect him to know me and I was surprised when he mentioned he had taught here many years ago," I admitted.

The Dean gestured politely that we should move toward the exit. "There are many rumors about those two months. The fact is, he had to cancel his last classes because no one would attend. Everyone was shocked by his views, which were radical even back then. He is an honorary professor, which gives him full access to the University, so it's no surprise he knows about you. We'll talk more at tomorrow's meeting. Are you ready to start teaching at one of the best universities in the world?" he asked, peering closely at me.

"Absolutely! I have been looking forward to doing this and feel ready to take this important step."

"You do know that you are the youngest person to hold this chair, which you earned amongst other worthy candidates. You should be proud of yourself. Many scientists do not get this kind of recognition in their lifetime. Science owes a debt to you and your research, as well as your discoveries. I would like to think you would continue on that track. We will support you in all your endeavors."

I must have blushed because he looked surprised. I took a deep breath and said, "I reassure you I have no intention of slowing down, sir. I sought this post not just because I love teaching, which I do, but also for the opportunities it provides."

We had reached the outdoor area where the reception was being held. It was getting dark and a cool breeze had risen. The Dean shook my hand and moved away to greet the other guests. I hadn't met many people yet, so I stood awkwardly, glancing around.

The music playing and a glass of wine I hastily snatched from a passing waiter, made me feel a bit more at ease. The alcohol would help me wind down and, taking a long sip, I became absorbed in my own thoughts.

I thought back to Athora and what had happened there a month ago. It was no exaggeration to say that Lukas had been snatched from the jaws of death. When the helicopter had arrived, it had struggled to land due to the strong winds that were picking up speed. Deep inside me, I was convinced that Sophie's murky concoction was what had saved him. He was recovering in an Athenian hospital and I intended to visit him the following week when I would be passing through the capital. I would then visit the island of

Ikaria to attend an anthropology conference and then Athora for a few days. That would be my brief summer vacation before I returned to California to start my new life as a professor.

Life on the island had returned to normal, as the intense and unusual weather phenomena had stopped. The superstitious among the locals insisted that what had happened on the eve of the feast day of the Dormition was a bad omen. The following day's festivities were canceled while Lukas remained in critical condition. Father George had asked only for Mass to go ahead.

Another reason I was anxious to return to the island as soon as possible was to clarify the situation with Petros. We had never managed to complete that interrupted conversation. Despite being aware of the difficult practicalities of our relationship, he had tried to propose once more, the day before I was due to fly to the US. I had not let him finish. I pleaded stress about the upcoming journey and said we would talk about everything in a week, when I would return.

Despite being impressed by his response on the day of the accident and his efforts to find a helicopter to airlift Lukas, my feelings remained the same and I stood by my intention to refuse. My work took up most of my life, I lived out of a suitcase and I wanted to focus on teaching and my research, which I had started to neglect.

I lifted the glass to my lips and realized that it was empty. For a few seconds, I wavered between a second glass of wine and leaving. It would probably be best if I returned to the hotel. Two difficult, busy days filled with meetings lay ahead, after which I would be on a plane back to Greece.

I placed my glass on a table and turned to go, running into a man who was standing right behind me. I jumped, but words came easier this time. "Professor Marcus! I'm so sorry, I didn't see, are you okay?" I asked, touching his hand solicitously.

Smiling, he smoothed down his jacket. "I'm fine. It's my fault for creeping up on you. I was about to speak when you turned around. Our synchronicity was exemplary." Even though he was still smiling, there was something inquisitive in his piercing eyes, as if he were trying to read my thoughts. He cheerfully added, "I must admit, I feel a bit shaken."

He was now smiling broadly, a sign that whatever had preoccupied him a second ago was gone. I returned his smile and once again apologized for my clumsiness.

"Are you leaving?" he asked.

"Yes, I have a couple of very busy days ahead and I should get some rest," I replied. "That doesn't mean I need to leave immediately," I added hastily.

He looked at me playfully, understanding that I wanted to stay and talk to him. "The truth is that this is too boring for anyone to want to stay," he commented, casting a look of disdain over the assembled crowd. "You'll be in Ikaria next week if I'm not mistaken."

Despite my surprise at his detailed knowledge of my schedule, I did not want to ask him why he was so interested. As it turned out, he answered my unspoken question immediately, lowering his voice to a near whisper. "I stay up to date you know. The discovery in South Africa by the team you were part of is too significant to go unnoticed. A human skeleton that lived two million years ago and that could be the first of our species—that is obviously the result of many years of hard work and research."

"Yes, *Homo Naledi* was the result of hard teamwork, which bore fruit in the end."

"I have been following your work and must confess that I was very happy when you were given the Paleontology chair. You deserve it. You will make a beautiful, valuable addition to the staff here."

Although I smiled at the compliment, I felt my cheeks burn, as I did not expect a man of his temperament to be flirtatious, albeit discreetly so. Unstoppable, he carried on singing my praises in a flowing mix of flattery and information. "In the beginning, I would look at the wonderful pictures circulating online, from the expedition site. Then, another piece of news came up. Your home island in Greece, in the middle of the Aegean Sea, and the strange meteorological phenomena that have manifested this summer in the wider region..."

The man was a series of constant surprises, and I honestly did not know whether to feel flattered and proud or worried that some kind of obsession lurked behind his following up everything connected to me, no matter how tenuously. "I'm trying to see the link, Professor, but I'm afraid I can't," I said keeping my tone as polite as possible.

"There is no secret link beyond the fact that you are an attractive woman who happens to come from an island which has caught my attention; not just *my* attention, to be precise. I just happened to see something you posted on the

University website on the same day I received information concerning Athora, so I made the link, nothing more. Everything else is the usual pursuit of a lifelong investigator of any strange occurrence in the Universe."

A woman, who had been hovering discreetly nearby for the past two minutes, interrupted our conversation with an apology. She whispered something in the professor's ears and left us.

"It is time to say good-bye. I assure you that you will both be in my thoughts—you and your island."

I still had a thousand questions to ask, but they would have to remain unanswered. "I would like to keep in touch, if you wish so, too." His face lit up.

"That could be interpreted as a sign of more than an academic interested in me, Miss Meliou," he joked. "I'm joking, you understand, but yes, I hope to speak to you again, perhaps once you are back in California. In the meantime, there is the University site, there is e-mail, and so you may write to me...My phone number is easy to remember. It is the date of the supposed end of the world, without the first zero."

I looked at him trying to decode what he was saying, but he waved goodbye. "Au *revoir!*" he cheerily said. "I hope it all works out."

He turned to walk away, but I was faster, wanting an answer to at least one of the many questions that were swirling in my mind. "Professor, what did you mean when you said that my island and the wider area have caught your attention, about the unusual phenomena?"

He wearily turned around, as if he no longer felt like talking, and silently waited for me to finish.

"I was told the unusual weather is now over and everything is back to normal. Whatever it was, it's over," I said in one breath.

"I'm sorry, Miss Meliou, but it is not over. On the contrary, it has only just begun," he solemnly replied. Leaving me no room to ask for clarifications, he walked away.

Nonplussed, I watched his back as he moved through the crowd. It was true that the unseasonal weather had caused much debate among scientists, but the consensus seemed to be that it was a random event, a one-off.

I cast an absent-minded look at the crowd and decided that it was time to leave. I wanted to return to my hotel and look up any relevant information. The conversation with Professor Marcus had me worried and anxious.

My hotel was only a few minutes away and, despite the somewhat late hour, I decided to return on foot. I let my eyes wander over the houses I passed, looking more closely at the buildings I liked in case I spotted any "for rent" signs. I still had to sort out the details of my move here in a month, and finding a place to stay was my top priority.

The new prospects opening up before me stirred something I hadn't felt in a long time: indescribable joy for what the future held. From the moment I had decided to make this my new home, everything had been exactly what I had hoped for. This university post had been a lifelong dream. Not only would I be holding the Paleontology chair and teaching this semester, I would be joining many excavations around the world. Medicine may have been my original choice, but paleontology had won me over, pushing me to set my previous studies aside...

The sound of my heels interrupted the silence of the night, and it was the first time I was enjoying the rhythmic tap of my feet on the pavement. A bright red glow was faintly discernible over the mountains, a sign that the fire that had been ravaging California's forests for days was still pursuing its destructive path. The prolonged drought, precursor and ally of the relentless wildfires, was paving the way for more fires, turning hundreds of thousands of hectares to ash and chasing thousands of people from their homes. Maybe it was the sight of the flames, but I could feel the smoke in my nostrils.

I was nearing the hotel when I became aware of someone closing up behind me. I was walking through a lively neighborhood and people were still out, so I didn't worry. I just slowed down so he could take over; he did not. I realized that the stranger had fallen into step with me, a few short paces behind. When I accelerated, he would accelerate. When I slowed down, he, too, would slow down.

Walking as lightly as I could, so that the sound of my clicking heels would not drown out his movements, I instinctively took out my cell phone. Trying to keep my cool, I pretended to dial. I stopped, supposedly to talk, and sharply turned to face the road, so that I could catch a glimpse of the man who was following me.

My abrupt stop must have startled him. Lowering his face, he hid his features under the bill of his baseball cap before I had a chance to see his face.

I was on high alert, my pulse racing and my adrenaline skyrocketing, as he came nearer. He wore headphones and I could faintly make out the lyrics to the song playing, even at a distance. Keeping a steady pace, he indifferently moved past me and walked ahead.

I stood still, cell phone glued to my ear, until he was much farther ahead. He did not look back once.

Feeling my heartbeat return to normal, I realized his presence had been accidental and that, evidently, he was not following me. Maybe he only meant to make a pass at me, seeing me walk alone at night, but my determined stance had dissuaded him.

I put my cell phone back in my bag and, carefully observing what was happening around me, hurried toward the hotel, now visible just around the next corner. Memories from many years ago started to stir inside me, but I refused to surrender to fear. I took a deep breath and released them into the cool summer breeze, so it could blow them far away.

Back in my hotel room, I pulled off my clothes and flung them onto an armchair. In my underwear, I moved to the bathtub and turned on the taps. While the bath filled, I turned off the ceiling light and moved to the window, where I carefully scanned the street below. It was empty. I pulled the heavy curtains shut and returned to the bathroom.

As I let the warm water soak my tension away, the lyrics of the song I had heard through the man's earphones came to me. *Nevermind.* Of course, that was it! I picked up my cell phone and pressed play. As the tune filled the bathroom, I sang along, accompanying Leonard Cohen's incredible voice with a whisper.

I had to leave
My life behind
I dug some graves

Athora *

You'll never find
The story's told
With facts and lies
I had a name
But nevermind
Nevermind
Nevermind…

* * *

The professor's words concerning the strange weather phenomena on the island and the wider area of the Aegean, which were supposed to continue, did not preoccupy me any further; the updates reaching me from the island giving me no cause for concern.

Nor did I pay particular attention to what the dean confidentially disclosed to me when we met on the day following the reception, namely that Professor Jose Marcus was part of an international committee of "wise men" that observed and discussed unusual occurrences on the planet, not necessarily meteorological.

I eventually managed to find a house I really liked and make all the necessary arrangements for my stay. I completed the round of meetings that had been set up and everything was ready for me to start teaching in about twenty days. All that was left was for me to enjoy my vacation back home and I couldn't wait.

* * *

It was still warm in Ikaria. My father had told me that the sea had been unusually calm these past few days. Sitting on my hotel balcony, I could now see for myself. Only the fishing boats returning to the harbor and the occasional dive of a seagull hunting for fish rippled the tranquil surface of the water, as still and smooth as a mirror.

It was too early for me to have any chance of enjoying a strong cup of coffee and a hearty breakfast—nothing seemed to happen on this island before nine o'clock.

I had arrived late the previous night on the last ferry from Piraeus and my brief exchanges with the locals seemed to confirm the island's reputation for a laid-back attitude, to which their exceptionally long life expectancy was attributed. In fact, life expectancy was the topic of that afternoon's conference.

Feeling my stomach rumble, I decided to go down to the dining room to see if, against all hope, breakfast was being served.

The corridor was dark and, before my eyes could adjust to the feeble light, a man holding a suitcase suddenly appeared before me. His unexpected presence startled me and a small, frightened cry escaped my lips. I heard him whisper, "I'm sorry" in English, hastily apologizing for giving me a fright.

Realizing that it was just another hotel guest, I fumbled along the corridor wall to find the light switch. The man remained standing in the corridor and a strange expression came over his face, as he looked at me in the bright, artificial light. I smiled and moved toward the stairs, feeling somewhat puzzled. As I walked downstairs, the sound of a door being unlocked echoed down the deserted hallway.

The reception was bathed in sunlight. I noticed all the details I had missed the night before when, in my exhaustion, I only thought about getting to bed. Old nets dotted with seashells, starfish, and driftwood alluded to the main activity of the islanders and added a touch of sea freshness to the room.

The young woman sitting behind the reception desk greeted me and let me know that breakfast would soon be served.

I was the first person to arrive in the dining room, so I picked one of the best tables, enjoying the spectacular view and the double espresso the waiter brought over. In just a few minutes, the dining room was heaving with people carrying plates to and from the buffet tables.

"Excuse me, may I join you?"

Startled, I looked up to see who was addressing me and realized all the other tables were already full. Holding a tray, the man I had crossed in the corridor just moments ago was asking me if the seat across the table was taken. Without hesitating, I gestured that he could sit and with a rather curt "Good morning" turned back to my laptop and my correspondence. I felt awkward and thought that maybe I was being rude to him. At the same time, I did not want him to think that I was looking for company just because I sat on my own.

The sweet coconut smell of his sunscreen hit my nostrils and I peeked at him over my laptop. He did not look to be over forty and his slim, athletic frame made him pass for an even younger man.

The few words he had spoken were in an accent that I couldn't place. His black hair, closely cropped, accentuated his high cheekbones, a detail I always found attractive in men. He turned to watch the sea and I admired his sculpted profile, with its angular, broad strokes.

My inquisitive gaze must have rested on his face longer than I thought, and before I could look away, his dark brown eyes met mine when he abruptly turned toward me. He gave me a tight little smile and carried on eating his breakfast.

Despite his discretion, I found his presence distracting and could not concentrate on what I was writing. I logged out of my e-mail and started browsing through the news.

A headline caught my attention. It referred to the Harpies and I instantly recalled Sophie's words at the time of Lukas' accident. I could tell from the opening sentence that it was a very interesting article and I didn't want to read it in a rush, pressed by the presence of the charming man sitting across the table. I saved it for later and turned my gaze toward him with studied indifference. He was looking at the sea and sipping his coffee with evident enjoyment, as if I was not even present.

I had finished my breakfast, so I decided to resume work on my balcony where there would be no distractions. I gathered my things and rose from the table, feeling his eyes take in every movement I made. I saw him smile, and, just as I was about to say goodbye, he turned to the young waitress to ask for some more coffee.

I hovered for a couple of seconds, but he carried on ignoring me. Feeling bilious indignation rise inside me, I turned my back to him and moved toward the dining room exit.

Walking up to my room, I felt angry with myself for getting so annoyed. What did I expect? That he would be overawed by my beauty, succumb to my charm, engage in flirtatious banter as if we were starring in some romantic comedy? Then again, I did feel the need for at least one small sign of admiration on his part. The realization hit me hard. Wanting a man's attention was something I had not felt in a long time. The past ten years spent with Petros had dulled any such desire. Now here was a man, a complete stranger, who had managed to rouse it without actually doing anything.

Petros had informed me that, as soon as the tourist season was over, he would be coming to America for a month. It was a decision I would be overruling in a few days' time. We had not really been in touch lately, but I wanted to put an official end to the relationship. I was more upset about not having had the time to see Lukas. My flight had been delayed and I had narrowly managed to catch the boat to Ikaria. Luckily, his condition was improving, slowly but steadily. I wondered whether I should find some time to visit him before returning to America. Once on US soil, my visits to Greece were sure to become more infrequent.

I finished replying to all my e-mail and contacted the conference organizer. He asked me whether I wanted to join some of the other participants in a guided tour of the island he was giving. I preferred to spend the day by myself and simply asked that someone pick me up from the hotel in the afternoon. I wanted to relax and enjoy whatever little free time I had at my own pace.

Anthropologists from all over the world would be attending the conference. I would be commenting on the locals' longevity from a paleontologist's perspective, examining the phenomenon through the millennia based on the paleontological finds on the island and the Aegean. I went over my speech and, having made sure everything was in order, prepared to go out.

The receptionist was willing to help me find a place for a quick swim. The beach she recommended was called *Armenistis*, and she stressed that the water there was rarely as calm as that morning and that it would be "a great shame" for me to miss such rare tranquility and the unparalleled view from the peninsula. To underline her claims, she mentioned that the locals had nicknamed it "the washing machine," because it was always choppy there.

When the taxi dropped me off, I realized how right she had been to insist. Like a retouched photo, the shades of blue merged so harmonically on the water's surface and were so transparent that I could make out the tiny pebbles on the sandy seabed.

I could not wait to feel the water wrap around me. I flung my clothes onto a lounger and rushed to its welcoming coolness. I lay on my back, feeling my long hair spread around me like a loosely woven mantle. Taking a deep breath, I dove under; eyes wide open, I watched the tiny fish flitting fearlessly around me.

I had swum in similar waters before, on the remote shores of Athora. Its mountainous landscape and sharp cliffs meant that most of the beaches could only be reached by boat. There, I used to swim naked. I looked around to make sure that no one was near and took off my bathing suit, slinging it around my shoulder. I felt my body become one with the sea. How I'd missed that feeling! I had forgotten how uniquely, delightfully free being in the water felt.

I closed my eyes and turned my face to the sun. The warm sunrays burnt my skin and dried the salty droplets on my face. Their glow spread under my eyelids, turning everything bright red. I remembered my mother telling me, when I was young, that if you did that and then suddenly opened your eyes, you would go blind. Although I had never really believed it, her words seemed to have stuck—I had never dared.

When I turned to face the beach a few moments later, my eyes were blurry. With difficulty, I noticed a man bending over my things. I blinked trying to focus on the figure, but for a few seconds it was impossible. I hastily pulled on my bathing suit and swam toward the shore, seeing the man's silhouette disappear behind the beach bar.

As soon as I stepped on the sand, I ran to my lounger to check whether anything was missing. Everything seemed to be in its place. Cell phone, wallet, laptop were intact. The only thing that troubled me was that my bag was unzipped. Had I left it that way in my hurry to get to the water?

I walked to the end of the wooden deck trying to spot the man but had no way of being certain whether one of the dozen people on the beach had just gone through my things.

I returned to my lounger perplexed and then noticed a cold bottle of water on the table under the umbrella. The waiter must have dropped it off just when I had turned to look at the shore and I had misinterpreted what he was doing.

I soon forgot about the incident as I relaxed, sipping a mild cocktail. This *is the life*, I thought, stretching luxuriously on my lounger and enjoying the tranquil view before me.

Strains of salsa music burst through the beach bar's speakers, adding an exotic hue to the ambiance and luring a couple to the deck, their steps following the beat of the bongos. The woman, feet slightly apart, swayed against her partner, who followed her movements with similar sensuality, turning their dance into a seductive, erotic dialogue between their dancing bodies.

Soon enough, a bacchanalian, ecstatic scene started to unfold before me, as others followed the example of the first couple and joined them on the dance floor. The louder the music got, the more intense the swaying movements became, merging in a rising crescendo.

I could not take my eyes off the couple that had roused everyone from their loungers. I envied the way the man led his partner. He held her almost trapped against him, expertly synchronizing his rhythm to hers. It was hard to tell who set the pace or led, as every move was a wave of absolute synchronicity. Their coordination showed intimacy and familiarity since they both seemed to know what they were doing, but the passion between them was that of a couple meeting for the very first time.

I closed my eyes and pictured myself in the woman's place but the song ended abruptly before I could complete the image in my head. I wished I could dance like that, even though there was no way I could let myself go in front of so many people.

I drained my glass in a single gulp and, despite being tempted by the thought of a second cocktail, decided to pass and return to my hotel. I was on the island for purely professional reasons, so my head had no difficulty ruling my heart once again.

The taxi driver recommended a pretty *taverna* near the hotel where I could grab a quick bite and, an hour later, I was back in my room. I closed the blinds and stretched out on the big bed, feeling the sea salt rub into the sheets. I could not get the couple dancing at the beach out my head, only this time I was the man's partner...

Chapter 3

The sudden storm had forced pedestrians to seek shelter under the shop awnings. They had merged into a single mass of bodies as they tried to squeeze under them and protect themselves using whatever was at hand. The provident among them had unfurled their umbrellas, but even they did not dare walk in the torrential rain.

The weather had been prone to sudden outbursts lately. Although such outbursts were not uncommon around Lake Como, they had recently increased in frequency, intensity, and duration.

An elderly man slowly approached one of the shop awnings, under which the startled pedestrians had packed themselves like sardines, trying to keep dry. His long, shoulder-length white hair was dripping wet, further soaking the collar of his trench coat.

People shifted right and left to make space for him to join them. While the small crowd rearranged themselves as best as they could, he stood on the edge of the pavement, getting drenched but seemingly not caring about the torrential pounding of the heavy raindrops.

In the meantime, a young man wearing a black baseball cap and holding an open umbrella appeared behind him like a guardian angel, protecting the elderly body from the rain, which kept getting stronger.

He gave a look of surprise at his unexpected savior and smiled when he realized the young man was just being polite. He started walking along the edge of the pavement, making his way through the throng, in the direction of a large house a few meters away. Now and then, he glanced at the stranger who still held the umbrella above his head and was gently pushing away those who stood in the old man's way, to allow him to reach his destination faster.

A short while later, the old man stopped before the front door and wiped the water from his face. Then he turned to his escort and, with a smile, spoke in Italian. "This is where I live. That was very kind of you, thank you."

The other man nodded without a word, half his face still hidden under the black cap.

"I would invite you in for a cup of tea until the storm blows over, but maybe you are busy. Although you, too, are drenched, by the look of it," he added, pointing to the wet clothes.

The young man looked around him, troubled by the prospect of walking away in the downpour and asked in a low voice, "Do you speak English?"

The elderly man nodded yes.

"A cup of tea sounds good, but I don't wish to impose on you..."

"Not at all! It's rare to meet a true gentleman these days. I'd be happy to return your kind gesture. Tea will be ready in a minute," he replied in excellent English and, without waiting for a reply, turned to punch in the entry code on the panel by the door.

The young man, standing behind him, raised his head ever so slightly to align his line of vision with the wrinkly fingers slowly touching the number keys. A few seconds later, a soft beep indicated that the door was open and the old man held it open for his guest to pass through. The young man furled his umbrella and entered the hall, head bowed.

The loud, sharp bark of a dog came from somewhere farther inside. Before his owner had a chance to restrain him, a small beagle launched itself toward the stranger. With great difficulty, the old man bent over and picked the growling dog in his arms, trying to sooth it. "He does this with everyone he doesn't know, but he'll calm down in a little bit, don't you worry about him. Come on in... Take a seat while I make the tea. The weather has gone crazy these days. The lake will overflow if it keeps on like this. Imagine what will happen when winter comes," he said moving inside the kitchen.

He opened a door, placed the dog inside, and clicked it shut. He slowly removed his trench coat, shook it out and draped it over a chair. Then he busied himself preparing tea.

The man in the cap was still standing near the entrance as if needing permission to take the first step and move farther inside. The house was rather dark and the air stifling with the scent of artificial pine.

"Are you going to stay there?" his host called out without turning to look at him.

His guest slowly raised his head and watched the old man shuffle around in the kitchen. He placed his umbrella against the wall and took out a pair of black gloves from his pocket. Pulling them on, he crept toward the old man.

As if sensing something strange was happening, the white-haired man sharply turned around. For a few seconds, neither man spoke. "So you didn't just happen to come across me," he said calmly.

The dog's bark sounded louder, followed by a menacing growl.

The cap still shaded the stranger's features as he stood silently, his chest rising with every breath. Looking at the floor, his voice calm but filled with tension, he replied. "No, it was no accident."

The old man remained pensive for a moment as if trying to process every possible scenario in his head. "All my cash is in the top drawer of my desk. Take it and go," he finally offered.

"I didn't come to rob you."

"What is it you want then?" asked the old man sharply.

"For us to dig up your past. Together." He took a step forward.

Terrified, the old man shouted, "You have no idea what you are getting into. I advise you to leave, while there's still time..."

Seething with anger at what he had just heard, the man in the cap lunged at the old man and grabbed him by the throat. With a swift, controlled movement, he plunged a syringe that had been hiding in his pocket into the man's neck, between the long white hair. The cup the old man had been holding crashed onto the floor, spreading porcelain fragments everywhere. Like a fish caught in a net, he feebly tried to react, but to no avail. Seconds later, he slumped against his assailant, who dragged him to the living room through an open arched doorway. He dropped the old man onto the couch, turning the man's head on the armrest to face him.

The immobilized man's eyes were wide open and he seemed to be conscious, though unable to make a single movement. He could only move his eyelids, which fluttered in an effort to focus on the stranger who was staring down at him.

From the small room beyond the kitchen, the dog frantically scratched the door, trying to get to his master. Annoyed at the noise, the assailant moved to the door and slammed it hard with his fist. The dog whimpered in fright and fell silent.

He returned to the living room and fixed his gaze on his victim, who was panting heavily. Without a word, he pulled his gloves sharply over his wrists, almost ripping the thin leather as it stretched tightly across his fingers. He pulled the heavy curtains shut, blocking the gray natural light, and turned the light on.

He moved to the couch and repositioned the old man, who was beginning to slide off. The numb, inert body was like a helpless puppet in a clumsy puppeteer's hands. The young man then moved to the desk across the room and sat on the chair before a glowing computer screen.

"I imagine you use the same code," he muttered, entering the combination he had seen the man punch in before.

A grunt that escaped the old man confirmed his suspicions. The assailant smiled and turned around. "I know you can't see me, but you can hear me just fine. In a few moments, I will have accessed your files. I think you know what will happen next. If you want it done peacefully, start thinking about what you are willing to reveal. Otherwise, prepare for a slow and torturous death." Without waiting for a reply, he turned back to the screen and resumed his search, his brow furrowed in concentration.

A few minutes had passed since the two men had entered the house. Very slowly, the old man was beginning to stir, raising his hands ever so slightly, with great difficulty. The other man, lips pursed, kept tapping and clicking, evidently searching for something, the fury in his eyes betraying that he was not finding it.

He suddenly got up, reached the couch in two great strides, and sharply pulled the man's shirt open, with such force that he tore it on one side. He lifted the limp right arm. A small tattoo was noticeable under the man's armpit. He saw it and his face lit up. He leaned in, trying to read the writing etched at the base of the tattoo. "Well, this is a surprise," he mumbled under his breath, letting the man's arm drop heavily by his still body.

He returned to the computer and, without sitting down, leaned over the keyboard and typed a code once again. The glow that appeared on the screen signaled that he had finally found the key to unlock the files. Now, he just had to be patient while the data loaded.

Satisfied, he walked back to the old man and stood over him. "Smart of you to combine the codes, but the tattoo betrayed you. I thought it was going to be harder," he said. "You obviously did not expect to be found out."

The old man tried to utter something but failed, still under the influence of the drug. Only his eyes spoke of his terror.

"You are one of many I'm looking for," said the stranger. "I have spent the last twenty years tracking you down, all of you. I guess you don't understand what I'm talking about because you have no idea who I am and what you've done to me."

"I don't know..." The old man croaked the words with great difficulty, almost inaudibly.

"You knew a few minutes ago when you advised me not to mess with you. You understand your time has come, whether or not I find what I'm looking for. You can just make it easier for yourself by telling me everything you have organized with such care and precision."

"I'm telling you... I don't know what you are talking about..." The old man was now speaking more clearly, a sign that the effect of the drug was starting to wear off. "I tried to be nice to you... I invited you into my home..."

"I may not need any details from you in the end. I will know everything when the information you have hidden so well shows up on the screen."

A beep from the desktop, followed by the sound of violins, filled the room, announcing something important.

"Here we go then," said the man in the cap and moved toward the desk.

Standing before the screen, what he saw compelled him to sit down dumbfounded. He started clicking, opening files and scrolling through their contents, before taking out a USB flash drive from his pocket and starting to transfer the files.

In the time that had elapsed, the old man slowly and painfully moved his hand to his chest, as if he was having difficulty breathing. The music drowned out the barely perceptible rattle in his throat, so it went unnoticed by the man in the cap. When the violin stopped playing a few moments later, he heard the dying man's gasps.

He jumped up and saw the old man was choking, foam spilling from the side of his mouth. The young man quickly wiped it away and placed his hands on the man's chest, pumping rhythmically in an effort to resuscitate him.

It was too late; the man had taken his last breath. The assailant placed two fingers against the stiffening neck looking for a pulse and then pulled the eyelids apart to check his pupils. The dog's timid whimper echoed once again.

He sighed and turned to look at the computer screen. The file transfer was speeding along and would soon be complete.

He moved to a large dining table behind the couch and cleared it, leaving the polished wood bare. He then stripped the old man bare, throwing the clothes carelessly on the floor. Pulling him by the armpits, he dragged him to the table and placed him on it, as if he were about to perform an autopsy.

He reached into one of the pockets of his raincoat and removed a coil of rope, which he placed next to the lifeless body. Then he made his way to the kitchen and fumbled through the drawers. He selected three large knives and carefully aligned them next to the coil of rope.

A beep sounded from the computer and he returned to the desk once more. He looked at the screen and his face clouded over. He could tell that, despite what he had managed to access, something was missing.

Hastily, he started searching through the house. He emptied out drawers, rummaged through everything, even pulled the paintings down from the wall. He ended up before the room where the dog was locked up, helplessly staring at the door. Sensing the intruder's presence, the beagle growled more ferociously.

He turned the handle and flung the door open, sending it slamming against the wall. The small dog sprinted past his leg, desperately seeking a place to hide. The electrical appliances that filled the room showed that it functioned as a laundry room and storeroom.

His gaze immediately fell on a painting on the wall. It depicted the death of Achilles, an arrow stuck in his heel. Just like the tattoo on the old man's armpit.

He turned away disappointed, stepping on the broken cup fragments that lay scattered all over the kitchen floor. Back at the dining room table, he leaned heavily against it, pondering what to do next.

He suddenly gasped and slowly raised his head, eyes fixed on the corpse's feet. The coil of rope and the knives were lined up beside them. He examined them one by one and picked one, testing its sharpness against his thumb. He lifted the right leg and felt the sole and heel. With nearly surgical precision, he made a careful, shallow incision along the curve of the heel. A few drops of blood dropped indolently onto the wooden surface.

He peeled off one of his gloves and inserted his fingers into the wound, feeling around. Seconds later, he pulled them away and brought them up close to his eyes. Between the bloody bits of flesh glistened a tiny box, the size of a SIM card.

He dashed to the kitchen sink, opened the tap ever so slightly and rinsed it under the trickling water. He patted it dry with a paper towel and placed it on a kitchen bench. With the point of a blade, he pressed a tiny groove and prized it open. The tiny box was a capsule that housed a memory card. He gingerly picked it up and examined it for a few seconds before returning to the computer. He found the memory card adapter in a stationary box on the desk and attached it to a USB port. An icon flashed on the screen. He clicked it and a map of the world slowly appeared.

His features hardened as he watched the emerging image, mesmerized. Tiny red dots blinked on various locations around the world. His eyes narrowed in on a small Greek island in the middle of the Aegean. The cursor hovered above it, and another file opened on the side of the screen. He clicked transfer and waited until it was completed. Then, he stood up and returned to the table. "It's a shame you won't feel the pain," he said as if the dead man could hear him.

He picked up the same sharp knife he had used on the heel. Bringing it up to the victim's right hand, he cleanly sliced off the thumb.

Half an hour later, the man in the baseball cap exited the house, hunching under the weight of a bulging rubbish bag he carried over one shoulder. In his other hand, he held a leash. At the end of the leash, a small beagle obediently followed him, hungrily sniffing the pavement.

The sun had set, the rain had stopped and darkness was enveloping the foggy lake.

Chapter 4

The pilot's announcement that the plane had just crossed the Atlantic and was now flying over Europe woke the man traveling in business class. He removed his sleeping mask and pressed the button on the side of his seat to bring the backrest upright. In around three hours, the plane would be landing in Athens.

He stretched, trying to get the blood flowing through his limbs, which had stiffened after sitting in a cabin for so many hours. Glancing at his wristwatch, he pushed the flight attendant call button.

A young woman appeared and he politely asked for a cup of coffee. He unfastened his seatbelt and stood up, stretching once more. He opened the overhead compartment and brought down a thin black case.

Back in his seat, he pulled out his laptop and placed it on his knees. He connected it to his cell phone, which he promptly hid down the side of his seat. He glanced around and, entering a code, activated the computer. In the middle of the screen, a message appeared informing him that the satellite connection was in progress.

From the corner of his eye, he spotted the approaching flight attendant. He pressed a button on the keyboard and a game of chess immediately appeared, masking the previous screen.

He smiled his thanks and took the porcelain cup and saucer in his hand. Once the attendant moved away, he brought up the original screen. The satellite connection was successful and a world map appeared on his screen.

Zooming in, he focused first on Istanbul and then Como. He brought up and quickly scanned various reports on the two murders that had taken place there. He studied police statements for a moment and then, after checking no one was coming down the aisle, he entered a website, which requested a series of codes and passwords before allowing access.

A few seconds later, he opened a folder containing a number of photos showing the naked corpses of the two men as found at the scene of the crime, from all possible angles. It was a horrifying sight, but he did not seem shocked. On the contrary, he zoomed in and peered closely, taking in every small detail, studying them.

He returned to the world map and clicked on a small Greek island, where three red dots blinked like buoys in the deep blue sea. Clicking on each dot, in turn, brought up the generic outline of a face marked by a red question mark.

He pulled his eyes away from the screen and looked out of the window at the million bright lights of a city somewhere in Europe. He picked up his coffee cup and, his eyes still on the ground far below, took a pensive sip.

* * *

The ferry had just docked at the port of Athora and around thirty passengers were making their way down to the luggage area.

In the open-air waiting area, a man sat on a bench under a small wooden canopy holding a newspaper. He was flicking through it with a bored expression, evidently killing time while waiting for someone.

As soon as he saw the first passengers emerge, he stood up and, flinging the newspaper on the bench, raised a piece of cardboard on which the name "Carlo Liretto" had been carelessly scribbled.

The newspaper sheets fluttered onto the tarmac, but he didn't even notice. By his feet, the foreign news section ruffled aimlessly. "Is a globe-trotting serial killer on the loose?" screamed the headline with the subheading "Murders in Istanbul and Como shockingly similar. Interpol on high alert for possible new attack."

A dark-haired, athletic-looking man of around forty stepped off the ferry carrying a small suitcase and walked to the man holding the cardboard sign high above his head. He took off his sunglasses and stretched out his hand, enunciating slowly and clearly. "Hello, Carlo Loretto."

The waiting man looked at the writing on his cardboard sign and, realizing his error, apologized in heavily accented English. "I am Kimon. The business partner of Petros. I also am your driver. How was the journey?"

"Well, considering I have been traveling by plane and boat for twenty-four hours non-stop..." He let his words trail off and pointed to the exit, indicating they should get going.

Kimon immediately made to take the leather bag slung over the newcomer's shoulder, but Carlo politely declined, saying there was no need. Kimon then firmly grabbed the man's suitcase without giving him a chance to refuse and set off toward his car, which was parked nearby.

Soon they were on their way to the hotel, following the seaside route. The sun had just set and the tranquil sea was reflecting all the colors that tinted the early evening sky.

The visitor, staring at the enchanting view, willingly answered all of Kimon's questions. All the while, he kept the leather bag firmly wedged between his legs, refusing to part from it even for a single moment.

Kimon's English was poor and a certain amount of divination was required on the part of the listener to make sense of what he was asking. "So how you decide to invest Athora?" Kimon asked, giving the man seated in the passenger seat beside him a sly look.

Carlo didn't seem to have any difficulty understanding the question. Keeping his face turned to the sea, he replied, "We haven't decided yet. I represent a big American company that builds wind farms, and your island is one of the areas we are looking at. I came here to see if there is any potential."

Kimon, his attention now fixed on the winding road, evidently considered it his duty to give the man a mini-orientation and started giving him the guided-tour. "Down there is ancient city of Athora," he said pointing to a spot where two large marble columns could be made out against the sea. "Remains of ancient temple," he clarified.

The speech that followed had evidently been memorized because Kimon switched into fluent English for the first time. "The rest of the ruins are now buried under water. Archaeologists speculate the city was destroyed in a big earthquake. Sea levels have risen in the past few years, completely covering what few ruins remain, but if you look down from the surface you can see it all very clearly. According to an old legend, the Egyptian goddess Athor had built a city on the same spot."

"Hathor," Carlo corrected him absent-mindedly.

"Hathor, I always make this mistake," said Kimon and resumed his recital with undiminished zeal: "Most of the houses you see on the left side of the road belong to foreigners who came to our island and bought land. More than three hundred people. Some came with their families, others on their own, from all over the world, seeking the peaceful isolation you can only find far away from the mainland..." He nodded to the tall stone houses flanking the road on this part of their journey. Set wide apart in estates separated by tall dry walls, they all looked out to the east, facing the sea.

The passenger leaned forward to get a better view and slightly lowered his dark sunglasses as if his curiosity had been piqued by the presence of so many foreigners on the island.

"We are so alone here, is like another country," commented Kimon and laughed at his own joke. He pointed across to the bridge that appeared as they drove around a bend. "Our bridge—the pride of Athora and the Aegean. It was built fifteen years ago and covers the three hundred and fifty feet of saltwater that split the island in two. The part we are on is where the *Chora* stands, literally meaning 'the Town'. The half of the island across the bridge is called *Pera Mera*, meaning 'the far side'. Where I take you now, eh?

"Even though the water level is low at this point, the bridge was built on tall pylons so that the waves raised by the northerly wind cannot reach it. About a month ago, there was big storm, and many waves came over the bridge. But nothing happened. Luckily, no cars were on it...Geologists speculate that, in the old days, both pieces of land were joined, but—"

"After a great earthquake that part of the land sank." The man sitting next to him smiled pointedly.

"Errr...yes...very good," stammered Kimon, at a loss as to how to take that comment.

As they crossed the bridge, Carlo rolled down his window took a deep breath. His face instantly took on a peaceful expression, as if the sea breeze had swept away every care.

Once they had crossed the bridge onto Pera Mera, Kimon turned up the slope leading to the hotel.

On the stone wall surrounding the property, its name had been carved on a large white slab of marble: "Borasco." The visitor took in the sign and a sarcastic smile flickered on his lips. "Borasco," he said. "A thunderstorm or violent squall, especially in the Mediterranean."

Kimon noticed and laughed. "Yes, we love wind here." He stepped gently on the brakes and the car came to a stop before the main entrance. The two men exited the car and Kimon removed the suitcase from the trunk, handing it over to the young bellhop hurrying down the steps to welcome the guest. Carlo once again slung his bag over his shoulder and turned to look across the bridge, squinting at a barely perceptible chapel perched on the mountaintop.

"*Panagia I Pyroessa*," Kimon volunteered. "A small church. On August 14, it was so windy Lukas fall in the cliff. First time no fire was lit in the evening."

"Is it that windy up there?"

"It is always wind on Athora, but not like this. We almost lost our mind. But now, weather is good and Lukas is fine.

Athora is great for wind turbines," he added in a conspiratorial whisper as if revealing a big secret.

Indifferently, the visitor took a banknote from his pocket and proffered it to Kimon, who crumpled it in his palm, thanking him. He then handed Carlo a set of car keys and pointed to an old jeep parked nearby. "This is your car. It looks a little worn, but there is no road on this island that it can't travel. I don't think you need me any more..."

Carlo took the key and, casting a glance at his new mode of transport, said goodbye and walked into the hotel lobby.

Kimon waited until he was gone and then got back inside his car. As soon as he was back on the main road, he picked up his cell phone and made a call. "Hi, Petros, it's me, Kimon. I've just dropped him off at the hotel...No he didn't say much, just that his company is thinking of investing on the island. I don't know, he seemed very secretive. We should keep an eye on his movements."

He was struggling to change gear on the upcoming turn, so he added hurriedly, "I'm hanging up now... I'm on my way to the Chora...we'll talk in person."

He had just driven onto the bridge when something on the water's surface made him suddenly pull up. He jumped out of the car and ran to the railing, leaning over to get a closer look. "What is this?" he gasped, staring at a pod of dolphins trying to cross under the bridge.

The sea level was low and the bed littered with sharp rocks, which cut the flesh of the dolphins turning the water a deep red. The air was filled with an eerie sound, like the sound of babies crying. Kimon shuddered and started crossing himself.

He stood there for a while, anxiously watching as the dolphins tried to navigate the shallow passage. Once they were all under the bridge, they all disappeared into deeper water, even the wounded animals.

The sea sucked in the blood and dispersed it, and soon resumed its normal shades of blue. Stunned, he returned to his car and started the engine. The look on his face was that of a man who had just seen a ghost.

* * *

A large raft, overflowing with people, was sailing toward a beach on the east side of Athora, its engine straining under the heavy load. As it neared the shore, the orange life vests worn by its passengers became visible, bright against the monochrome stretch of blue.

Many locals were already waiting on the shore, having been alerted by a fisherman who had spotted the vessel in the open water, moving toward the island.

Everyone seemed tense. It was the first time refugees were landing on the island. Athora was not a favorite destination for refugees or traffickers, who preferred the islands closer to the Turkish coastline.

Suddenly, a man on the boat barked an order and two men, perched on opposite sides of the raft, pulled out large knives and started frantically stabbing the sides of the boat. The air hissed out as the boat began to collapse and sink.

Panicking, the passengers jumped into the water and tried to swim to the shore, some trying to hold onto their small children, whose frightened cries and sobs reached those waiting on the shore. In response, many waded into the sea to help. Luckily, it was a calm, windless day and the beach was shallow. Under different circumstance, many would have drowned.

As the first of the shipwrecked struggled onto the sand aided by the locals, a coastguard speedboat appeared around the small cape, horns blaring and causing widespread panic. Those still clinging onto the half-sunken boat let go in a hurry.

On the beach, the rescued kissed the locals' hands, tears streaming down their cheeks in silent gratitude. Dehydrated from their long journey, they grasped the proffered water bottles and drank in great, thirsty gulps, explaining in broken English that they had spent a day at sea and arrived on the island by accident.

Amidst the chaos, one of the newly arrived men quietly crept behind a cluster of rocks. He was carrying a backpack wrapped in nylon. Removing the makeshift waterproof casing, he pulled out dry clothes and shoes, hastily discarded his wet garments, and changed clothes. He took out a ziplock and extracted a passport, a wad of cash held together with an elastic band and a cell phone. He switched the phone on, dialed and wedged it between his raised shoulder and ear, hastily buttoning up his shirt. He looked around forty, dark-skinned, sporting a closely trimmed beard. His hard expression softened only when he whispered, "I'm here."

He then hung up without another word. He fished out a baseball cap from the bottom of his bag and pulled it low over his forehead. He hurriedly shoved the wet clothes into the backpack and hoisted it on his back. He removed the SIM card from his phone and replaced it with a new one, then put it in his pocket without switching it on.

Tying his shoelaces, he looked out toward the road where people were pulling up in their cars, carrying food and clothes for the unexpected arrivals. Spotting at once the two taxis waiting to carry some of the refugees to the port, he walked briskly to the road. He approached one of the drivers, and in perfect English asked if the man would give him a lift—just him.

The taxi driver, hoping to make more money, asked him to wait until the taxi was full. The man opened his palm discreetly and showed the driver a bank note that more than covered the journey fare times five. It was enough to convince the driver, who got back behind the wheel, glancing around him suspiciously.

No one paid any attention to the taxi making a u-turn and heading to the port, raising a cloud of dust as it departed.

As soon as the beach was out of sight, the driver put the banknote in his pocket and stretched out his hand. "My name is Manolis, welcome to Athora."

The man looked at the driver from under the brim of his cap and shook his hand. "I'm Azim." Without another word, he turned his face away and spent the rest of the journey looking out of the window, making it clear that any further conversation was out of the question.

Chapter 5

The conference had just begun. Seated alongside the other speakers at the front row, I was attentively listening to the mayor of Ikaria's welcome, when a man hurried past, head bowed, to a seat farther down the row.

Curious, I turned to see who the latecomer was. With a jolt, I recognized the man who had shared my table that same morning. He cast a quick, puzzled look in my direction, gave me a fleeting smile and turned his attention back to the speaker.

Well, I'll be damned! I thought to myself. *What is he doing here?* I was dying to find out. Not only was I surprised to see him, I was even more rattled by his evident indifference. I could not manage to shake off the feeling of a woman scorned.

In the past, I never paid attention when someone would flirt with me, but, as I realized with a pang, that hadn't happened in a very long time. The past ten years, spent in the shadow of my relationship with Petros, had snuffed out any need for validation, though not because I felt complete in my relationship. I constantly filled the emotional void with work, travel, and the ambition to establish myself in my field. Now that it had finally happened, the idea that my time had passed scared me: I would be turning forty in three months.

I couldn't even remember the last time I'd felt pleasure making love to Petros. That too had become almost a formality over the years, although it hadn't started out that way; things had been different in the beginning.

I felt grateful for the way he had stood by me at the most difficult time in my life and helped me get over the shock, but I couldn't carry on pretending to have feelings for him when they were no longer there.

I could not pinpoint when it had happened, why I now felt as if I was getting old all of a sudden. The truth was that in recent years I had forgotten how to live.

The round of applause that followed the conclusion of the mayor's speech brought me back to the present.

The conference chair invited the first speaker to the podium, a Japanese anthropologist who came straight to the point, saying that the inhabitants of Okinawa, famous for their longevity, regularly followed a healthy diet, making sure that every day they ingested one produce from the sea and one from the land.

I had recently read an article and automatically started to recall the impressive data cited regarding the locals' extraordinary life expectancy.

My attention drifted back to the room to hear the next speaker, a French doctor, who stressed the other two factors affecting wellbeing: an easy pace of life and quality sex accompanied by an emotional bond. As could be expected, his words were greeted with applause and ripples of hilarity. *If that's the case, my chances of reaching a ripe old age are pretty slim*, I thought. At the end of his speech, he raised his glass of water to toast us, saying *cheers* in Greek and announcing we were all invited to a local *panegyri*, a traditional Greek festival, that same evening. *There's my chance to boost my life expectancy a little,* I joked to myself. I had heard lots about Ikaria's all-night festivals and wasn't planning to let this chance pass me by.

While I mulled over these thoughts, the next speaker had been announced, an anthropologist with a Hispanic sounding name. That's when the stranger who had managed to cause me such turmoil left his seat and hurriedly walked past me in the direction of... the podium. *So that's who it was!*

I hadn't managed to catch his name properly, but as soon as he was up, he leaned into the microphone and, as if answering my question, introduced himself. "Good afternoon. My name is Gabriel Martinez. I'm a physical anthropologist. I was born in Cuba but grew up in Boston..."

The spotlight falling on him made him glow from head to toe. It's true, his white shirt contributed to the luminous picture I had before me, but I still had the sense that it was mostly due to some internal light that seemed to emanate from him.

His voice was warm and self-confident and his speech showed a knowledgeable man at ease with his subject.

No matter how hard I tried to catch his eye, he kept his gaze fixed on the far end of the room. Without looking at his notes, he cited research and all the fascinating insight it had revealed about Ikaria. "An Australian journalist once said, 'there is a beautiful island in the Aegean, where people party until dawn, don't take medication, do not work out, and do not watch their diet. And yet, many of them live to be a hundred, are healthy, and make love to death'." The way he delivered the last few words and the double entendre got a loud laugh and a round of applause.

Athora *

He wiped a small bead of sweat from his forehead with the back of his hand and waited for everyone to settle down. Then, with a serious, earnest expression, he started to approach the conference topic from an anthropological point of view, at times wandering into my field of expertise. "Physical Anthropology examines the biological aspects of human existence and activity. An anthropologist, such as myself, will study the evolution of humans and their adaptation to their environment, examining skeletal remains and fossils, while observing the behavior not only of different population groups or races but even individuals over time..."

At this point, he paused rather abruptly and turned in my direction, gazing at me intently as if he had just noticed something important about me. I felt awkward, as the people seated beside me tried to understand what was going on, turning to stare at me.

He addressed the audience once again, making his small pause appear to be a momentary incident of academic absent-mindedness. I was convinced his glance had been more than that. It was a piercing look and I felt sure there was nothing accidental about it. It was as if he was trying to communicate some kind of message to me.

"As I was saying," he continued without missing a beat, "our main preoccupation is the study of human behavior, which for centuries has determined the evolution of our species; an evolution that has self-destructive tendencies. Humankind, as an entity, started to evolve these last three thousand years alongside the knowledge it acquired, simultaneously developing the communities it lived in. It started to manifest pathogenicities that ruled its actions.

Man started to kill, not for domination or food, but to satisfy instincts that, as far as we know, were not part of primal nature. There are humans that behave with unbelievable cruelty toward the weak. So, I wonder, what instincts and what needs push someone to rape and kill a child? What kind of instinct is satisfied by such an act? What impulse makes a man in Africa, or anywhere else in the world, raid a village and slaughter women and children in the name of some racial and religious dispute?"

He grew more and more agitated and the cool rationality of his earlier words gave way to a pithy diatribe. I felt everyone freeze. However, these were not views I did not share, and I found myself nodding along to both his thoughts and sentiments.

He paused once again and it was as if time had stood still. Everyone was hanging from his lips. So was I, captivated by the man's frankness and passion.

After a few moments of silence, where you could hear a pin drop, he spoke again, in a calm and peaceful voice, as he had at the beginning of his speech. "No matter what has happened on this planet for millions of years, one thing is certain...Life will still go on," he concluded.

I was startled because those were more or less the closing lines of my speech. I mechanically clapped along with the others, who were enthusiastically applauding, and prepared to take the podium. It was my turn.

* * *

Night had descended in all its darkness at this late hour. High up on one of Athora's mountains, a few scattered lanterns and the stars sparkling in the heavens were the only source of light. If one looked carefully, one would note that a couple of those lights came from the interior of a cottage snuggled between the rocks. Two small windows and a wooden door were all that made up its tiny façade. The rest of the house stretched like an oblong dome a few feet into the slope, nestling in the mountain's belly.

The occupier of the small cottage stepped out onto the narrow path. Sophie or Athora, as some called her. The nickname bothered her; even angered her.

She wore a long, frayed shirt that reached almost to her knees. Years of sunshine had faded and bleached it, and it was impossible to tell what color it had once been. Long wide black trousers and a pair of canvas shoes that looked hand-made completed the outfit.

Like a sponge, her white hair absorbed what little light there was and stood out in the inky darkness that had spread its tentacles all over the island.

Holding a stone in each hand, she approached the windows and tried to see if they fit in the opening, wishing to seal them shut at some later point.

After a while, she placed the stones on a pile near the wall. She had carefully selected the flat-surfaced stones so they would easily fit into each other, like bricks.

Used to the darkness and the landscape, she moved fast. She entered the house through the open door, where an oil lamp diffused a brighter glow than the lanterns scattered in her front yard.

The house only had one room, a single long space. On a smooth part of the rocky wall, she had painted a landscape dominated by a great tornado in its center.

A nook had been carved into the rock on one side to make a bed. A wooden shelf filled with old books stood above it.

Across the ceiling and high on the walls hung dried, aromatic herbs, filling the room with their scent. Jars filled with crushed herbs lined the walls in neat rows, carefully labeled in ink with a distinctive, cursive hand.

A bulky, flat stone served as a table. On it stood a clay bowl filled with purple grapes. Passing by, she picked a grape and put it in her mouth. As she crunched it, she grabbed a woolly jacket and went back to the exit.

She put out all the lanterns bar one and pulled the door shut. She then walked along the rocks and stepped onto the narrow passage that led to the canyon. She bent down between two large stones and sipped the water trickling down from a small spring. The water pooled and then ran in a small, narrow creek down the slope.

At that altitude, the sound of the sea gently brushing against the rocks below was but a faint murmur.

Sophie slowly followed the rough, tapering path as it wound its way up the mountain. Looking ahead, she could just about make out the shape of the chapel of the Virgin Mary perched higher up on a nearby mountaintop.

Far below, a cluster of lights sparkled—newly built houses, with a view of the narrow sea passage that split the island in two.

After a short, arduous trek, which at times forced her to climb up the steep slope on all fours, Sophie reached the peak. The cliff dropped down sharply, stopping close to the spot where one end of the bridge stood.

She untied her jacket from around her waist and pulled it on. The wind was chilly at this altitude. She stood at the highest point and looked at the large boulders, which lay scattered around her as if an invisible hand had flung them from the skies. *Anemotafia*, the locals called them— Tombstones of the Winds. They said that the dangerous winds, the ones that brought disaster to the world, lay buried beneath the stones and no one must ever release them.

She sat cross-legged on the ground in front of a large stone, pulling her legs ceremoniously beneath her. She had carved the stone herself—a wide-open eye, its iris another open eye, standing guard at the highest point of the island, watching over the sea.

She slipped her hand into her shirt pocket and when she brushed against what she was looking for she gripped it tightly in her fist. She fixed her eyes on the horizon and sat still, staring into the darkness. She then closed her eyes and started whispering something that sounded like a rhythmic incantation.

Her features took on the wilderness of the landscape around her, and her words grew louder and louder. A violent gust of wind suddenly hit her chest, trying to throw her back. Instinctively she thrust her free hand onto the ground, and a sharp rock became her painful anchor. She enunciated the last two words slowly, opened her eyes and fixed them to the east as if waiting for a signal. All she saw was a thin black line, which slowly swallowed up the light of the stars as it moved across the sky. It was so far away that she couldn't tell whether its darkness would reach the island.

She closed her eyes again for a moment, dropping the white stone she had been gripping so tightly back into her pocket. She got up slowly, religiously, and dusted down her shirt and trousers. Turning back to the path, she began to make her way down the slope.

Forked lightning tore through the dark clouds to the east. Sophie jumped as if the current had passed right through her. She turned to look behind her. Her gaze became one with the night, but no matter how intensely she searched the sky, all she could see was the dark, brooding horizon.

* * *

The moment I stood behind the podium, a blast of light pierced the room through the large bay window, blinding everyone. I thought someone was taking photos using a flash, but the clap of thunder a few seconds later and the rattling windowpanes left no doubt it was a thunderbolt, striking nearby.

I paused for a minute before beginning my speech, waiting for the rising murmur of astonishment to settle. Soon, everyone was quiet. I thought back to how clear the weather had been just a couple of hours ago. The whims of the weather that summer never ceased to amaze me.

"No matter what the weather is like, we are still going to the festival," I joked, trying to lighten up the atmosphere.

It worked. Everyone laughed, and I seized the moment. I opened my laptop and looked at the screen. However, I found it very difficult to utter the first few words. I stared at the silent audience and my gaze settled on him. His eyes were glued to his cell phone, once again oblivious to my presence. I tried to mask my annoyance and plowed on.

"If we try to understand the place occupied by the eldest inhabitant of this island in the vast space-time continuum, we might understand his influence, as well as his imprint on the Universe.

"As the renowned paleontologist Jose Marcus once said, 'if we wish to formulate, by approximation, an idea of our place in the Universe, both in terms of time and space, we must realize that we are nothing more than a few lines on the page of a book on the shelf of a library that is larger than Europe and filled with books'."

"So, in this vastness, right now, we are not even a letter of those few lines on the page," Gabriel Martinez shouted out from the front row, interrupting me with a smile.

Normally, I would have felt annoyed at the interruption. Instead, it felt good to have his attention at last and so I returned the smile, saying, "Man is not interested in the vastness because he is condemned to live in the moment, or at least pretend he is." We looked at each other for a few seconds, and I realized he got the hint.

Spurred on by his interjection, I turned back to the audience. "We all passionately seek the hidden secrets that will decode the reason for our existence and, furthermore, the creation of our world as it is. Those few lines in the book of our existence have been erased and re-written many times for millions of years. However, this does not deter us from constantly seeking our origin and trying to plan the future, based on our history. Long-term and at times catastrophic natural changes have led to this," I said, pointing at the room.

Outside, another flash of lightning lit the windows. This time the crack of thunder was louder and even the glass of water on the podium before me shook.

Ignoring the weather, I carried on. "If the dinosaurs had not become extinct, for example, none of us would be here. The meteorite that probably destroyed a large part of the world then, is in some way our 'ancestor'."

I could feel some in the audience tense in disagreement at what I had just said. As far as I was concerned, I was content with finally holding the attention of the man who had intrigued me. Feeling encouraged, I carried on. "All of these astonishing events, which happened on earth millions of years ago, had one and only outcome. Us.

"Isn't it magical? Does it not surpass every science fiction scenario we could possibly come up with, this script written by God, according to some; Nature, to others, or whatever name one may wish to give to the creator of what we have been part of for many thousands of years?"

I realized I was veering from what I had planned to say, which approached the subject of longevity from a more scientific point of view, but I did not care. I felt good about the way I was expressing myself.

Nonetheless, I spent some time analyzing certain scientific terms that concerned the geological history of the island and how it had been shaped by various natural disasters.

Concluding that part of my presentation, I reverted to the style with which I had begun my speech. "Today I followed local custom and took a nap at lunchtime. I can't even remember the last time I slept during the day. Here, people observe their siesta religiously. They encourage those who come to the island to follow their pace, which they refuse to abandon for any reason.

"What is remarkable on Ikaria isn't just how long people live but how they choose to live. At festivals and all social gatherings, everyone is present; centenarians and babies alike. Like one big family... no one feels neglected, they all feel part of a tightly knit community.

"So, in conclusion, I suggest we all meet up at tonight's festival, so that we may shore up our time reserves with a few more minutes of good, quality life. If the weather allows it."

I stepped down to the sound of warm applause. Looking at me, he applauded until I returned to my seat. Only then did he turn to look at the podium and hear the mayor thank everyone.

For the first time, a sense of triumph swept through me.

* * *

The storm did not last long but filled the air with a humidity that seemed to stick to our every pore.

The minivan dropped us off near the square. The noise coming from that direction indicated that the party was already underway. Initially, the organizers had told us the festival would be canceled if it continued to rain. Luckily, nature proved generous enough and allowed us to enjoy this unique experience.

Despite looking hard for Gabriel after we left the conference, I didn't manage to spot him. I hoped he would at least turn up for this.

I had spoken to my parents earlier in the evening. They told me that a boat of refugees had washed up on the island because they had lost their bearings. It seemed strange to me, as something like that had never happened before, but I did not dwell on it. I yearned for a carefree evening.

As soon as the mayor saw us, he came over and led us to a table near the band. All the conference speakers were present, except for Gabriel. I wondered whether he hadn't realized we'd set off, whether he'd somehow been left behind. But how could I ask without showing that I was interested in him?

All the tables in the square were full. What impressed me the most was that I was now witnessing what all the research had shown: people of all ages, laughing, eating, and drinking as if they had no other care in the world.

In the empty space at the center that would later serve as a dance floor, children were already twirling to the sound of the band. A little girl stumbled repeatedly as she tried to follow the steps, falling over, but always getting up determined to dance.

I had been to many local festivals on our own island and I was curious to see what was so different about Ikaria. The following day I would be departing for Athora and from then on things would follow their course.

I suddenly realized that the orderly life that awaited me was suffocating me. I had spent so many years traveling all over the world. Being a part of a team that made so many significant discoveries had made me feel like I was a small part of the planet's modern history. However, I had neglected my personal needs and watched my life flow before me like some kind of road movie. Loaded with luggage, I moved here and there like a chess piece on a board.

Since my arrival on Ikaria, I had been in turmoil. My feelings had shifted and all the joy I had felt at the prospect of teaching at one of the most reputable universities in America—indeed, in the whole world—had somehow dimmed. I needed to loosen up, let myself go. To leave my old self behind, test my limits, explore all these new feelings that were welling up inside me.

The mayor filled my glass with red wine. Tonight, I would drink. We all clinked glasses and I downed my drink in a single gulp. It left a sweet, tart taste in my mouth. I liked it... both the wine and the warmth that began to spread through me. I drained the last dregs and the mayor, seated beside me, looked at me in surprise. "Is that how you drink your wine on Athora, Miss Meliou?" he teased.

Wiping a drop of wine from my lips, I smiled and replied, "Truth be told, no. But tonight I decided to do it the Ikaria way." I held out my glass for a refill.

He readily did so, at the same time explaining: "The wine you are drinking is a blend of two varieties called *Fokiano* and *Begleri*. They say that if you drink it in one gulp you lose your mind and everything you keep hidden inside you bubbles up to the surface." He took a sip of wine and continued, "Now that I have the chance, I'd like to tell you how proud we all are to see one of our own rise to such prominence."

"I'm very honored and I will try not to let you down," I replied, raising my glass in silent toast to everyone seated around the table.

All the foreign speakers were looking around them in astonishment. Chatting with them on the bus, I realized that none of them had ever been to anything like this before. I appointed myself Greek tourism ambassador and explained a few things about Ikaria festivals, referring to the mayor whenever any questions I could not answer came up.

I was drinking more slowly now, as it became clear that the night ahead would be long. Despite my self-restraint, the first wave of haziness had already washed over me, but it felt so good I really did not care. Every now and then, my eyes would wander over the square looking for him, wondering where he was, what had become of him.

When I saw him walk across the square in our direction, I felt a spark of delight and sat up straighter. The spark went out as suddenly as it appeared, when a young woman who had been walking a couple of steps behind him came and joined us at our table. Everybody started shifting their chairs to make room for them and then they sat together across from me.

My attention was inevitably drawn to his companion, a beautiful brunette who could not have been older than twenty-five. Like me, she wore a long white dress, only hers left very little to the imagination.

No matter how indifferent I tried to appear, my eyes would shift toward the two of them, trying to figure out exactly what the relationship was. I wondered if they were a couple, but I heard the mayor speak to her as if he knew her well because she was a local, so their relationship could only be recent... and fleeting.

The voice of reason in my head kept shouting at me to stop it. I was still involved with Petros, and Gabriel Martinez was a man who liked to fill his spare time pleasantly by the look of it.

I took another long sip and banished my jealous thoughts.

Suddenly, the music stopped and everyone began to rise from their seats and move toward the empty space between the tables. One man even held the little girl who had been stumbling around the dance floor in his arms and she giggled in delight.

I stared at them wondering what this sudden mass migration to the dance floor was all about, when a sudden hush fell over the square. Everyone had turned to look at the band. I followed their gaze and saw a young man appear, holding a violin. He sat on a tall chair and after exchanging silent glances with the other musicians, placed the violin under his chin, holding it at an angle. With his other hand, he raised the bow toward the crowd, as if giving a signal.

What then happened made the hairs on the back of my neck stand on end. The clamoring exclamations of enthusiasm and the whistles burst my eardrums and I instinctively put my hands over my ears. The mayor beside me laughed at my reaction, telling me this was when the real fun began. Most of the crowd had already formed a circle, draping their arms over their neighbor's shoulders, and were ready to dance.

With the first scratch of the bow on the chords, the familiar melody of Ikaria's folk tunes burst out, igniting an unbelievable outburst of joy.

I felt all its energy pierce me to the core. Leaning over the table, I impulsively clinked my glass with Gabriel's, forcing him to turn his attention to me and stop talking to his companion. The young woman jumped back in alarm, as a few drops of wine landed on her dress, staining the white cloth like blood drops.

I loudly shouted out "I'm sorry" and tried to excuse myself for my clumsiness. I handed her my napkin in an attempt to appease her, but nothing I did seemed to improve her mood. She cast me a thunderous look and stood up to go remove the stain.

Gabriel moved to let her pass through and, as soon as she was some distance away, looked at me with a sarcastic smile, as if accusing me of doing it on purpose.

The loud music rendered all verbal communication impossible, so our eyes did the talking, each trying to detect the other's intentions. My intentions, in any case, were perfectly clear. Luckily, no one else seemed to have divined them, only him. He kept his glass close to his lips and took small sips, his gaze shifting between the dancers and me.

I was not trying, nor did I wish, to hide anymore. As a future university professor, I should have been more careful, but the fire I felt burning inside me and which the wine had momentarily extinguished, was flaring up once again.

Meanwhile, the party was now in full swing and the mayor was spurring us on to join the dancers. One by one, everyone at our table stood up, pulling their neighbor along.

I was the last person to get up and I determinedly pulled Gabriel's hand to follow me. Unhesitatingly, he entered the improvised circle that coiled like a serpent, joining all the dancers together.

As soon as he placed his right arm on my shoulders, his soft touch filled me with delicious warmth. Of their own will, my lips started singing along to the song and I immediately turned to look at him as he fruitlessly tried to figure out the steps to the dance. Singing loudly along with everyone else, I signaled to him with a nod that he should not care about steps but let the music and its frenzied rhythm carry his feet. He did so and gradually seemed to get swept up in this almost mystical ritual. It was as if everyone's energy had merged, creating a force I had never felt before.

"Is this what you meant at the conference when you said we should live in the moment?" he shouted in my ear.

"Exactly," I shouted back, hungrily gazing into his eyes.

The crowd spun around, following the repeating beat, and so did my head. For the first time in a long time, I felt content, caught in a rare, single moment when I had all I needed.

We danced for quite a while, the band playing over and over the same lively tunes. Gabriel followed, transfixed, letting his serious professor image slip for a moment.

When the music stopped, everyone applauded and downed a round of shots that someone was distributing on a massive tray.

The pause did not last long. Almost immediately, the violinist's bow touched the chords again, sending the crowd into a renewed frenzy.

Gabriel did not even notice his companion who had returned a few minutes earlier and now sulked at the table watching everyone dance, all alone. On the contrary, he placed his arm on my shoulder and, looking at me, rejoined the dance.

I felt as if I was in a dream. Without thinking about it, I took Gabriel by the hand when the music stopped and, walking through the crowd, I led him beyond the square, toward the church.

I could not understand what led me to do something so unlike me. Maybe the haze brought on by the wine or my adrenaline, skyrocketing with the exultation of the dance, had defeated my inhibitions. The only thing I can be certain of is that, for the first time in my life, I acted impulsively.

I did not even turn to look at the man following me. I could only feel, as I held him, some slight hesitation. I intended to pull him into the darkness, where my embarrassment would not make me lose my courage. I heard his voice ask me where we were going, but I didn't reply, pulling him toward the most secluded spot I could see, just behind the sanctuary.

Before we even got there, I felt him put an abrupt stop to my relentless course with all his strength. I turned to face him, out of breath and tingling with excitement. My ragged breath was almost splitting my chest in half and my legs shook.

I tried to guess his mood, and before he had a chance to react, I fell into his arms and my mouth sought his. I did not even hear the words he uttered, but just when I could feel his soft kiss, he put his arms between us and gently pushed me away saying, "Please stop."

I thought he was dithering and took his arm and placed it on my breast, then guided it further down. I demanded his caress but he resisted. "What are you doing?" he hissed, grabbing my wrists and holding me at arm's length.

His eyes blazed with anger in the dim light. Like a house of cards blown down by the wind, everything inside me started to collapse. The way he spoke and looked at me made it clear that he did not like what I was about to do and I suddenly froze. I tried to say something but my trembling chin made it impossible to turn sound into words. I felt tears roll down my cheeks and then a sob escaped my throat. I bowed my head defeated by my own self and freed myself from his grip with all the strength I had left. "I'm sorry..." I stammered and turned away, feeling all the shame in the world land on my shoulders.

"Don't go!" he shouted. He gripped my arms and turned me to face him. "I'm sorry too, but I can't do it. I'm with someone. Please don't cry. You were so happy just a few moments ago..."

"I'm so sorry. You have someone and I've behaved abominably," I said. "I got carried away; I don't know what happened to me... I've never done anything like this before!" I tried to excuse my inappropriate behavior.

"I believe you," he reassured me and turned toward the square, where the party was in full flow. "Let's go back, they'll be looking for us."

"Go back to your girlfriend and I'll join you in a bit. I don't want them to see me like this... I am so sorry."

"I'm responsible too, I let myself get carried away... And she's not my girlfriend," he said drily and left.

I wished the ground would swallow me up. I squeezed my temples trying to understand what had just happened. I couldn't believe I'd plummeted to such depths of ignominy. I had never felt more humiliated in my life. How could I face everyone, when they may have realized I had disappeared with Gabriel down some dark alley?

I sat on a stone bench by the church wall and looked at the light of a candle flicker through the stained glass window. I could not have thought of a more terrible place to try to seduce him.

The noise from the festival drifted to where I sat and I could not summon the strength to return there. A few minutes later, I stood up and struggled to stay upright. I hated myself for the way I had behaved, brazenly going after a brief desperate encounter with a random man. I had debased myself trying to catch his attention.

I took a deep breath and decided not to reappear at the festival. I could not pretend to enjoy myself while feeling the tension between us. Somehow, I would manage to make my way back to the hotel.

I walked around the church and took a sloping road trying to walk in a straight line. I knew I was too far away to return to the hotel on foot, but I was hoping to meet a car along the way.

I had only been walking for a few minutes when I saw headlights approaching behind me. I instantly turned around and raised my hand.

It pulled up beside me and I leaned in through the open window to speak to the driver. "Could you please give me a lift to a place where I could find a taxi?"

The man looked puzzled for a moment but then nodded that I should get in.

As soon as I sat in the passenger seat, he smiled and said, "Weren't you sitting at the mayor's table?"

"Yes. Something came up and I had to leave. I didn't want to inconvenience anyone," I replied. His raised eyebrow showed that he did not believe a word I said.

It suddenly hit me that there I was, in the middle of the night, sitting in a car no one had seen me get into, beside a total stranger. I was still behaving recklessly; what was happening to me?

"I'll drive you to Agios Kyrikos," he said and took a sharp turn left, leaving the main road. "It's faster this way," he added and I felt myself freeze, assaulted by terrible memories.

My fears proved unfounded. The man truly was a kind person, who not only helped me but also dropped me off where I was staying.

Just before we reached the hotel, I discovered I had left my bag back on the table. I did not say anything. During our long drive, I'd gathered that my Good Samaritan was so obliging he was likely to drive back all that way just to bring me my handbag. I was sure the mayor or one of the other guests would notice the bag when they started wondering where I was. The pressing problem was that my room key was inside it and the dark reception area indicated that no one was around to let me in with their spare key.

I took off my shoes and held them while I walked down the steps leading to the rocky beach beneath the hotel. I still felt dizzy. The winding road had made my stomach heave, but I had managed not to humiliate myself in front of yet another stranger. I had had enough embarrassment for one evening.

The heat had dried off the sudden storm, so as soon as I arrived at the beach I stretched out on one of the loungers lined up on the flat surface of the rocks. Absolute silence engulfed me. Only the sounds of the festival I had just escaped from kept ringing in my ears.

Looking out at the still waters, I felt their tranquility steadily spread inside me. I turned to look in the direction of Athora, seeking some comfort, anticipating my return the following day.

I wished I could be magically whisked away to my island that very moment, close to the people who loved me. Luckily, my cell phone was still back at the square. In the depths of dark despair, I was capable of foolishly calling Petros and asking him to set a date for our wedding before my return to California.

I never made any important decisions in the heat of the moment. I always waited patiently for my emotions to subside. The only time I had allowed my heart to rule my head had been that evening, when I had flung myself at Gabriel and got rejected in return. I still could not believe I had behaved so foolishly, so vulgarly.

My bad mood and the cool Mistral rising from the northwest made me shiver. I picked up an abandoned towel and covered myself. My father used to tell a story of how Mistral was a prince whose lover had been abducted by pirates. Enraged, he had asked the god of the sea to turn him into a wind. His wish granted, he blew so violently he sank all the pirate ships and inadvertently drowned the woman he loved. Ever since, he has been wandering the seas asking for the spell to be broken, to be a man again, to no avail. He rages when he remembers his lost love and blows softly when he whispers songs to her, in the hope that she might hear.

I took refuge in my memories, trying to erase the events of the evening. My heavy lids would close and then open with the rustle of the wind. I was balancing on that imperceptible line that separates sleep from wakefulness, until I finally, sweetly, drifted off to sleep.

The throbbing sound of a speedboat passing near the beach made me sit up with a startle. I couldn't tell how long I had been asleep.

I looked around, dazed, and saw a light on one of the hotel balconies. I took it a signal to get up and return to the hotel, hoping to somehow find a way to get back to my room.

I crossed the dark lobby, which was deserted as expected, and slowly walked up the stairs. I fumbled for the light switch in the corridor and then...

Surprise was soon followed by a sense of relief, when I saw my handbag hanging on the doorknob outside my room. A folded note peeked out from one of the side pockets.

It was from the mayor, who had dropped off my bag and was asking me to message him as soon as I got his note and let him know that I was well. They were all worried about me and if they did not hear from me soon, they would contact the police.

The corridor light switched itself off. I tiptoed farther down the corridor, where Gabriel's room was, and gingerly put my ear to his door. Nothing. Absolute silence. The "do not disturb" sign dangled from the door, as if personally addressed to me. Was he alone? Was the girl who had accompanied him to the festival with him? I pictured them sleeping in each other's arms, satiated with pleasure. Although he had made it clear he was not interested in me, I felt a pang of jealousy at the thought.

I snuck back to my room as quietly as possible, trying to keep my presence a secret and spare myself any further embarrassment. I fished out my key and let myself in. The first thing I did was send a text message to the number the mayor had left on the note, saying that I was okay. Then I slowly removed all my clothes and headed for the shower.

The bathroom mirror reflected back the telltale signs of my attempt to seduce Gabriel. A red mark stretched from my chest to the area below my belly button, reminding me how roughly I had pressed his hand against my body to guide him there.

I abandoned myself to the water's embrace and, trying to find some release from the tension that had built up inside me, tenderly caressed my body.

Athora *

Chapter 6

A male figure slowly crossed the Chora late at night. The hump formed by the backpack he was carrying disfigured his form and cast a terrifying shadow.

Winding his way through the narrow lanes, he reached the square. The church of St Porphyrios loomed over it, dark and gloomy at this hour. The vigil oil lamps burning at the *templon* barely shone through the stained glass windows.

The sudden sound of approaching voices shattered the silence and the shadow hid behind the thick bougainvillea, its branches stretching like bloodstained fingers all the way up the bell tower, staining the tall façade red all the way to the top.

Two nighttime strollers paused before the church, crossed themselves and moved on, loudly debating the weather's recent whims.

Silence once again descended on the square as the echo of their voices vanished between the walls sheltering the sleeping town. Not another soul stirred. All the shops were closed, to reopen in a few hours with the early morning sun.

Ensuring he was all alone, the man cautiously crept out of his hiding spot and walked alongside the church until he reached the stone house standing behind it. An enclosed passageway connected the house to the church.

Casting furtive glances around him, he approached the front door of the house and paused, alert to any sound that might be coming from inside. It was deadly quiet. He placed his backpack on the ground and removed a pair of gloves and a small blade. He pulled on the gloves and gingerly inserted the blade into the lock, with stealthy, practiced movements. A few seconds later the faintest of clicks showed the lock was no longer an obstacle.

He pushed the door open and, picking up his backpack, tiptoed inside pushing the door shut behind him. The dim light of a lampshade on a dining room sideboard cast a yellow wreath on the wall, enclosing the icon of St George astride his horse, slaying a dragon with his spear. Beneath it stood a framed photo of a priest surrounded by a gaggle of smiling children somewhere in Africa.

As soon as he heard the snores coming from the bedroom, the intruder opened his backpack once again and fumbled inside. Holding a syringe, he crept into the room and up to the bed. He forcefully pressed his open palm over the face of the sleeping man and jammed the syringe in his neck.

The man woke up with a start and instinctively tried to sit up, but the intruder's grip held him fast against his pillow. The drug rapidly spread through his body and instantly paralyzed him. A few spasms and the man lay still. Only his eyes flickered about trying to spot his assailant, who had slowly pulled away his hand once he was certain that everything was going according to plan.

When he was sure that his victim could not move and that all he could do was utter low, strangled cries, he switched on the bathroom light and left the door slightly ajar, just enough to dispel the darkness in the bedroom.

He removed a roll of masking tape from his backpack, cradled the immobilized man's head, and wrapped the masking tape around it twice, sealing his mouth shut.

"If you know the woman's name I might let you die without too much pain," the man said in English. "You can't speak right now, so blink to let me know whether you are willing to cooperate."

The man could not blink—his eyes were wide with fear and despair, and his nostrils flared as he struggled to breathe through his nose.

"You must be wondering who I am," said the intruder. "You will go to your grave wondering that. It took me many years to track you down. Now you are revealed to me, one by one, and the day of reckoning is here. Were you ever really a priest or was it a part you've been playing so well all this time? You must have had a lot of help to be in this position today. Help from those who otherwise pretend to be men of God. Their time will come too. As for you, know this: there is no escape from me now. Your torment will be long. Unless you tell me what I want to know."

He turned to look at a door to the side of the bed and walked toward it. He opened it and stood before the dimly lit passageway that joined the vicarage to the church. He walked to the end of the arched passageway, unlocked the door at the other end and pushed it open. The dim light of the votive oil lamps spread down the dark corridor, along with the lingering scent of incense.

He made his way back to the bedroom and approached the bed. With precise movements, he began to undress the helpless man until he lay naked on the bed. He lifted him up and flung him over his shoulders with the ease of a farmer lifting a sack of potatoes. Then he carried him to the church.

He paused for a moment down the aisle and looked up at the dome, where the almighty stretched out his hand, holding a large, bronze chandelier. He adjusted the man's limp body over his shoulder to spread the load better and moved toward the sanctuary.

The whiteness of the naked body made it look almost translucent, as it lay stretched on the red silk cloth that covered the altar.

The perpetrator had carefully removed all the holy vessels and instruments, piously placing them wherever he could, as if he did not want to cause the slightest damage. Holding a knife he had taken from his backpack, he stood beside his victim, who was shaking as if a small electric current was coursing through his body.

"I'll give you a chance to talk," the assailant said. "You can try to shout for help as loudly as you want, but no one will hear you. Blink twice if you agree."

The man on the altar, who had started to regain his consciousness, blinked twice. Slowly, his assailant removed the tape, waiting to hear the man's answer.

As if he were drunk, his victim tried to mumble a few words but his mouth was still numb from the anesthetic. He struggled to ask, "Who are you? Why are you doing this? What have I done to you?"

"There is no point in us introducing ourselves; our acquaintance will be brief. You don't know me. However, I am sure you know exactly why I am here. It's because of your past."

The man tried to protest, but a gloved hand covered his mouth and stifled his words.

"All I want to know is if you know anything about the woman on the island. I'll find her anyway, but I thought you might make it easier... *Father George*." He sniggered sarcastically when he spoke the last two words and pulled his hand away.

"I swear to God I don't know any woman! I don't know who you are talking about or why you are doing this," the priest whimpered.

The man slapped him hard and brought his face close to the priest. "You dare take God's name," he hissed "after all you have done. It is blasphemy to do so in here."

He picked up his backpack and unzipped the front pocket. He pulled out a photo and almost stuck it on the semi-conscious man's face. "Does this photo remind you of anyone? Speak!" he commanded with controlled rage.

The priest's eyes widened and a sob choked his voice. "God will punish you for this," was all he could say.

"God never punishes anyone," the man replied. "Man punishes himself, playing with fire. You played with fire and now you will pay."

The priest desperately tried to call for help. The howl of a wounded, struggling animal escaped his lips before his tormentor sealed his mouth with tape once more and brought his fist to the man's head, knocking him out. He then paused and listened to the darkness outside. All that could be heard was the monotonous chirp of a cricket that had sneaked into the church, offering his own prayers to the Almighty.

Having made sure all was quiet outside, the man sat on a chair by the altar and removed his baseball cap, looking at the priest's chest rise and fall with each shallow, uneven breath. He remained pensive for a moment as if trying to gather his thoughts. He then stood up and spread the contents of his backpack next to the still body. A large needle threaded with thick black thread, a piece of rope, and a bin bag surrounded the sharp knife on the table. He was ready to begin.

He glanced around at the icons of the saints looking at him in silent judgment, and brought the candelabra close, lighting one of the candles with the flame of a vigil oil lamp. He picked up the priest's right arm and lifted it. There was no tattoo on the armpit, just a dark stain like an old burn mark, which betrayed the presence of something that had been erased. He straightened his gloves and brought the knife to the priest's thumb.

The oil ran out in one of the oil lamps and the flame hissed as it touched the water, where it died with a shudder.

Chapter 7

I slept restlessly all evening, despite the silence that reigned in the hotel during the night. I was due to leave for Athora at three, and I did not want to venture outside until then, to avoid running into him. I called room service and asked them to bring breakfast to my room. I stepped out onto the balcony while I waited, and sat gazing at the sea.

A soft breeze stirred its surface, leaving a flurry of indistinct shapes in its wake, as if a fairy was touching the waters here and there with her magic wand.

The weather was changing once again, I noted with surprise. The forecast had been clear skies for the next few days. I picked up my cell phone and went online to see what nature had in mind and stared at headlines of a sudden tornadic waterspout wreaking havoc on the Turkish coastline the previous evening, leaving behind scores of dead and missing.

Here, the weather was calm and sunny, except for a few distant clouds on the horizon. The forecast, however, announced sudden weather changes in the Aegean that evening, with strong winds and rain.

I wondered what was going on. The words of Professor Marcus that something unusual was happening in the region echoed in my ears. I hadn't paid attention then, but now, with the weather behaving so strangely for this time of year, I felt my chest tighten.

Just then, Gabriel appeared on the path that led down to the beach. I tried to sink low into my chair and hide, but he saw me. He raised his hand in greeting as if nothing unpleasant had ever happened between us.

I waved back and shifted my chair out of his line on vision. I found my hide-and-seek routine ridiculous. When I heard a knock on my door a few moments later, I instantly decided to stop hiding and feeling uncomfortable simply for expressing my feelings… however clumsily or rather more passionately than the object of my desire could withstand.

I opened the door and asked the waiter to take my tray back to the dining room, apologizing for the inconvenience.

An hour later, with still no sign of Gabriel, I decided to return to my room and pack. As soon as I walked in, I stepped out onto the balcony to check I had left nothing there. That is when I noticed the sharp change.

I stood gaping at the horizon; I had never seen anything like it before. The sky had split in two, one half bright blue sunshine and the other dark grey with rapidly amassing heavy clouds. A conspiracy of ravens cawed noisily as it flew up and turned south, bickering which way to go. They seemed uncertain, changing direction abruptly every now and then as if trying to circumvent obstacles visible only to them.

I hastily stepped back into the room and started to gather my things, my mind still filled with this bizarre sight.

* * *

Outside the vicarage, an elderly woman persistently knocked on the door, patiently waiting for someone to let her in. One last, stronger knock and the door shifted ajar. She gently pushed it open, calling out the priest's name. He should have been at the church already.

Receiving no reply, she decided to walk in, casting anxious looks around her. She brought her hand to her mouth and stifled a startled cry. The house had been ransacked, the floor littered with the remnants of a frantic search. In the bedroom, the closet and all the drawers gaped open. The priest was nowhere to be seen.

Instead of turning back and going to summon help, she walked through the open door into the passageway that led to the church. It, too, was deserted.

Feeling truly frightened, she desperately cried, "Father George... Father George!" The echo of her voice in the empty building was her only reply.

Realizing that something must have happened to the priest and that she should alert everyone, she walked to the exit as fast as her legs could carry her. At the church door, she started waving her arms and shouting at those sitting in the coffee shop across the square.

As soon as they saw the old woman, they jumped up in alarm and ran toward her. Trembling, she described what she had seen. One of the men ran to the priest's house to check what was happening.

In the meantime, neighbors who had heard her cries started to gather at the square and the news soon spread. The man who had dashed to the priest's house walked back in a rush, speaking loudly on his cell phone. From what they could make out, he had called the police to tell them about the burglary. He hung up and informed everyone that no one was to approach the priest's house. Evidently, those were the police instructions.

Worried, the gathered crowd spread in every direction looking for the priest. They soon returned to the square as perplexed as they had left it. The priest had not been found.

They stood around discussing all the possible reasons behind his disappearance, when the old woman who had alerted them pointed to the craggy outcrop of rocks rising high above the Chora. At its peak, a woman was strolling, unaware that she was being observed.

As if sensing all eyes on her, Sophie turned and looked in their direction. Indifferent to the gathered crowd, she kept walking along the path, her white hair streaming behind her.

The people at the square exchanged a few glances, but no one commented on her presence. Instead, they resumed their conversations after this brief silent pause.

It wasn't long before two police officers appeared on one of the narrow streets leading to the square, followed by Petros, Kimon, and Efthymis, Fotini's father.

Most of the Chora's residents had arrived at the square by then, troubled by the burglary, and worried about the priest's disappearance. Many visitors to the island wandered among them, drawn by the unusual gathering and the tension that filled the air. Carlo, the visitor Kimon had transported to the hotel the previous day, was one of them. As soon as he spotted his driver, he approached him to find out what had happened, showing his surprise.

The two police officers made their way through the crowd, which parted to let them through and walked to the back of the church.

"I bet you anything the priest has downed a few drinks and we'll soon find him snoring in a corner," Kimon said insolently.

"Watch your words, Kimon. People can hear you," scolded Petros turning to look at Carlo who was standing nearby.

"That one doesn't speak a word of Greek," Kimon confidently asserted.

Efthymis was about to say something but stopped when he saw one of the officers return from the vicarage. Petros went up to him and tersely asked, "What happened, did you find the priest?"

"No, but the house has been turned upside down," he announced and went running toward the police car parked at the end of the cobbled square.

Carlo calmly observed the unfolding drama. Excusing himself, he followed Efthymis, who broke away from the group and moved to the church. He crossed himself at the entrance and walked down the nave, where he paused and looked at the Beautiful Gates in the center of the Templon, which separated the sanctum from the nave. Closely behind, the foreigner gazed at the murals covering the church walls.

Unaware of the other man's presence, Efthymis hesitantly approached the Temple in awe and spotted the red stains on the steps leading to the sanctum. He stopped breathing for a moment. He sharply turned to head for the exit, aware that he had just discovered an important clue but froze to the spot when he saw the other man standing close by. "I'm going to get the police," he said in a shaky voice in Greek, forgetting the visitor spoke no Greek.

Carlo stayed fixed to his spot, waiting for events to unfold.

A few minutes later, the sound of approaching voices grew louder and a group of people burst into the church on the heels of Fotini's father and two uniformed officers. One of them cast Carlo a suspicious look and headed straight to the sanctum. He cautiously swung the two carved wooden panels outwards, revealing the altar, which was covered with its purple cloth, and moved inside. A loud curse escaped his lips as he stepped into the pool of blood by the table.

He carefully lifted the cloth and dropped it as if he had just been stung, stepping back aghast. He looked at those gathered outside the sanctum, as if waiting for the priest to come out and give communion. A look of horror on his face, he opened his mouth to say something but no sound came out. He lifted the fabric once again and looked at the sight beneath it more calmly this time. He let the cloth drop and ordered everyone out whilst hastily dialing a number on his cell phone. All business now, he started reporting what he had just seen.

The last man to remain in the church was Carlo, curiously looking at the sanctum, but he, too, returned to the courtyard after the second police officer curtly pointed out that he should leave. Efthymis, though upset by what was happening, was discreetly observing the curious visitor, trying to understand who he was and what he was doing there.

Farther down the square the news was already spreading, shattering the peaceful life of the island.

* * *

The ferryboat had just left the port of Ikaria and I felt my spirits rise as soon as I set foot on the gangway. Travel always revived me.

I found a nice spot in the ship's lounge and sat looking toward the windows, which let in the warm sun rays and showered me with light.

The mayor himself had escorted me to the ferry, thanking me for participating in the conference. I, in turn, promised him and myself that I would vacation on the island the first chance I got. I had been impressed by the locals' carefree attitude and self-deprecation. They displayed their flaws first and then their virtues, a rarity among our species.

I took out my cell phone and laptop and looked for a plug to charge them, as they were both out of battery. The TV screen kept showing scenes from the disaster zone in Turkey and all the damage caused by the waterspout, while meteorologists warned of severe weather phenomena in the Aegean, due to last for quite a few days.

That was all I needed—to be stranded on the island and miss my flight to the US. However, I desperately wanted to see my parents before I left and clarify the situation with Petros. So there I was, in the middle of the sea, traveling to Athora.

In three hours at most, the ferry would dock at the port. I had plenty of time to think seriously about my relationship. There was no point in extending it any further, even if I had briefly entertained that option after the Gabriel fiasco. Life was pulling me in another direction, so not making the decision to end it now would only be prolonging the inevitable. I absolutely did not want to end up like those women who marry at some point simply to avoid a single life and then spend the rest of their lives lonely within a marriage.

The events of the previous night had opened up a chasm in me. Not just the rejection I had experienced, but because I felt, more than ever, the years drifting past and pushing everything I wanted to experience out of my reach.

In my confused state, I even thought of resigning for a moment, before I even had a chance to perform my new duties at the university. *Just because a man had not responded to my flirtatious overtures!* It was becoming obvious to me that I had been harboring many repressed feelings, which were now pouring out like a torrent, forcing me to deal with them. At least the anger that had been boiling inside me now seemed to subside.

I switched on my phone and saw I had many missed calls from my father. I tried to call him back, but it was impossible. There was no signal and, as one of the crew informed me, it would be so for the next couple of hours. It made sense, there was no other island on the way to Athora and the closest islands, Chios on one side and Andros on the other, were too many miles away for the signal to reach the boat.

I had no choice at present other than to admire the sea and drink the coffee I had bought at the bar.

As I sat daydreaming, a shadow fell on me, obscuring the sun rays I was basking in. I thought it was a trick of the light. A few steps from my table, Gabriel stood staring at me, equally dumbstruck.

He walked up to the table and sat beside me, explaining how he was planning to visit Athora for a short break and exclaimed, "what a coincidence!" when I informed him that I came from there. I tried hard to appear relaxed and hide how thrilled I felt. Wanting to dispel any clouds of discomfort between us, I looked around to make sure no one was listening and told him, "I apologize for last night. I could come up with a lot of excuses for my behavior, but..."

He touched my hand lightly and interrupted me. "You don't need to apologize for anything. We had been drinking, and I have to confess that I was not as unmoved as I appeared."

The way he looked at me sent shivers of pleasure through me. Unaware of the effect he was having on me, he continued, "As I told you, I'm not single. I don't mean the girl whose dress you ruined. I met her after the conference and she offered to give me a ride to the festival. Nothing else happened between us. I'm getting married in a couple of months. You are an extremely attractive woman, but I am happy with my wife and I'm not looking for anything else... anyone else."

I felt flattered by his discreetly flirtatious manner, which nonetheless left no room for misunderstandings. He was the kind of man I wanted to be with, faithful and reserved, able to resist any temptation. Petros thought I hadn't caught on to his little adventures with other women while I was away, but I simply never cared enough to bring it up, even though I had remained faithful- at least until the previous evening. If the man sitting across from me had responded, that would have been the first time I had ever cheated on anyone.

Just then, the strains of a song rang from the speaker, so perfect I could have picked it myself as the soundtrack to that moment. "Nevermind" by Leonard Cohen, and before I had a chance to say how much I loved that song I heard Gabriel say the words for me. "I love that song."

I smiled and didn't comment. I preferred to hide that we shared the same taste in music, worried that he might interpret it as me making another pass at him. I was being very cautious, even though what I felt was exactly the opposite of what I showed.

"How come you picked Athora for your vacation?" I asked, trying to change the mood of the moment. "It's not your typical tourist destination."

"The seclusion of Athora intrigued me. As an anthropologist, I wanted to observe the way of life and the behavior of the locals on such a location. This is my first visit to Greece and I thought I would make the most of this opportunity to visit a couple of islands. I'll move on to Lesbos afterward, to meet my wife. She is on the island, recording the refugee situation. She is an anthropologist, too."

A soft tenderness crept into his voice every time he mentioned her. I was impressed by the fact that he referred to her as his wife despite not being married yet.

While I drifted off on the waves of my own thoughts, Gabriel kept the conversation going by asking me, "Are you alone?"

He obviously wasn't referring to the present moment.

"The right question would be am I in love?" I replied waiting for his reaction, which was immediate.

"Are you?"

"I don't know if I've ever been..." I replied with unusual candor. This was the first time I discussed my personal life and I was doing it with a total stranger.

He looked baffled. "Love is like magic," he said with great warmth. "When you don't believe in it, it simply doesn't exist. People who try to analyze the magic of love suffer from incurable cynicism. When you fall in love, you have to let yourself go, to stop being afraid. To experience it, even when you know it will not lead anywhere."

It was one of the most beautiful and apt explanations of love I had ever heard. His point of view left me speechless and, to hide my awkwardness, I teasingly asked, "Did you come up with this or is it a famous saying?" *Incurable cynicism...how true in my case!*

He just smiled and changing tone and subject, said, "I really like the name of your island." He removed a laptop from his bag and turned it on.

"You get reception?" I asked watching him try to log on.

He looked at the screen and sighed. "No, no reception. I was trying to Google the origin of the name Athora to try and impress you, but..." He shrugged.

I watched his lips every time he spoke. Not only did he have a slight, imperceptible Spanish accent when he spoke English, I liked the way every time he ended a sentence his lips stayed slightly parted, as if waiting for a kiss. I hurriedly dismissed my thoughts before they once again led me astray and took on a more serious tone. "In antiquity, the name of the island was Hathor. According to the legend, the Egyptian goddess landed on the island during a terrible storm. To thank the locals who gave her and her companions food and shelter, Hathor built a small town, on the spot where the ancient Greeks later built theirs. A massive earthquake, around two and a half thousand years ago, destroyed it and most of it sank into the sea. That's when the island was split in two."

I realized I had piqued his interest, because he shifted slightly toward me, as if he did not want to miss a word. Encouraged by his attentiveness, I embellished my narrative and enjoyed his undivided attention. "Hathor was the goddess of love and rebirth, that's why she is compared to Venus, or Aphrodite as the Greeks call her. The Egyptians worshipped her as the Great Mother, who gave birth to all gods and mortals. However, she was also the goddess who led the dead to whatever lies after the body's death. So she simultaneously represents both sides of love and lovemaking: life and death."

"Man has always invented myths to try to explain the creation of the world and to reconcile itself with the idea of death. The element of love is present in nearly all ceremonies of worship," he observed looking at me intently. "Now that you are telling me all this, I remember reading a book on the subject. I think it's called *Death in Egypt.* Is that right?"

"*Love in Egypt,* if it's the same book we are talking about. I've read it."

"Yes, of course. I'm sorry, I interrupted you. Please go on."

I could feel his leg touch mine under the table, now that he had moved closer. I tried to disguise the effect it was having on me and keep my concentration. "In other words, Hathor is half-responsible for the name of my island. The other half of its origin is rather obvious. The fact that the island is lost in the middle of the sea made people call it "the island out of *thoria*," sight in Greek. Athora became the prevalent name, a blend of the ancient myth and the islands invisibility due to its location. Generally speaking, it is an island brimming with legends and stories."

"A-thora," he enunciated slowly, looking for my approval that he was pronouncing it properly.

I didn't have a chance to compliment him because the boat suddenly shuddered. My coffee cup tilted and Gabriel grabbed it in one swift movement to stop it from falling onto the floor. The weather had turned and the ferry rocked to the rhythm of the mounting waves. I looked at my fellow passengers. They all looked shaken at this sudden change in sailing conditions.

Gabriel stood up, trying to keep his balance. "I' m going to my cabin to lie down," he announced.

I was surprised that he had booked a cabin for such a brief journey, but I did not comment on it.

"I would invite you to come if you wanted to rest—"

"No thank you, I'm fine here," I interrupted him before he could finish his sentence. It was a knee-jerk reaction; I did not want him to think I wanted to be with him.

He picked up his bag and smiled, although I thought I could detect a worried look in his eyes. Swaying back and forth, he made his way to the corridor that led to the cabins. I followed his progress down the corridor until he reached a door at the end and turned to smile at me before going inside.

In the meantime, the waves had gotten stronger and the boat was now rocking wildly. I leaned my head against the back of the couch and tried to fight off my mounting nausea.

Athora *

Despite being an islander, I suffered in choppy seas. I wanted to sleep until we arrived, but every time I closed my eyes, I saw myself knocking on his door, going in, and in my fantasy, he responded with ardor. I wasn't about to censor my own imagination.

Chapter 8

The police had cordoned off the area surrounding the church with a yellow ribbon, but the crowd remained on the square talking loudly. The coffee shop's doors were closed, an unusual sight so early in the afternoon. Inside, Athora's chief of police had summoned the old woman and the man who had gone inside the priest's home, as well as Efthymis and Carlo, who were present when the body was found. He had asked all four to make a statement and each one of them had described what they had seen and done that morning.

The door suddenly swung open and one of the police officers entered brandishing his cell phone. "I've taken a lot of photos, sir, from all angles."

The chief of police looked at the photos and swallowed hard, disgusted. "Send them to Headquarters while we wait for the criminal investigators to land. They're taking a helicopter."

He pulled the police officer aside and spoke softly, so as not to be overheard. "This is very serious and we must handle it carefully. I have never seen anything like it. People high up on the chain of command were very interested in this, it's caused a stir. No one is to approach the scene of the crime without my permission. Okay, now go do as I said, Athens has been pestering me for those photos."

The police officer busied himself dispatching the photos while his superior approached Carlo and addressed him in English. "So you were at the square by accident and you decided to go inside the church just to see what was happening?"

"That's right. I didn't get the chance to see much, we were told to step outside. I only found out what was there later," he replied calmly.

"Where were you last night?"

"I was in the lobby until late at night. Then I went up to my room and came down for breakfast around eight. The staff can verify my movements."

"They already have," the chief stated drily, in a tone that implied he knew what he was doing and needed no instructions. He pursued the interrogation nonetheless, impassively observing Carlo's demeanor. "And how long do you intend to stay on our island?"

"As I already told you, I have a few meetings lined up concerning an investment in wind farms that the company I represent is considering. Here, on the island. A few more days, I can't exactly say. It will depend on how my meetings go. Now, if you don't have any more questions, I'd like to go."

The chief squinted at him, as if evaluating his request. Then, looking at the others standing by, he said, "You may return to your hotel for now. When the Athens team arrives, I'll call you back in. As you understand, I would not want you to leave, so I will ask you to hand over your passport until things become clearer. Also, to leave your phone number with the officer so we can contact you."

"I will do it, although I am not legally obliged to. My passport is in my car. I can go fetch it—"

"No need. My colleague will escort you to your car and you can hand it over to him."

It was plain he did not trust him, but Carlo pretended not to notice. "I hope you find the man you are looking for. I am at your disposal for anything you may need," he said with an eager smile.

The chief asked the remaining civilians to be patient for a little longer and walked to the police officer who had just finished sending the photos. He bent down and whispered in his ear, "There's something I don't like about that man. Watch his movements and I'll let you know to bring him in when the others arrive. Talk to the hotel, see if he goes there. I hope the port authority doesn't let anyone leave the port."

"No, sir. An Australian tourist traveling by sailboat made a fuss over the weather ban on departures, but when they threatened to lock him up, he calmed down. The ferry from Ikaria will be arriving shortly. Other than that, nothing comes in, nothing goes out."

"I was also told that they saw that crazy woman, Sophie, on the rocks just after the murder. We must find a way to talk to her."

"No objections, sir. But it will take me ages to get to her house and we are all needed here right now."

"Fine, leave it for now. I'll ask one of the locals to go get her. We need to question the refugees, too, but that can wait."

The police officer seemed perplexed by the idea that the refugees might have anything to do with the murder, but he did not have a chance to comment. His chief ordered him to escort the foreigner to his car.

Their appearance on the square caused a momentary hush. They moved through the silent, expectant crowd and down the narrow street that led to the car park. Like the chorus in a Classical Greek drama, the crowd followed their every move, vainly trying to detect some meaning in their words or gestures.

The sun was a pale haze of yellow, obscured by a bank of heavy dark clouds. The wind hissed and groaned as it fought its way through the winding streets, carrying the first drops of rain with it.

As soon as they turned down the path, the silence lifted. Timidly at first, the crowd resumed its speculations.

* * *

In a state of shock, I listened to the latest news from Athora. We were near the port, and the signal was better. The sea was calmer now, but I still felt dizzy and disorientated. My father told me the police had let him go home, but they would probably call him back once the detectives arrived from Athens.

I was so absorbed in what he was saying that I only became aware of Gabriel's presence once he was standing very close to me. He could tell from the look on my face that something was wrong. He turned to walk away but I motioned for him to sit down and wrapped up the call, not wanting to appear rude. In any case, I would shortly be able to talk to my parents in person. I hung up and gave Gabriel, who could not have understood a word of that call, a troubled look.

"Is everything okay?" he asked with genuine concern.

"I have bad news from Athora. Last night the priest was murdered at his house in the Chora and the island is gripped with unrest."

"Murdered? By whom?"

"They don't know yet. My father just happened to be there when they discovered the body and he told me it was a horrifying sight."

"Why would anyone want to kill the priest?"

"I have no idea. I'll find out more once we're on the island."

"Did you know him?"

"Not very well. He seemed to be a peaceful man and he helped all those in need. I can't imagine why anyone would want to kill him—inside the church, on the altar! He came to the island a few months ago, when the old priest died... of natural causes."

Gabriel stared at me in wide-eyed shock. "Inside the church?" he gasped. "That can't be random; there is symbolism in such an act. Do people of other religious persuasions live on Athora? In some cases the motives are religious."

"Many foreigners have moved to the island in recent years and yesterday a boatload of refugees arrived. But why point a finger at them?"

"It's just one of many possibilities. Now that I think about it, maybe I shouldn't disembark on Athora."

"What do you mean?" I cried out in alarm before I had a chance to control my reaction.

"It's not a good idea to have a vacation on an island where a tragedy has just happened. I'll move on to Lesbos, meet my wife a few days earlier."

As if magically wanting to grant my wish for Gabriel to stay, the captain's voice rang out from the speakers, announcing that due to the sudden change in weather the ship would spend the night at the port of Athora. A ban on departures had been issued across the Aegean.

"Man plans and God laughs," Gabriel said with a smile. "I guess now is an apt time to say that."

I felt a big grin struggle to escape my lips and it took all my self-control to stifle it. I raised my shoulders in what I hoped was a show of nonchalance, implying that nature had made that call.

"The way things have turned out, I would appreciate any recommendations about what I should do during my stay," he continued.

"Don't worry; I won't let you get bored. Where are you staying, Chora or Pera Mera?"

"I don't really know. The hotel is called "Vendaval," like the gusty southwest wind," he explained and I felt a wave of relief wash over me that he wasn't staying at Petros'. "Is it any good or should I move elsewhere?"

"It's one of the nicest hotels, especially if you get to stay in one of the secluded little villas."

"I think that's what I've booked. I noticed most hotels have wind names."

"Yes, they tend to avoid the usual names on Athora. Winds seem to prefer our island, so we thought we'd return the honor. They have wind names from all over the world, just like the island has residents from every corner of the earth." I suddenly remembered what he had said earlier, about the murder motives and a shadow flickered across my eyes.

"I'd better leave you. I can see you need a moment," he observed. "You could do without me making your head spin with all my que—"

"No, no, it's no trouble," I interrupted him. "The waves are doing a far better job of that," I joked and touched my forehead. The boat was still rocking back and forth, although the sea was calmer now that we were entering the port. "Please stay; you are helping me forget it."

I don't know whether it was my imagination, but I could detect something different in the way he looked at me. I broke the momentary lull by changing the subject. "Tell me about your work. I saw that you collaborate with a large research center."

"I do, in Sweden. Mostly, though, I work independently. My base is in Washington. Like you, I spend most of my time traveling and lecturing on my subject. I admire you paleontologists. Although our fields are connected, I always had an interest in that area."

"It's never too late. I love anthropology." Just then, I noticed a man who was staring at us. I raised my hand and waved; he was an acquaintance of my father. Ignoring the indiscreet looks he was giving us, I turned back to Gabriel.

"When do you start teaching at Berkeley?" he asked, showing that he had gone to the trouble of finding out some things about me.

"I should be at my post in two weeks, so I can prepare for my classes and coordinate future research."

"You were quite the talking point in our circles: the first woman to teach paleontology at Berkeley. The discovery of *Homo Naledi* by your team is a great find, but for me, the highlight was the discovery in Patagonia, when you guys found Dreadnought."

It was clear that his research had extended beyond reading my resume in the conference brochure. That discovery was truly important, bringing to light the largest dinosaur that had ever lived. I hastily pointed out that I was simply one of the scientists on the team, not the excavation leader.

He smiled at my modesty and said, "I would have loved to have been there when you made the discovery."

I could barely hold back from saying that yes, I would have loved that too. Instead, I switched gear and became the remote, matter-of-fact, scientist. "The excavation took a very long time, as did all the research. It really is an amazing feeling, to stand before the fossil of the greatest living thing to have walked the earth. An adult weighed as much as a herd of elephants. Its tail alone was thirty feet long. It is called Dreadnought because obviously, it had nothing to fear. What other dinosaur would dare mess with it?"

Gabriel nodded and gestured at the ferry. "I guess it must have been as big as this...only steadier." He paused and looked at me intently once again, lowering his voice. "Thank goodness these creatures became extinct; otherwise we wouldn't be here now...right?"

There it was again, that ambiguous look; as if the more time he spent in my company the more he liked me. The way he spoke that last sentence made him sound like an actor in a soap opera, but it did not bother me in the least. I was enthralled by the possibilities that seemed to open up before me. "That's right. Besides, our very existence is the result of a series of random events," I replied flirtatiously, feeling emboldened.

Before I had a chance to say more, the announcement that we were arriving at the port clipped my wings, as did the text alert coming from my cell phone. It was Petros, letting me know he was coming to pick me up. Talking to Gabriel, I had forgotten what was waiting for me on the island.

Gabriel produced a business card from his pocket and handed it to me. "I'm going to get my things," he announced. "If you have any free time during the next few days, I would love to see you again. If not, it was very... adventurous knowing you. I hope you find what you're looking for."

He did not linger to hear my reply but made a sharp turn and walked back to his cabin. His sudden rush to say goodbye puzzled me, but I imagined that he was in an awkward position too. It was a nice wish anyway, even if it did not sound plausible to me. I was afraid I would grow old without even having a chance to look.

I still had about ten minutes to wait, so I switched on my laptop to check my e-mail. I had saved the article on the Harpies and I thought now would be a good time to read it and see if I could make any sense of what Sophie had said that day at the cliff.

In Greek mythology, the Harpies were the half-human half-bird personification of storm winds. Also known as the hounds of Zeus, their twilight dance was likened to the end of the world. They snatched the spirits of the dead and led them to Hades or delivered those who had committed atrocious crimes to the Eumenides, the infernal goddesses of vengeance, for punishment. The article contained a host of interesting information, none of which shed any light on Sophie's words. What did any of this have to do with Lukas' accident?

I sat looking at the screen perplexed when a mail notification popped up in the corner. It was from Jose Marcus. The connection was slow. Waiting for the e-mail to appear, I gazed at the heavy clouds that seemed to have completely obscured the afternoon sun. When I looked at my screen again, I thought only part of the message had arrived. A single stark sentence stared at me from my screen.

It has begun.

* * *

As soon as I set foot on land, I was greeted by a blustery, wintry landscape. Dense dark clouds hung low over the hilltops and a squally wind drenched my face with sparse heavy droplets. It was as if the seasons had changed in the space of a few hours.

I saw Petros walk toward me hunched in a windbreaker and I unzipped my suitcase and fumbled around for a light linen jacket, shivering in the cold.

"Welcome," he said, and picked up my suitcase.

I kissed him on the cheek and turned to see whether Gabriel was coming down the gangway, but I could not see him in the small group that was making its way out of the ferry.

"Are you waiting for someone?" Petros impatiently asked.

"One of the speakers at the conference was traveling on the same ferry, but..."

"Who? Do I know him? We can wait for him if you like."

"No, there's no need. I might see him later since the boat is not leaving."

"Unbelievable, right?" Petros gently put his hand on my back and guided me in the direction of the car. "There is a ban on sailing and the weather is supposed to get worse. Everyone is having a go at the weather people for failing to predict it would turn."

I thought back to Professor Marcus' e-mail and wondered exactly what he meant. How did this message tie-in with what he had told me at Berkeley? I decided to write and ask as soon as I got home. "Tell me what happened to Father George," I said, anxious for more detail.

"What your father told you on the phone. Someone cut him up like an Easter lamb."

The man's raw bluntness never ceased to amaze me. Unperturbed, he continued, adding more and more hair-raising detail as he drove me home. "They found him naked on the altar with his balls chopped off."

The tires screeched as he suddenly stepped on the brakes. A dog had wandered into the middle of the road and stood there, growling and barking at the sky as if trying to warn it off. Peter honked, and as soon as the animal moved aside, he set off once again. "They've caught a couple of immigrants and they're interrogating them."

A feeling of outrage started to burn through me at the thought that the first people to be accused were the weakest, as if cruelty had a nationality. "Aren't they jumping to conclusions?" I asked, looking out at the trees bowing to the force of the wind in a strange balletic game of cat and mouse.

"I don't know. A group of detectives is flying here by helicopter, all the way from Athens. There's a rumor there have been other murders like this one."

"Where? On Athora?" I cried out, startled.

"Don't be silly! Other parts of the world. I don't know where and when. It all sounded very confusing. I guess we'll find out soon."

"Is my father okay?"

"He was kind of shaken, but he took a tranquilizer and is fine now. Actually, he was the first one to arrive at the scene of the crime. Luckily the priest was covered up, so he didn't see the whole mess."

"I can't believe it..."

"Never mind all that now. Did you have a good time on Ikaria?"

The question made me uneasy, but I managed to hide my awkwardness. "It was fine," I drily replied. "Didn't have much time to do anything."

"Sure you did! You went to a festival, didn't you? Your father told me." He looked at me with a sarcastic smirk.

For a moment, I thought he knew. Luckily, I reasoned that that was impossible. On the other hand, I hated feeling guilty about it. I deserved better than that and I chided myself for feeling any guilt toward Petros. "Yes, I went after the conference. The mayor invited us."

"So you had a good time, don't complain. Was the friend who traveled with you there too?"

"Yes."

"I see..." he said, his voice loaded with meaning. "An American is here," he said breaking the awkward silence that ensued. "He represents a company that builds wind farms. I've put Kimon on the case. If all goes well, they'll buy everything up on the hill, where your family has land too."

I was in no mood to talk about this. Petros kept a finger in every pie on the island, things I was not remotely interested in. I crossly put an end to the matter. "My father deals with these things. Talk to him if you are interested."

He did not seem to like my reply and sulked, staring fixedly at the road ahead. I chose not to say another word and we spent the rest of the drive in chilly silence. When we pulled up outside my house, Petros opened his door to get out, but I took his hand, forcing him to turn and face me. "It's better if you don't come in."

"What do you mean? Are you mad at me because I asked whether you had a good time?" He stared at me, incredulous.

"No, it's not that. I'd just like to be alone with my parents. We'll meet and talk as soon as possible."

"I can't wait to hear what you could possibly have to say."

"I need to rest, Petros, and we can talk about things tomorrow, calmly. I'm tired from the journey."

"And the partying," he snapped.

Even though I knew it was bad timing, I couldn't stop myself. "This is neither the time nor the place, but..." I paused wanting to make sure about what I was going to say. All the thoughts I had kept bottled up were about to burst out, right here, in a car that was being shaken by the strong gusts of wind. I took a deep breath and summoned whatever reserves of strength I had left. In a slow, determined voice, I spoke a single, simple sentence. "I'm ending our relationship."

Silence followed my declaration. Petros was stunned and looked at me as if I had just lost my mind. He was trying to decide whether I meant what I said. Before he had a chance to recover, I boldly continued. "I appreciate everything you've done for me, Petros. But I don't see how we can have a shared future. I am leaving to start a new life in just a few days. These past few years, we have seen each other every four months, briefly and pressed for time. Do you like that?"

"It doesn't matter what I like. What matters is what you've decided." His voice was cold. "I intended to give up everything for you, follow you to America. You should have at least let me know you were planning this. I'd made plans. Heck, I made an announcement about the two of us! What am I supposed to tell people? Everyone knows we're getting married soon."

If there had been any lingering chance that I might change my mind about Petros, it died with his last words. All he cared about was what people would think, not the essence of our relationship. I did not intend to bring up his infidelities. I just wanted this oppressive situation to be over as soon as possible. "We don't have to fight, Petros. Let us part in a civilized manner and get on with our lives. In any case, we won't be running into each other in the future."

He looked toward the house, where my mother stood in the doorway looking at us with a puzzled frown. She was probably wondering why we sat chatting in the car instead of going inside.

"Go now and we'll talk later," he said through gritted teeth. "You know, life is not as simple as you make it sound."

His white, pursed lips showed how upset he was. Not because he loved me or because he was devastated to lose me, but because his ego had received a blow, as had all the plans he had been making for the both of us.

"I won't be changing my mind. I'm asking you to respect my decision," I insisted. "We have nothing to gain by becoming enemies."

Putting an end to the discussion at that point, I opened the car door and turned away from him. He grabbed my arm in a tight grip and stopped me from getting out. "I was the one who helped you get back on your feet. Have you forgotten how you desperately tried to pull yourself together again? Who helped you then?"

I thought I had managed to bury the trauma deep inside me, out of reach. His words unearthed it in one fell swoop and brought back the nightmare of that man, ten years ago. I angrily pushed him away, grabbed my suitcase from the back seat and got out, slamming the door behind me.

He did not make a move, just watched me walk up to my mother, who took me in her arms. "Why isn't Petros coming?" she asked watching the car make a u-turn and speed away.

"He had some business..." I stammered, not wanting to tell her that we had just broken up.

"Sweetheart, why are you crying?"

"I'm not crying mum, it's the rain." I hurriedly dried my eyes and stepped inside the house.

"But...it's not raining," she said, looking at the dark sky.

* * *

The man in the baseball cap carefully picked his way through the rocks on Pera Mera. The strong gusts of wind hindered his progress, but he was determined to reach the sea passage that split the island in two and nothing was going to stand in his way.

The bridge in the distance was barely discernible, obscured by the thickening clouds. Visibility was poor.

He walked further down, trying to find a sheltered spot. Glancing up at the mountain across he spotted the chapel of the Virgin Mary bursting through the dense clouds, as if trying to fight them off. The waves echoed the groans of the swirling water below, as if the sea were writhing in agony with every violent knock against the rocks.

The sun was setting, and the grey sky grew gradually darker.

The man put down his backpack and took out a pair of binoculars. He wedged the backpack in a crevice and scanned the mountain across the bridge. It didn't take him long to find the pale light that escaped from the open door of the tiny house wedged into the mountainside. He pressed the record button in the binoculars' camera and zoomed in. The clouds made the image even grainier, but he went ahead and recorded the place anyway. Examining every inch of the wall with a slow, sweeping movement, he focused on the long knife hanging beside the entrance.

The owner did not seem to be around, but he spotted her a few minutes later. She was walking toward the house carrying a large stone, which she added to a tall pile by the front door.

The image was fuzzy and he could barely discern the woman moving outside the house like an elf; a long, slim silhouette, white hair and loose clothing billowing behind her.

A thick, silver cloud hindered his field of vision for a while. The small house disappeared in dark, misty vapors and only reappeared when the wind blew stronger than before. All signs of life had vanished. The door had closed and the lantern no longer shone.

The weather conditions were not conducive to a stakeout and it was getting darker with every passing minute. Soon he would not be able to see anything on his way back. The man looked at the sky and accepted that it was time to go. He picked up his backpack and, casting one last glance in the direction of the house, started to climb back up, letting the fog swallow him up as he moved away.

* * *

The coffee shop at the square had been turned into a makeshift police station while the officers waited for the homicide squad from Athens to arrive. Until that time, the local chief of police had let the witnesses return to their homes and would be recalling them when they needed them.

It was getting dark and the bad weather had forced most people to reluctantly leave the square. Serious crime was unheard of on Athora and the murder had excited and alarmed people in equal measure. A curious few remained, waiting to see how events would unfold.

A laptop had been brought in, and the chief of police had spent the afternoon online. Athens had informed him about the murders in Istanbul and Como and he tried to find as much information about them as possible.

Evidently troubled, he paid no attention to his cell phone, which had not stopped ringing all day. That changed when he saw the number. It was a call from headquarters. He scrambled to take the call and a disappointed look came over his face. Shaking his head from side to side, he asked for further instructions. A terse conversation followed and he soon hung up, beckoning one of the officers to approach. "We have a problem. The helicopter almost crashed because of the wind and had to turn back. Nothing flies until tomorrow lunchtime. It's going to reach 10 on the Beaufort scale in open waters."

"The body will start decomposing. What are we going to do? It's still in the sanctum; we can't leave it there any longer."

"They said the doctor should perform an initial autopsy. She will be guided by the coroner in Athens."

"I'm sorry sir, but I don't think a graduate on her service year is experienced enough."

"What do you suggest? I don't think there's another doctor on the island."

"Why don't we ask Meliou to help us? I heard she is here."

"But she's a paleontologist, not a doctor!" snapped the chief.

"She kind of is. She studied medicine in the US. I know Fotini well. Do you remember that Italian who cut his head open on the rocks three years ago? She stitched the wound. She gave Lukas first aid. We should call her and not risk embarrassing ourselves. I can't see another solution right now."

"You're right, I'd forgotten all about Meliou. Go get them both and we'll see. We'll use your cell phone to call Athens, the camera is better. The coroner can see what they are doing that way... if the signal is strong enough inside the church. In any case, we can't leave the body there any longer, for many reasons." He pointed to those who still lingered outside. "After the autopsy is done, we should video the crime scene. They want a video, all the details. Apparently, we need to take more photos. I don't understand why they want so many. Then we have to carry the body to a fridge, without contaminating the crime scene."

The police officer scratched his chin. "What about the funeral home? They have a mortuary fridge. We should move it there, there's no other choice."

"Okay. Call them to make arrangements, make sure nothing goes wrong. Call me when everyone is here, we all go in together. Post a guard at the funeral home. No one will be allowed in."

"Yes, sir," replied the police officer, but more instructions followed.

"Be careful, all of you. We can't mess this up. We need to find out if the priest had any family, notify them. I had a look, but couldn't find any relatives. Ask around in case one of the parishioners knows something. We've notified the metropolis in Chios, but still no reply. They must be in shock."

The police officer nodded he understood. Before leaving to carry out the orders, he stood by the laptop and curiously examined the screen. A page detailing the two other murders was open. "Exactly the same way, huh?" he asked, quickly scanning the document.

"No pictures, as you can tell, but yes, if the description is accurate, the method used was the same."

"So we have a serial killer on the island?"

"Maybe," replied the chief of police. "If one person did it."

* * *

I had barely had a chance to exchange a few words with my parents when I heard a knock at the door. I thought it was Petros, coming to demand an explanation. When I opened the door, I was taken aback to see my friend Stelios standing there, in his police uniform. He hastily told me that the homicide squad from Athens could not come and asked me to join the doctor to evaluate the crime scene and describe the condition of the body to the coroner because they had to move it.

I accepted without hesitation and, within half an hour, the three of us arrived at the church. The funeral home people were already waiting to transport the body when we would be done. They stood at the corner of the square closest to the church, surrounded by the few locals who were waiting to find out more about the heinous crime.

I buttoned up a wool jacket my mother had loaned me, feeling the cold wind pound through me. From the corner of my eye, I spotted Petros and Kimon outside the coffee shop. He was looking at me angrily, but I paid no attention. I had not felt this free in a long time and I was not going to abandon my newfound freedom by going back on my decision.

The chief of police came up to us and thanked us. The young doctor looked terrified. On the drive to the church, she had confided that this was her first corpse since qualifying. Stelios comforted her, telling her all she really had to do was sign a death certificate.

As for myself, I felt perfectly calm. My eyes had seen many horrors, especially on our expeditions in Africa, so I did not think the sight of a corpse would terrify me. Digging for fossils, we had often come across the mass graves of victims whose bodies were still decomposing. I was mostly upset by the fact that I had known the priest. We had talked on the trek to the chapel on the eve of the feast day and he had seemed like a kind man, eager to improve the life of the parish.

We entered the church and walked toward the Beautiful Gates of the Templon. The doctor walked beside me. I felt her grip my hand and stumble when the amputated corpse came in sight. She turned a deathly white and looked like she was about to faint. I held her up for a moment, then advised her to stay back and just confirm my observations from afar.

I pulled on the surgical gloves she handed me and walked up the nave. Taking a deep breath, I entered the sanctuary. The *avaton*, the prohibition on entry for women, had just fallen—for such a tragic reason, too.

The acrid smell of burning oil from the hanging vigil lamps filled the stuffy church, making me want to gasp for air; or, maybe, it was the view before me that made me feel like I was choking.

Stelios held a cell phone up close to my face. I could barely make out the blurry image of the coroner on the screen. I could hear his voice, but then sound and picture started to break up and suddenly disappeared altogether. I didn't know whether the bad weather or the thick stone walls were to blame, but we'd lost connection.

We exchanged glances filled with despair. Time was pressing. The priest had died hours ago and the body was starting to smell. With a nod, the chief of police gave me to understand that I was in charge now. That is how in the blink of an eye I found myself at the center of these gruesome events.

Realizing that everyone was counting on me, I shook off the tiredness that was numbing my mind and body and asked them to turn all the lights on. Then I focused on the task at hand.

From what I had managed to grasp during the brief conversation with the coroner, and what the chief had previously told me, Homicide needed details as to the kind of wounds the priest had suffered, as well as the cause of death.

Even with an initial, cursory examination, I could tell that the murderer's method had to do with some kind of ritual. Deaths accompanied by amputation were not uncommon in ancient religions. Often, during excavations, we would unearth skeletons bearing such marks. However, I had never seen anything like what lay on the altar table before me.

As I recounted the injuries in a loud, clear voice, I tried to fathom what kind of sick mind could have conceived such an act, even though the motive was clear: revenge. The crime was an act of vengeance. The amputated genitals, the removal of the thumbs and the stitched body parts showed the murderer's wrath toward the priest.

Stelios recorded my every move on his cell phone as I moved around the Altar. The corpse had started to turn purple and some faint bruising around his neck and on his face, like smudged finger marks, showed that the murderer had applied pressure on those points and that maybe death was due to asphyxiation.

Taking a closer look, I discovered a small prick mark on the carotid and a few drops of dried blood. He had probably drugged his victim to subdue him; he would have struggled to carry him here otherwise.

The knife that pierced the Achilles tendons was a plain kitchen knife, but with a long sharp blade. Bending down, I noticed another open wound close to the blade's point of entry on the priest's right ankle. While it seemed like a failed initial attempt to insert the blade, it was actually a completely different kind of cut. It was as if the murderer had looked for something in there.

I moved my hand toward the knife handle, and Stelios whispered that I should not touch it, to protect any possible fingerprints. I stood up and asked him to zoom in, and spent some more time examining the scene of the crime. When I felt I had covered everything, I asked if they needed anything else from me.

The chief of police held out his cell phone so I could speak to the coroner. Having tried to get through to him countless times while I was examining the body, he had finally succeeded.

I described the corpse's condition in detail and had to return to it a couple of times and look even more closely, to answer the coroner's questions. I could hear someone talking in English at the other end of the line, translating what I was saying to another party. I seemed to be in some kind of conference call. So foreign police were also involved in the case, I thought and remembered what Petros had told me. This was not a single case of murder.

Before returning the phone to the chief, I asked the coroner if they knew who the killer might be or what the motives were. He replied that it was not his place to answer, so I did not insist.

My part here was almost done. There was only one thing left to do. Before the funeral parlor people could come in and remove the body, I carefully pulled out the photo that was wedged under the priest's hands, where they had been sewn together. I had to get very close to the body to do that, and the stench of the cut-off genitals forced me to hold my breath for a few seconds. I placed the blood-drenched piece of evidence into a plastic folder that Stelios handed to me and delivered it to the chief.

We then covered the body with the sheet supplied by the funeral parlor and they carried it out on a stretcher. We all left the church except for Stelios and another officer who secured the area with tape.

The curious few who had remained gathered at the square watched our somber procession, dumbstruck as the events of the day sank in.

All of a sudden, a strong, swift gust of wind gripped the sheet and sent it high up the sky like a feather. I thought of the Harpies snatching the souls of the dead and a shiver ran down my spine.

Screams of horror escaped everyone's lips at the sight of the butchered body. Some of the women turned away, covering their eyes. The funeral parlor people dashed to the van and pushed the stretcher inside as quickly as they could, but the intervening few seconds were enough for everyone to understand that the murder that had taken place on the island had dimensions they would never have imagined.

Sheltering from the wind in the coffee shop a few minutes later, the police officers and I discussed what had taken place before my arrival. They would soon be returning to the police station at Pera Mera. The chief thought it necessary to fill me in on the two similar murders in Istanbul and Como. The doctor was not with us. She had preferred to return home and recover from the shock. She still looked so shaken when she had left us, I felt sorry for the poor girl.

"Do you think the murderer is still on the island?" I asked, feeling goosebumps at the thought.

"It's highly unlikely he managed to leave. The only vessel to dock at Athora today was the ferry from Ikaria, the one you were on, and it's not leaving until the weather improves. The port authorities have informed me that no ship left today, so the guy must still be out there." He paused to take a sip from a cup of tea. "I must leave you now. I still have things to do before the homicide team from Athens arrives—people to call, to question, to check who has recently arrived on the island and lots more. Thank you for your valuable help, Miss Meliou. You would have made an excellent coroner. I watched you in there and you seemed to know what you were doing. May I contact you again if I need to? Although I hope I won't have to."

"Please, don't hesitate. I'm shocked by what's happened and I hope you manage to solve it."

We all exited the coffee shop together. The owner was in a hurry to lock up and go home, exhausted, as he said, by the day's events. The people outside had returned home. There was no reason to stick around now that the body had been removed.

Saying goodbye to everyone, Stelios put his arm around my shoulders to shelter me from the cold wind. We walked to the police car so he could give me a ride home. Another car was parked behind it. The door swung open and Petros stepped out. "Shall I take you home?" he offered.

I looked at Stelios, who pulled away and stood at a loss. I asked him to get in the car and wait for me, then strode up to Petros. "Thank you, but I don't feel like talking right now. I'm too tired."

He opened his mouth to reply but I turned my back to him and walked off, speaking over my shoulder. "You shouldn't have treated me that way, Petros."

I hurried into the police car and left him standing there, staring at me open-mouthed.

An hour later, having explained to my parents what had happened, I took a bath and sat at the small desk in my room to send an e-mail to Professor Marcus, asking him to explain the meaning behind his message. I wondered what Gabriel was up to. Looking at the time, I was tempted to call him and ask him if he had settled in at his hotel, if he needed anything... any excuse would do.

* * *

Lying on the couch of the small, isolated hotel villa, Gabriel gazed out at the dark, angry sea that stretched beyond the balcony doors. The first drops of rain licked the glass and everything indicated a storm would soon be raging over the island. The wind whistled and howled and lightning bolts split the sky with ever-increasing fury, like skeletal fingers trying to touch the ground.

He slowly swirled a glass of white wine in one hand, he enjoyed watching nature's violence from the safety of the villa. Lost in his own thoughts, he looked expectantly at the threatening skies, as if waiting for some revelation, when a sound from the laptop perched on his knees interrupted his train of thought.

He looked at the screen, downed his wine in one long gulp and placed the glass on the floor, then hurriedly entered the address and the code that the page requested. Soon, a map of Greece appeared on the screen, nearly obscured by clouds. He moved the cursor over the Aegean and clicked on Athora. He could just about make the island's outline.

He typed some more and three small dots appeared in the nearby waters: one in Turkey, behind the island of Chios, one on the island of Limnos, and another one over the Cyclades.

He pressed play on a news video from an American TV network. The presenter was pointing to the same three dots on a similar map, facing the camera. "An unprecedented weather front has been developing over the Aegean Sea in Greece during these past few hours. Violent storms accompanied by gale-force winds are lining up in a wave of destruction and have already hit the Turkish shore and the wider area, disrupting transport and communications. Three ships in the region are already reported missing. It is unclear whether they were unable to reach a port in time or they disregarded weather warnings."

Gabriel sat up and placed the laptop on the coffee table in front of him, leaning into the screen, absorbed by the weather forecast. "The front is expected to improve in the coming hours. If not, the Aegean islands and the wider area may be facing the greatest storm on record."

He turned down the volume and looked outside, troubled by the turn of events, which were throwing his plans in disarray. He shook his head as if trying to shake off gloomy thoughts, and turned his attention back to the laptop, pressing a key. A photo covered the entire screen. He reached out and gently stroked the glass.

The crack of lightning striking nearby made him jump. The loud clap of rolling thunder almost drowned the buzzing sound coming from the coffee table. He picked up his cell phone and looked at the unknown number with a puzzled expression. He hesitated, but answered the call, speaking softly.

* * *

I guess I woke him up. I told him who I was, apologized for the late hour, and asked him if he preferred we hang up. He assured me I wasn't bothering him and that he was glad to hear from me.

His voice, as soft as a gentle caress, made me feel calmer and I lowered my voice in response. It felt like a hushed conversation, a secret only we two shared. I told him everything that had happened since we had last seen each other on the boat. He fell completely silent when I mentioned being asked to carry out an autopsy at the scene of the crime. I guess he was surprised.

He wanted to know the details, but I was in no mood to revisit the harrowing scene. I asked him what he was going to do now that he was stranded on the island and he told me there was nothing he could do other than wait. He had no choice.

We chatted for another five minutes. I did most of the talking, recommending things he could do, where he should eat, and how to kill time. The conversation then took a more personal turn.

I pictured his lips moving and staying parted at the end of each sentence, just as they had on the boat. I had retained such a vivid image of him I felt like he was sitting on the bed beside me and not at the other end of the line. I felt so attracted to him, even at a distance, and I wondered whether his sudden presence in my life was the trigger that had finally pushed me to tell Petros everything I felt was wrong with our relationship. I searched inside me for any residual feelings of guilt and found none.

He sounded like he was starting to relax and enjoy the conversation. He told me about his life. About his parents leaving Cuba for the US while he was still a baby. Both his parents had been scientists but had taken any job they could find to make a living after the move. He lost both parents and his twin sister in a car accident many years ago, while he was still in college.

I heard the catch in his voice and kept quiet, waiting for him to regain his composure. He spoke again to ask me about my life. I realized he did not wish to say more about his and didn't insist. I told him how I grew up on the island and won a scholarship to study medicine in the US, where I discovered the hidden world of paleontology and followed a different path.

As I spoke, I heard the beep of an incoming e-mail. Gabriel sensed my momentary distraction and offered to hang up, but I asked him to wait for a moment and opened Professor Marcus' e-mail, which I hurriedly read.

Athora *

Dear Fotini,

The weather in your part of the world will turn very violent. I see that you are unfortunately stranded there. I am about to join a teleconference with a group of scientists from all over the world. I guess you can imagine what the topic is. No, it's not your priest's murder.

I realized he was exceedingly well informed about everything, but had no clue as to how he managed that. Getting over my shock at seeing him mention the murder, I anxiously read on.

The weather you are about to experience is unprecedented in your region. Meteorologists forecast storms and gale-force winds, but my sources say it will be much, much worse. I hope they prove unreliable. I will know more after the teleconference, so you can expect another e-mail. I ask you to handle the information I have given you carefully, to avoid spreading panic.

This hurricane-like weather phenomenon will probably last for a few days. Do not be fooled by the 'eye of the storm', the initial indication that the storm is weakening. Take cover until the authorities tell you it is over. I will keep you posted. Goodnight and be careful.

* * *

Over at Pera Mera, two coastguards were holding a handcuffed man wearing a baseball cap by the elbows, escorting him to the police station.

The wind blew strong, whipping up the leaves that had fallen to the ground, whipping up the soil, and raising it all to the sky. It was very late and they made their way carefully through the dusky winding alleys. The sudden fog all but obscured the streetlights and all the windows had been shuttered against the bad weather.

Stelios met them at the entrance and told them to go straight into the chief's office. He was waiting for them there along with the taxi driver who had picked up the man at the beach and taken him to the port. The taxi driver had turned up at the police station an hour ago to inform the police, saying he had thought the man was acting "suspiciously" at the time. As soon as he heard about the priest's murder, he thought his passenger might have had something to do with it.

The foreigner raised his handcuffed wrists and shouted in English, "You have no right! Are there any charges against me? Am I under arrest so you bring me here in the middle of the night? I am a French citizen."

The chief asked one of the coastguards to remove the man's handcuffs and, as soon as they were off, pointed to a chair across his desk. "There has been a complaint against you by this man here. He broke the law transporting you after the shipwreck," he said, glaring at the taxi driver. "Your arrival has not been recorded and, as you understand, you have entered the country illegally."

The man pulled out his passport from his back pocket and placed it on the desk. "As I told you, I am a French citizen, therefore, a citizen of the European Union."

The chief picked up the passport and turned its pages slowly. "Mr. Azim Kadar, I see that you have recently visited Syria, as well as Istanbul about a month ago."

"I am of Syrian origin and I was in Istanbul on business."

"Have you visited Italy recently?" The chief walked around his desk to where Azim sat.

"No. I don't understand what any of this has to do with my arrest."

"If you are a French citizen, why did you not enter the country legally? Why did you come in with the refugees?"

"I don't think that is why you handcuffed me. Yes, I admit I entered the country illegally, but I had no other choice. That is all I can tell you right now, and if you insist on keeping me here, I would like to speak to a lawyer. I would also like to know the real reason you've brought me here."

The chief perched on the edge of his desk. "Your fellow passengers informed us that you were at the helm of the raft. So I could very easily charge you with—"

"Yes, I took over when the Turkish trafficker abandoned us in the middle of the sea and jumped onto another vessel that pulled alongside," Azim loudly protested.

The chief hushed him with a raised palm. "We know all that and we will get to it when the time comes. You are here for another matter. A priest was murdered last night at the Chora."

"What's that got to do with me?" shouted Azim, realizing the reason for his arrest.

"Where were you last night between 11 pm and 6 am?"

"I see...I see... Something happens in the world and of course Muslims are to blame," he said sarcastically, but changed his attitude when he saw the other man's eyes narrow. "I was at my hotel. I went out earlier, had some dinner, then I returned to my room. You don't think I had something to do with it?"

"These are difficult circumstances, Mr. Kadar, and we are only trying to do our job. We need to follow up and check everything. Since you will not tell us why you are here, we can only suspect—"

"I had nothing to do with the murder. I haven't even been to the Chora since I got here," he protested and then fell silent.

One of the coastguards spoke up just then, in Greek. He informed the chief that no one at the hotel had seen the man leave. The chief stood up, holding the passport. "We have confirmed that you were in your room last night," he explained. "Although of course, you could have snuck out without anyone noticing. You have managed to sneak onto the island after all. Your passport will have to stay here until Homicide arrives, from Athens. In any case, you won't be needing it in the next few days, not unless you are planning to swim away." He ignored Azim's displeased frown. "I will ask you to inform us of all your movements."

"My movements where?" Azim shouted, pointing to the flashes of lightning lighting up the windows.

The chief nodded in agreement and asked the two coastguards to escort Azim back to his hotel. As soon as they left, he told the taxi driver that he could go too and called Stelios into his office. "I don't know if he is involved in the murder," the chief answered his questioning look. He peered at the passport photo closely. "I'm sure he is hiding something, though, and we need to keep an eye on him. I'm willing to bet he isn't who he says he is."

He flung the passport in his desk drawer and picked up his jacket, motioning to Stelios to follow him outside. One of the roads leading to Pera Mera had collapsed under the weight of the debris the water was carrying down from the mountain.

* * *

Professor Marcus' words had disturbed me. I sat down to reply that I would impatiently wait for more news, apologizing to Gabriel. He wasn't at the other end of the line. I thought he must have got annoyed with the long wait, but then my phone rang. I picked it up hurriedly, without seeing the number and felt relieved when I heard him say we had been disconnected.

I didn't want to tell him exactly what I had just learned but spoke more generally about the bad weather. I lied that a meteorologist friend in the US had told me to be very careful in the coming days. He told me that he had already seen the weather warnings online and that he was upset to see his vacation plans go up in smoke.

We did not linger on the subject and quickly reverted to our previous conversation about our lives. Gradually, the conversation moved onto our personal lives, on love.

"On the boat, you told me that you didn't know if you had ever been in love."

"No, at least not the kind of 'in love' you were describing," I replied curtly, forcing him to make a long pause. I heard him blow out his breath, as if he had been disappointed.

"I hope it happens someday," he said and changed the topic, asking me about my parents.

He seemed very interested when I told him that my father used to work at the Town Hall Registry and that he kept an archive in our basement of everyone who had arrived on the island after the war, as well as any other interesting documents that he came across. He had records dating back to the time when the few Turks living on Athora collected taxes for the Ottoman Empire.

He asked to meet my father in the coming days—he was sure to learn many things that might interest an anthropologist, such as the composition and evolution of the population, social structure and much more. Mostly, though, it would keep him entertained while he remained trapped here by the weather.

We talked and talked about all sorts of things. As the hours passed by, I discovered that not only was he an attractive man, but a very sensitive human being as well. Gabriel knew when to probe delicately and make me open up and when to give me space. Like an expert tightrope walker, he could alternate between being distant and effusive, to the point where I often felt he was flirting with me but in a way that prevented me from making a move. That made things difficult for me, as the physical attraction I had initially felt was now compounded by a mental and spiritual connection, a feeling of...falling in love? No, I would not even contemplate that.

Outside the storm was intensifying. The screeching wind, the claps of thunder, the rain hammering the windowpanes all but drowned out the knock at my bedroom door. I asked Gabriel to hold the line once again and opened it to see my mother, who had anxiously come to check up on me. I told her I was fine, that she should go to bed.

As soon as she left, I returned to our phone call. I stretched out on the bed and, comfortably snug, resumed our conversation, savoring every word.

I felt so relaxed and at ease; without even realizing, I started to tell him what had happened in New York. It was a trauma in my past I was usually reluctant to revisit; an event I had shared with very few people. Had the police not arrived when they did, I would not be here today, I told him.

Silence followed the end of my story and I realized we had been disconnected once again. I had no idea how much of my confession he'd heard. It had all come spilling out of me, from the depths of my heart, an outpour that left no room for him to comment.

All my efforts to call him back proved fruitless. When the little envelope flashed on my screen, I knew the message was from him.

"I'm trying to call you but I can't get through. If you see this, text me. G."

Like an enthralled teenager, I immediately texted back. "Me too. It looks like we can only text."

The minutes went by with no response. Just when I became convinced he had gone to sleep, he texted back.

"Yes, it will be nice to talk in writing too. You had started telling me a story, but I only heard the very beginning before the line got cut. Would you like to text it?"

"It's a long, difficult story and I'd rather share it up close... or at least have you listening."

"Hahaha."

I stared at his reply, puzzled. "What does that mean?" I typed angrily.

"Whatever the three dots after 'up close' mean."

I felt thwarted. I did not know what to reply. As if sensing my unease, he texted first. "It's late and you need to rest. So do I. You had one tough day today..."

I could see he was still typing and couldn't wait for the words to show up.

"Let's go to sleep and come morning, we'll talk. We are stuck on the same island, we are sure to run into each other."

"You're right," I typed. "It's getting late and much as I enjoy talking to you..." Before I could press send, his text arrived and I deleted what I had been writing.

"Goodnight, Fotini..."

"Goodnight," I texted drily, no three dots or emoticons this time.

I was upset it ended so abruptly. I looked at the screen for a little longer and when it was obvious he wouldn't be sending another text, I went to the window. The glass was foggy with humidity. I flung it open recklessly and the wind and rain hit me as if an invisible hand had suddenly pushed me back.

I stood there feeling a wild impulse to stand up to the elements of nature, but I quickly realized it was a lost battle. I closed the shutters and turned my back to the storm raging outside.

On my bed, my phone gave a quick buzz. He'd just sent another message. I dived onto the mattress and picked it up. "I want you to know that, if things were different, I would have loved to have you here with me... Goodnight."

Happiness flooded through me. I had felt the same way throughout that long phone call, despite the long, gruesome day I'd had. "Me too..." I typed but could not send the message. No signal. I even tried to call him back, but it was useless.

The thought that Gabriel was in a serious relationship, that what we were doing was wrong, crossed my mind. The truth was I did not feel guilty; not about Petros, not about the other woman. For the first time in my life, I thought of my own feelings, without caring if people got hurt.

Disappointed I couldn't get through, I removed my drenched clothes and got under the covers. Feeling safe and sheltered in my room, I let the sounds of the storm lull me to sleep.

* * *

Gabriel had got off the couch and was leaning against the balcony doors, looking outside. Sheet lightning lit up his face. On the laptop behind him, Fotini's photo filled nearly half the screen. It was evident that her life had piqued his interest and that he had been trying to find out more about her. The newspaper article beneath the photo read, "Perpetrator dead after taking woman hostage in Manhattan basement flat."

* * *

Lying down in his hotel room, Azim watched the wind slam the tree branches against the window. Upset at having been brought in for questioning, he lay on his bed, but sleep eluded him. He felt imprisoned by the weather, stuck on the island when all he wanted to do was get away from it as quickly as he could.

He picked up the cell phone from the bedside table and tried to send the text he had written. "In a few days it will all be over and we can be together forever." Once again, the screen informed him that there was no network connection. For now, his message could not be sent.

He tried a few more times with the same result. Downcast, he turned to look at the window once again. The shadow of the raindrops streaming down the window fell on his face, like tears rolling unstoppably down his hollowed cheeks, making the sorrow etched on his face seem all the more desperate.

* * *

Holding an oil lamp in one hand, Sophie nervously circled the room that was her house. She went from wall to wall, feeling the rock in an attempt to locate the leak.

She had been living in this house for years, but the rocky walls had never leaked before. Luckily, the ground was inclined and the water coursed to the door instead of pooling inside.

Although the weather was becoming more agitated outside, calm reigned inside. She had sealed the windows with large stones and secured the door so that it resisted the fury of the wind.

She spent a few more minutes checking the walls, shook her hands dry, and placed the oil lamp on the table. She then walked to the door and pulled away the crumpled rug sealing the crack beneath the door, to let the water flow out of the room. As if she had just turned up the volume of the chaos reigning outside, the howling whistle of the wind snaked into the room bringing its frozen breath with it. It wound through the room, shaking the bunches of dried herbs hanging from the ceiling and chasing the stuffy air out of the dug-out house.

Suddenly, a low, growling rumble rippled down the mountain slope, shaking the lamp on the table and building up to an ever-increasing tremor. Small stones and soil started to fall from the ceiling. Sophie looked up, wondering what to do. Stay in or get out?

She was about to open the door when the thundering sound of falling rocks stopped her. She realized it was a landslide. It sounded like a giant stomping down the slope, dismantling the mountain rock by rock. The safest place for her to be right then was inside. If she stepped outside, she could end up crushed by the falling rocks, some of which she could hear pass inches from her door. The whole place shook like an earthquake, and a couple of the glass jars slipped from the shelves and crashed to the floor.

The nightmarish sound stopped after a while, but the wind and rain still roared.

Gripped by an anxious, bad feeling, Sophie tried to crack open the door and have a look outside. To her horror, she realized the door would not budge, not even an inch. She leaned her shoulder against it and pushed with all her might, over and over, but like a sealed tombstone the door remained shut, evidently blocked by a wall of rocks that had fallen on the other side.

Staying calm, she moved to one of the windows and tried to open the shutters. Nothing moved. She tried the other window; still nothing. Just like the door, they had been sealed shut. She was a prisoner in her own home, and try as she might to think of a way out, all exits were blocked.

Peals of distant thunder broke the silence, showing the storm was passing over, even though it still maintained its full force.

Despite her peaceful demeanor, Sophie was troubled. She fully realized the gravity of her predicament. She sat on a chair and tried to think about what she should do. At least she could feel the air blowing under the door, so she would not run out of oxygen. Breathing was not going to be enough, however; she had to prepare for a possible long stay buried inside her home.

She gathered her loose, long hair and pinned it back. She then stood up, determined, and picked out a few glass jars. She emptied their liquid contents through the crack in the door, so they could trickle outside, then moved to the crack in the walls where the water was coming in and secured a short piece of hosepipe. She placed the other end of the hose into one of the jars, which started to fill up. She was collecting water, the most valuable resource she would need to survive.

For the first time since her arrival on Athora, her life depended on others. The only way she could be free would be if help arrived from the outside.

* * *

In the darkened room, the bluish glow of a laptop belied that some kind of work was in progress. A man pulled his face up close to the screen, the cool glare making his features look like they had been sculpted from ice.

He raised his eyebrows and impatiently tapped his fingers on the table as he waited for the photos to load. When they did, the screen was filled with the naked, lifeless body of the priest on the altar.

He carefully clicked through the photos, attentively examining each one as it appeared on the screen. The close-ups clearly showed all the details of the repulsive crime.

The priest's lips had been stitched together with black thread, as if someone wanted to zip them up. His severed thumbs peeked out from the corners of his mouth. The eyes had also been stitched shut, so that the skin above the cheekbones met the eyebrows. Black thread joined his hands, the palms tightly pressed together above the man's chest as if the victim had been forced to keep them clasped in prayer. Beneath them, bloodstains obscured an already blurry photo and the faded image of the faces depicted. Like lumps of fresh meat, the amputated genitals had been placed on his stomach and his feet were bound at the ankles with rope and skewered together with a knife that passed through the Achilles tendons. It had all been done very methodically.

The man looked up and slowly lowered the screen. Keeping the lights off, he moved through the darkness to the door and slid it open. The wind invaded the room through the opening in a menacing whistle. He opened the door fully, stepping outside, and the howl abruptly stopped, as if a greedy mouth had just gulped it down.

Chapter 9

When I woke up, before I even opened my eyes, I could sense that all was calm outside. No rain, no thunder. Unwilling to abandon the comfort of my bed, I pulled the covers over my head and huddled down into my cozy cocoon. It did not last long. Soon, all the thoughts pushed aside by the night's slumber washed over me, forcing me to get up and look out the window.

The weather had improved considerably and only a strong breeze shook the branches of my father's olives in the orchard. The gray sky still looked menacing, as if it was only catching its breath before unleashing the next round.

I looked at the clock and realized that, even though it was still early, I had had a long, uninterrupted sleep, so I felt rested. The pleasant sensation of happy dreams, whose images were still blurry in my mind, sent a quiver through me.

I opened my laptop and saw that internet connection had been restored at some point during the evening, and a backlog of e-mails had filled my inbox. Now, however, no connection was available. I picked out the one sent by Professor Marcus and opened it immediately. The introduction sent alarm bells off in my head.

Dear Fotini,

We just finished the teleconference. A "weather bomb," that is, a low-pressure system whose central pressure falls rapidly in a process known as explosive cyclogenesis, will hit the wider area in the next few days, with Athora at its epicenter.

One cause is the continued violent disruption in the upper atmosphere. More significantly, it is caused by the sharp rise in the Aegean's sea temperature, recorded these past few months by floating platforms monitoring it, which we have set up in collaboration with Greek colleagues.

What you've seen these past few days are like a handgun's bullets compared to the megatons that will be unleashed by the weather bomb tonight. You can expect many violent storms, accompanied by intense lightning, heavy rainfall and hail, and strong gale-force winds that could exceed 12 on the Beaufort scale. The authorities in Greece have already been notified. The Greek islands have suffered extensive damage and many people are missing, but I guess you already know that.

Seek shelter in the coming days. What will follow will be unlike anything you have previously experienced. Find a safe place and store provisions. It is better to pick bunker-like basements without any other buildings on top. Most importantly, organize yourselves and keep calm. These conditions tend to awaken people's most feral survival instincts, leading them to unforeseen actions.

We cannot tell how long this weather will last. It will pass, certainly, but I cannot stress its ferocity.

I see there are communication difficulties in the wider area already. I hope you receive this message. Soon, it will all pass and I will see you lecturing at your post.

Once again, I stress the need for careful handling of the information I have given you. Panic can cause greater harm than whatever ignites the panic in the first place.

All my best,
Jose Marcus.
P.S. Have they caught the killer?

I tried hard to reply to thank him and reassure him I had received his message but to no avail. What I did manage to do was land back in the grim reality of the present with a thud. I already felt caught in the eye of the storm. I couldn't believe it. Asking me about the murder too, as an aside. *What a strange man! Why was he so interested in the murder? Maybe, for some reason, it interested the "committee" he was a member of,* I mused.

My mother, hearing me move around my room, called me down to breakfast. I got dressed and went downstairs, intending to grab a quick bite and step out to see what the situation on the island was, as well as find out what the authorities were planning in the face of the coming storm, while the lull in the weather still held.

As soon as I stepped off the last step, I was met with an unpleasant surprise. Seated beside my parents, Petros looked up and smiled when he saw me. I still hadn't told my parents about my decision to break up with him, so I hid my displeasure and bid everyone good morning.

At first, we spoke about the priest's murder and the weather. Before I could prepare them for the upcoming "weather bomb," another bomb exploded around the kitchen table. "Petros told us the good news, Fotini," my father said with a happy smile.

"What good news?" I slowly asked, feeling my throat dry as I could already guess.

"Your wedding! At Christmas... why are you even asking?"

It took all my strength to hide my anger and distress. I looked at my mother. I could tell she noticed how upset I was. She had already witnessed the scene in the car and could tell something was amiss. I did not intend to get into a fight with Petros in front of my parents, so I chose to ignore the whole subject. "I think we should focus on what's happening on the island right now. There will be plenty of time to clarify things, later," I stressed, giving Petros a warning look that he should drop this.

He carried on, regardless. "After the wedding, I'll move to California and return to the island for the summer season."

I could feel my temples pulse. I slammed down my coffee cup and tried to put an end to the conversation. "We'll discuss this when the time is right, Petros. *Then* we'll let my parents know." I glared at him, fuming. "Agreed?"

As if all was well, he nodded in agreement. I tried to fathom what he hoped to gain by acting in this manner. This was the kind of thing that happened decades ago, when marriages were arranged and the groom was just brought to the house and presented to his future wife as a *fait accompli*.

A look of thunder still on my face, I turned to my father. "Remind me, the old shelter at the Chora, the one they turned into a gallery, what kind of state is it in?"

My father hastily swallowed and looked at me in surprise. "It's fine. We went to see a photography exhibition there the other day, about the sea around Athora. They've done it up nicely, why do you ask?"

"How many people can it accommodate?" I asked, ignoring his question.

"For an event?"

"No, to stay there... for a few days... to shelter," I said. Everyone looked at me as if I'd gone mad.

"Shelter from what, honey?" my mother stammered. "We're not at war."

"Maybe war would be easier. I'd least we'd know what we were up against."

"What do you mean?" asked Petros, suddenly serious.

I gave them a brief outline of Professor Marcus' e-mail, without naming him and asked them to be very careful about how they spread the news; especially Petros, who knew many people.

My father was skeptical, saying it was the usual experts exaggerating. In any case, our cellar was well protected, he added, and could withstand anything the weather could throw at it.

I asked them to stock up on water, food and everything else necessary for a short stay and got up to go to the Chora. The phones were still not working and I wanted to find out if there had been any developments in the murder case, as well as how informed the police were about the approaching storm.

"We don't have any time to lose. I'll take the car and be back by lunchtime," I told my father, getting up and giving him a quick peck on the forehead. "Don't leave the house. Let the neighbors know so they can prepare, without alarming them."

"I'll give you a lift..." Petros offered, but I cut him off. "No, I'd better take my father's car; I have a lot to do. If I'm not back for any reason, I'll be at the shelter, so don't worry about me."

I did not leave any room for discussion; I grabbed a coat and the car keys and headed to the door. I hugged my mother, who had followed me outside. She held my hand, looking very worried. "Fotini, please be careful..."

* * *

On the drive to the Chora, I saw the damage caused by the storm during the night. Cut cables, uprooted trees, collapsed dry walls and flooded fields... If those were just a warning, I did not want to contemplate what would happen next.

I already sensed an invisible threat in the air. Black clouds seemed to be scudding toward Athora from all four corners of the horizon, locked in a deadly race to reach the island.

I wondered what Gabriel was up to, but there was no way of contacting him other than driving to his hotel and finding him. I chased that thought away.

As soon as I reached the square, I saw Stelios by the church, gesticulating wildly to a group of people who had once again gathered there. "Hello Fotini, good morning," he said, still frowning as he left the group and walked toward me.

"Good morning," I replied and pulled him further away to a more secluded spot, where we wouldn't be overheard. "Have you received the weather warning?"

"Our only contact with the outside world is through military radio. That's how we are communicating too," he said holding up a portable two-way radio. "We got a warning at dawn that the weather would worsen tonight.

That's what I was trying to tell them over there, that they should take precautions, but they won't listen."

"I don't know what you've been told, but I was warned that it will get a lot worse. Maybe you should make an announcement for people to gather at the shelter, or find a safe place to hide. We have a good, solid cellar but most people, especially the foreigners staying in bungalows, should lock up their houses and go there."

Petros looked at me, puzzled. "Are you saying that we should declare a state of emergency? The mayor and most of the council are in Psara, for the local authority conference. A small unit of around ten soldiers is stationed in Pera Mera, so, for now, all authority lies with the chief of police."

"Let's move somewhere quiet where you can radio him so I can speak to him. We haven't got much time."

Without another word, we moved to a clearing and, once he got through, I reported more or less everything Professor Marcus had said, citing sources in the US. He revealed that a new message had just been radioed to them, confirming that as of this evening the weather would turn very nasty. He agreed that we should encourage all those who did not have a safe place to stay to come to the shelter, but felt that an official announcement would only spread panic.

We decided to all meet at the Chora around 11.00 am, to coordinate our efforts: civilians, army, and the port authorities. I then asked him whether there was any news about the murder, but I understood that under the present circumstances the murder was no longer a priority. The only thing that troubled me was that Father George's killer was circulating freely among us.

It wasn't long before people started to fill the square. Phone lines and the internet were still down, and the only means of contact with the outside world were walkie-talkies. Some people had managed to pick up some news on the radio—and they were all disheartening. Skyros, Chios, and Andros had been devastated by the intense weather. Many were missing and feared dead.

Following our conversation, the chief of police decided some measures had to be put in place. He announced that the shelter would open for all those who wished to stay there for the duration of the storm. A generator would be installed at the shelter, as reports of power outages were coming in from various small villages around the island.

While he gave instructions for the transportation of provisions there, I saw Gabriel arrive. He waved hello from afar, but I couldn't go greet him until the end of the briefing.

Many of those gathered were foreigners who had moved to the island in the past decade, choosing Athora as their home and hoping for a peaceful retirement. Here was nature, now, upsetting those best-laid plans.

An agitated woman in her sixties kept saying that her partner had gone missing during the storm. The couple lived in a villa by the road leading to Pera Mera. From her words, I gathered that they had met on the island and been living together these past few years. She had looked for him everywhere, she said, and now she was getting worried. A small search party quickly formed to go help her search for the missing man. I feared that he would be our first casualty.

An hour later, Stelios returned running to the square. He had been ordered by the chief to make a tour of the island and report on the damage. "There's been a large landslide further up the mountain," he said, out of breath.

I felt caught in a disaster movie. Sophie's house was on that slope, I realized with a start. "I know the way there well," I said. "We should head out there and see if she needs help." I felt a lot of sympathy for the strange woman after the incident with Lukas. More than likely, the potion she had given him had saved his life.

Gabriel, making his way through the crowd, walked up to me. "I want to help."

Stelios heard him and nodded his acceptance, then shouted for volunteers to step forward. A group of men left to help the woman search for her missing partner. Others dispersed to go home or stayed to help organize the shelter.

I kept looking up at the sky, where the clouds seemed to be mounting their ambush on the small island of Athora.

Stelios gestured to another man to come help Gabriel and me. It was someone I had never seen before.

"I'm Carlo," he said in English, holding my hand a second longer than necessary, as if he wanted me to notice him. I pulled it back with a smile, paying no heed to the gesture.

"Let's go!" Stelios shouted, walking fast to the police jeep.

The two men sat in the back seat and, after introducing themselves, fell silent for the rest of the journey.

Driving past the supermarket, we balked at the scenes that greeted us. Like a pack of angry animals, people had lunged on a container of bottled water, pulling at the plastic wrapping to get to the bottles and shouting at each other. Some seemed ready to start exchanging punches; others exited the store with trolleys filled to the brim or hastily flung their shopping into their cars.

Stelios slammed on the brakes and stepped outside. Everyone ignored him, as if he were invisible. He started shouting at the top of his voice. Only then did he seem to catch their reluctant attention, along with annoyed looks. He was telling them to calm down. While he tried to restore some order, I saw Petros and Kimon leave the supermarket, each pushing a trolley loaded with food and other supplies. Realizing who it was that had spread the panic, I felt annoyed with myself for speaking in front of Petros and believing he would keep his mouth shut. It was now evident that peace was hanging by a thread and things could easily get out of control.

Stelios returned a few minutes later. We made our way up the mountain. My eyes met Gabriel's in the rearview mirror, but he was silent and only spoke when spoken to. I could detect some sadness in the way he looked at me and I wanted to ask him what the matter was, but I didn't get a chance. We met many obstacles along the way and had to stop often to clear the fallen rocks or large branches we could not circumvent.

Stelios would stop and warn everyone we crossed of the coming storm. On a deserted part of the drive, we saw a man coming toward us from the opposite direction.

"Where do you think you are going?" Stelios asked him sternly, in English, once we were near. I realized he knew the man.

"I was trying to get to the Chora, but I think I'm lost," the man replied.

Stelios thought about it for a moment and then gestured at the man to get inside the car, telling him he was coming with us to help. Even though it sounded like an abrupt order, the stranger readily agreed and squeezed in at the back with the other two. "Hi, I'm Azim. Can anyone tell me what's happening?" he anxiously asked.

I gave him a quick update on the situation and then turned to look ahead. In the distance, the clouds had become one with the sea, as if some hungry vortex was sucking them down to the depths.

We had left the main road and followed a dirt path until it came to an abrupt stop. Removing a coil of rope from the trunk, we started to walk along the narrow path that led to Sophie's house.

I soon realized that it would be impossible for us to reach the house this way. Large rocks blocked the road ahead. We would have to climb up to the peak and, hopefully, manage to make our way down the other side, circling the rocks blocking our way.

Everyone agreed. Stelios, looking in the direction of the house, called out Sophie's name a couple of times hoping for a response. Unfortunately, the only reply was the echo of his voice.

I described the route we should take, and Carlo led the way with the assurance of an experienced hiker. I followed, Gabriel walked behind me, and the other two came last. I could hear them talk about Azim being summoned to the police station, but the wind scattered most of their words out of my hearing range.

We paused to catch our breath and drink some water.

"Will you tell us why you are here?" Stelios asked Azim in an accusatory tone. "If you have a French passport why did you come to Greece with the refugees?"

Azim gave us a despairing look. With a deep sigh, he began to tell his story. "I'm engaged to a girl from Turkey. Her father has been accused of being a conspirator in the coup. They arrested him and now the police are looking for us, saying we are collaborators. My fiancée managed to get to France with a fake passport, but I was trapped in the country, so I tried to cross to Greece with my compatriots from Syria. All I want is to get to France and be with her." He wiped a tear from his cheek.

"But they won't stop looking for you. You should have told the authorities all of this when you arrived," Stelios commented, all stern and official.

"And get deported to Turkey, where, as we all know, justice will prevail," he said sarcastically. "You've heard how they treat prisoners, right?"

I thought this was neither the time nor the place for this and said so, looking at Stelios intently. He seemed to doubt Azim's story. I couldn't help but wonder if he was harboring some kind of prejudice. I felt moved by the way Azim spoke about his fiancée and about how impatient he was to be with her.

We didn't stop for long. We kept climbing, the peak coming into sight. Sophie's house was not too far from there. Pera Mera was visible across the small channel separating the island, as was a part of the bridge in the distance.

The higher up we climbed, the more I felt the sky get nearer, weigh down heavier, with every passing minute.

Out of breath, we reached the highest point, where Sophie had carved the rock: a wide open eye with a smaller eye in its iris, as if gestating it. There had been an uproar when she had done that. People had wanted to tear it down, but no one had dared to actually do it. Thus the peculiar monument remained, watching the island like a vigilant guard.

Down the other side of the peak, the mountain looked like it had been raked over by a set of giant claws. Large rocks had shifted and tumbled down. The path was no longer there. We picked our way down carefully among the boulders, estimating the direction of the house.

The landscape was completely different and the ground, though solid rock, seemed to have subsided after the torrential rain and wind. Even the *Anemotafia*—the wind tombs—lay scattered in pieces, dotted remnants showing where they had once stood. They must have been swept down into the cliff. If the legend was true, the winds had now been unleashed to bring destruction on earth. *Maybe that had already happened*, I wryly thought looking at the destruction around me.

I stopped at a point I assumed was the small plateau in front of the house and carefully peered at the heap of rocks before me. Between two enormous boulders, I could just about make out the corner of a window. It would be hard to access and it would take a very long time to move the rocks. As for anyone exiting the house, that would be impossible.

Stelios gave me one end of the rope to hold and started to climb over the rocks. A boulder had stopped horizontally, leaving an opening like a magic gate. I told him to wait until I had a sturdy grip on the rope. Almost immediately, Carlo, Gabriel, and Azim came near me, helping me hold the counterweight as Stelios started to climb down through the opening.

Gabriel wrapped his arms around my waist as we pulled on the rope. We exchanged a look. The scene at the festival in Ikaria flashed before my eyes, as did our evening phone call. Carlo cast us a questioning glance and I felt awkward at the thought that he might suspect something was going on between us.

I hurriedly turned to look through the small crack at Stelios, who was trying to see how he could get closer to the house buried behind the rocks and the loose soil. I prayed that Sophie had been able to hide, that she hadn't been wandering outside the house at the time of the landslide.

I carefully listened for any sounds of life. The silence was strange—this spot usually teamed with birds and wild goats.

A knock on the wooden door and the hollow sound of her voice confirmed that she was inside the house. We all heaved a sigh of relief. Stelios asked us to be quiet so he could talk to her. I asked the three strong men to hold the rope and started my climb, without any great difficulty.

I descended toward Stelios, who was perched against an opening trying to figure out a way to get to the door and get Sophie out. I froze when I heard a rumble and looked up, terrified, fearing another landslide. Thankfully, it was just a gust of wind. As soon as it had blown over, I kept moving and reached my friend. Disappointed, Stelios told me he could not see a way to get her out without the right equipment.

I tried to look for a way, but he was right. Even if all five of us worked together, I wasn't certain we could shift all the rocks that blocked the front of her house.

I called out her name and her steady response showed that she was calm. Before I had a chance to explain how things were, the same rumble rang out. The worried cries of the three men standing above us made us run to the crack between the rocks and look outside.

A waterspout had suddenly appeared and was sailing down the channel like a ghost ship, raising a column of water up into the clouds. The strong wind rocked the rope, nearly flinging the other against the rocks as they struggled to keep their balance. Luckily, it died down quickly and the funnel vanished as suddenly as it had appeared.

It was now clear we could not stay here long, but how could we possibly abandon the poor woman in there?

As soon as all was quiet again, I told her there was not much we could do, but we were all determined to give it our best shot.

I asked for two of them to come down and a third man to stay up for safety. Gabriel came down first, followed by Carlo. Stelios looked at Azim, who had wound the rope around a protrusion on one of the rocks and was pulling at the other end using his body as a counterweight. He didn't seem pleased that we had left the refugee on his own and grumbled something between gritted teeth.

We started moving the rocks as quickly as we could. We had to be careful how we shifted them. One faulty move and the whole pile could come crashing down on us.

We worked for a while with our bare hands, as no one had thought to bring the gloves from the jeep. Covered in mud, we only paused to hear Sophie tell us she could finally see us through a crack in the window. Stelios declared that there wasn't enough time to free her today, we would have to leave soon. Gabriel disagreed and said we had to try a little longer. I was impressed by his stance. Sophie was a complete stranger to him and he was acting as one would for a good friend. Carlo followed the exchange without saying a word.

Suddenly it went dark as if someone had switched off the sun. Surprised by the sudden change I looked up and to my horror did not see Azim at his post. When the others realized it too, they dashed to my side. "Damn it," Stelios shouted.

As if she could detect our frustration, Sophie urged us to leave. She had enough food and water for a few days and maybe it was better to return to the Chora and come back for her when things were calmer.

To leave, though, we would need a sturdy rope. I tugged on the rope lightly to test it and felt no resistance at the other end. I felt it sag and pulled my hand away sharply, as if I had just been stung. Azim had wound it around the rock but hadn't tied it and now the rope was unraveling and could fall down toward us at any moment, trapping us outside Sophie's house.

Stelios' curse pierced the air, so loud I was sure it could be heard all the way to Pera Mera. We saw Aziz appear at the opening gesticulating wildly that we should get up in a hurry. I couldn't make out his words but I could tell something was terribly wrong.

I asked him to secure the rope and told the others to start climbing. Stelios climbed up first, eager to give Azim a tongue-lashing. Carlo offered his place but I said he should go ahead. Soon enough he was out too. Now they all three stood with their backs half-turned turned, looking in the opposite direction.

"You go ahead," Gabriel said, gently touching my hand.

Even though I did not want to leave him last, the look in his eyes and my curiosity at the strange posture of the other three won. I started to climb up. I thought I heard Gabriel say something to Sophie behind me, possibly trying to keep her spirits up, and then he gripped the rope and started to climb up as I pulled myself through the opening. I turned and started to pull on the rope to speed up his ascent. Soon, he was standing beside me.

I wanted to ask him what he had told Sophie but the shouts from the other three, who were already forging their way up the mountain, forced us to hurry up behind them. I did not even have time to look in the direction they had been staring at.

Panting, we caught up with them at the peak by the carved stone, trying to stay upright against the blustery wind that was trying to knock us off our feet. I wondered why they had stopped and walked up to them. What I saw coming in from the east turned my blood to ice.

* * *

Over at Pera Mera, a group led by the chief of police hastily walked down the alley that led to the caldera.

A man in visible distress took long strides trying to keep up with the chief, all the time waving his arms wildly as he tried to describe what he had found on the rocks.

It did not take them long to get there. They all lined up on the ledge and looked down the cliff toward where the man was pointing a shaky finger. In one voice, everyone let out an exclamation of horror.

A naked male body was lying a few feet below. He had fallen on his back and his body had been skewered by the sharp rocks, pieces of flesh hanging off it.

The caldera was one of the most enchanting parts of the island. The sunset from that spot rivaling the famous sunsets of Santorini. This time, there was no magic to the view.

A woman started screaming when she saw the butchered body. It was the man's partner, who had just recognized his corpse. Howling, she stretched her arms toward him and called his name, refusing to believe his terrible fate.

"Everyone step back," ordered the chief, signaling to the officer accompanying him that he should escort the poor woman farther away. Her desperate sobs moved him and he approached her, trying to calm her down. It was impossible.

Gripped with grief, she tried to break free and climb over the ledge, as if she wanted to jump over to be near him. They struggled to pull her away from the grim sight.

The chief returned to the spot, accompanied by the officer and some of the others. They stood there looking at the body of the elderly man. The chief leaned over to get a better look, keeping a tight grip on the ledge to resist the strong wind that risked pushing him over the precipice.

"Such a shame! He must have fallen during last night's storm," said one of the men standing beside him.

The chief pushed himself upright and still keeping his eyes on the body, muttered grimly. "I doubt he came out here naked and I doubt he cut off his thumbs, sewed them into his mouth and then jumped..."

Everyone froze at his words and instinctively turned to look back at the crushed body.

"Same methodology as the priest's murder," commented the police officer. "What are we going to do chief? The weather is turning bad and..."

The howling sound made him stop talking and turn with everyone else toward the small channel, where a waterspout was majestically proceeding toward the bridge.

The all stared at it dumbstruck until it disappeared. Then the chief turned toward the officer. "Call Stelios and Meliou. It looks like the murderer is on the island and still at it. I thought he would stop with the priest. Obviously, I was wrong. Go radio Athens from the barracks first. I don't think we can get down to the body in this wind, but we must take photos and find a way to lift him up. What are we going to tell the poor woman? You go tell her, and I'll see what we can do."

As soon as the police officer left, the chief turned to the others who were looking at him expectantly. The woman's heartbreaking cries could still be heard in the distance. It was a tough decision to make and he felt his temples throb with pain. He looked up at the angry sky and the clouds circling the island in a frenzied dance and wondered what else was in store for them.

The sudden cry of a man urging them to look across gave him the answer. In a direct line with the Chora, though still several miles away, what was coming toward them left them speechless.

* * *

At the top of the mountain, we stood stunned and stared east, where a waterspout extended from the base of an enormous cloud down to the surface of the sea like a massive tree trunk, coming steadily toward us. Everything we had seen so far paled before this monster; it slowly gobbled up water and sucked it up into a spiral formed by the black clouds. Lightning split the horizon, stabbing the surface of the sea, which received the fury of the elements and responded by building up its own arsenal of massive waves.

We could not hear any thunderclaps, a sign that they were still quite far away. It would not be long, though, before the sea tornado made landfall, as the swirling clouds fed the waterspout and pushed it toward Athora.

"We have to go," Stelios screamed and started walking fast toward the car.

Gabriel looked at me as if waiting for my response and the other two remained frozen to the spot, mesmerized by the nightmarish sight. I wanted to stay and watch, too, but I suddenly realized that this was real life, not some TV screen I was looking at. I turned and followed Stelios, who was running downhill despite the rocks and stones in his path, shouting at the others to get moving.

I turned and saw Gabriel and Azim follow me. Carlo had taken out his phone and was taking pictures like some tourist. I urged him to come down and he replied that we should go ahead and he would catch up with us. I was puzzled, but could not waste any time thinking about it.

Farther down the slope, as we slowed down to cross a narrow passage, I turned and cast one last curious look at Carlo. He was walking in the opposite direction, holding his phone up to his ear. Gabriel came near and asked me what was going on.

"Carlo is still back up there and I think he's talking on the phone."

"How? There's no signal..." Gabriel pulled out his phone and looked at it. Azim followed suit. Neither of them could get a connection.

Gabriel spoke emphatically. "He is a grown man, Fotini. If he doesn't want to come, that's his problem. Let's go, we can't waste any time."

As if he could hear his words, Carlo turned and ran toward us. We did not wait up but started to make our way down in a hurry. I thought of Sophie, who was probably safer than we were at that moment. There was no imminent danger of another landslide and the large rocks in front of her house had suddenly become transformed from a prison to a castle that protected her.

We reached the car and hastily got inside, our eyes fixed on the beast fast approaching us. Stelios was driving like a maniac; I had to ask him to slow down or we would find ourselves at the bottom of a cliff.

I asked Carlo about the phone call and he said that he could get a connection for a moment but could not get through in the end. For some strange reason, I did not believe him.

I had no chance to ask any more questions. In a scared voice, Azim told us to look to the southwest, where heavy clouds and another waterspout were moving toward the island. It did not look as large as the one already upon us, but it was clear that the two together would be devastating.

I could hear someone calling Stelios over the radio. We all fell silent, as we listened to his colleague detail the second murder. Despite my shock and the static, which drowned out half his words, I could tell that the murder was strikingly similar to the death of Father George. It was as if a curse had fallen on Athora; the island was being tested by both gods and daemons in every possible way.

The man's report ended and we fell into a somber silence. Stelios broke the silence once we reached the Chora, asking if any of the three men wanted to get off here, since he and I would be making our way to Pera Mera as the chief had requested.

They decided to come with us, swept up in the frantic events unfolding around us, so we all headed toward the other side. I was thinking there was little I could do and that maybe it would be best if I returned home, but said nothing.

The traffic heading in the direction of the Chora was heavy, as many families were driving there to seek refuge in the shelter.

Driving past the newer homes of the foreigners, we saw their owners boarding up windows and doors and gathering what they could from their gardens. Stelios kept pausing to let them know about the shelter, but most seemed reluctant to leave.

I could not believe what was happening. I kept thinking that I was caught up in some disaster movie; that it would all magically stop when the director yelled, "Cut!"

The bridge soon appeared ahead. We drove up and were about to cross it when Carlo shouted for us to stop, grabbing Stelios by the shoulder. Startled, he stepped on the brakes and the car came to an abrupt stop nearly flinging me onto the dashboard. Annoyed, Stelios turned to Carlo to tell him off, but Carlo kept jabbing his finger toward the sea. It took a while for the fact that the bridge was now impossible to cross to sink in. Rows of large, looming waves were making their way down the channel, bursting high over its banks. It would not be long before they hit the bridge.

Stelios put the car in reverse and backed up to higher ground. Feeling relatively safe where we had stopped, we got out and waved our arms wildly over our heads, trying to warn off a car driving toward the bridge from the opposite side. We screamed and jumped up and down, but we were obviously too far away.

Without thinking about it, I made to dash toward the bridge, but Gabriel grabbed my arm and held me back. I could only pray that the car would manage to cross the bridge before the waves hit and swept it off. Someone driving further up the hill realized what was happening and stopped, honking frantically.

The driver only realized what was happening once he was halfway across the bridge. He tried to brake and then reverse, instead of stepping down on the gas pedal and speeding across. In his panic, he crashed into the railings. He tried to move forward but the fender was caught. Desperate, the man stepped out and opened one of the back doors, picking up a small girl from the backseat.

My blood froze as I watched him desperately run toward the direction he had come from. His feet splashed in water. The waves had raised the water level and the sea was now flooding the bridge. I had seen many things in my life, but seeing the distressed father trying to save his child shocked me to my core.

We shared his agony as we saw him cross the last few meters at the end of the bridge, where the other car's driver stood waiting and motioned for him to hurry.

Under the pressure of the torrential waves, the bridge suddenly buckled and the man lost his footing and fell. The little girl stood up, sobbing, and stretched her hands to her father who summoned all his strength, picked her up and reached the end of the bridge.

The dent in the bridge now made it slope up toward the land at that point. It was impossible for him to climb up with a child in his hands. He lifted his daughter as high as he could for the other man to grab her.

I sighed with relief when I saw the girl change hands and a woman lead her back to the car and away from danger a few seconds later.

It was like watching a silent movie. The strong wind and the sound of the crashing waves drowned out any voices and filled our ears with a cacophony of howls and crashes.

The first waves now smashed onto the bridge, sweeping the car away. It bobbed down the channel like a small paper boat. They pounded the bridge in quick succession and pounced on the unlucky father, who was holding onto a protruding iron rod trying to make his way up the sloping edge of the bridge. He sank beneath the torrential waters.

The other man, who up until that moment had stood on the edge trying to grab the father's hand, stepped back at the very last second and managed to get away, running back to the woman and the shocked child.

I could feel the wind drying the tears falling down my cheeks. Gabriel's warm touch on my hand made me jump and ask that we search the waters carefully, in case we spotted the man among the waves.

I thought I saw something move. Believing it was the man's body, I started running to the water's edge, heedless of the danger. The hope that maybe I could save him spurred me on to run faster than ever. Behind me, the four men shouted at me to stop, but, as if propelled by a higher force, I reached the edge where the waves were breaking and stood to scan the waters.

I do not know how I ended up in the water myself; it happened in a split second. I tried to swim but the current was so strong I could not overcome it, so I let it swallow me up.

A sudden knock on my head sent a sharp shock of pain through my body, but then a strange calm flooded me as water filled my mouth uninhibited and everything around me became a blur.

Athora *

Chapter 10

A small bus was waiting to carry to the Chora the last people who wished to stay at the shelter. Fotini's parents were among them. Before they boarded the bus, they asked the coastguard organizing the departure to radio Stelios, so he could then let their daughter know of the change in their plans.

The clock was ticking and everyone was tense and agitated, so the man said it would have to wait, but promised to do so later.

Alarmed at the approaching weather, they climbed onto the bus and hoped Fotini would be safe. Efthymis was carefully holding an old, worn book with a plastic cover. On its cover, a print showed body parts laid out on a surgical table.

The coastguard threw a few blankets in the bus and closed the door. He shouted at the driver to set off and said goodbye to those who had decided to brave the storm in their own homes, urging them to return there.

Shortly the bus was driving down to the Chora, the vast waterspout reflected on its foggy, wet windows, the distant, otherworldly rumble of thunder ringing in the approaching wrath of nature.

* * *

The four men ran across the channel's banks trying to locate Fotini's body that had been swallowed up by the crashing waves.

Gabriel, gripped with despair, took off his jacket and, before anyone could stop him, dived into the choppy waters. He bobbed on the surface for a few moments looking around him and then, diving under, disappeared beneath the surface.

Stelios, Azim, and Carlo looked at each other, panicking as another row of waves broke into the channel. They shouted at Gabriel to turn back, but he could no longer hear them. If Gabriel did not find Fotini in time, both would be dead, swept away by the waves like the little girl's father.

With mounting anxiety, they scanned the murky water for some hopeful sign, and as the seconds ticked past their hopes sunk.

Suddenly, a head appeared on the surface. Gabriel was sucking in air hungrily, as if gasping for breath for the first time in his life. He was trying to swim to the shore, cutting through the waters with one arm. With his other hand, he was pulling Fotini, whom he had brought up to the surface. There was barely any time left; the next set of waves was rapidly approaching.

Azim waded into the water screaming at Carlo and Stelios to form a human chain to reach Gabriel, who seemed to be losing his strength and was struggling to keep his head above the water.

When they finally pulled him out, they grabbed Fotini's unconscious body and clambered up the sharp rocks. Drenched and exhausted, they reached a safe height where the massive waves could not reach them.

A few seconds later, the waves crashed through the channel, pounding the bridge until it collapsed. They carried its fragments along their wild course.

Carlo stretched Fotini down on a rock and kneeled next to her. He tilted her head back lightly and checked for breathing. Placing the heels of his hands on her chest, he started compressions. He then tilted her head back again, parted her lips and, covering them with his mouth, breathed oxygen into her lungs.

Gabriel, exhausted, was lying down on his back, arms widespread, trying to breathe, while Azim and Stelios knelt next to Carlo watching, worried, ready to assist him whenever he needed it.

Carlo, though, seemed to know what he was doing and fought on, struggling with hands and breath to bring Fotini back to life.

* * *

Over at Pera Mera, the chief saw the waterspouts approaching and realized that they were now entering the final countdown. He asked everyone to leave the caldera and seek shelter in a safe place. Anyone who wanted to could accompany him to the army barracks where the soldiers had readied a large basement. Most preferred to remain in their own homes, despite knowing the great risks involved.

He cast a final glance at the corpse down the cliff and strode off determinedly, followed by those who had decided to accompany him. The top priority right now was to find shelter from the storm. He would deal with the murders later.

* * *

I felt discomfort seize my body, which shook under an inexplicable, pounding pressure on my chest. Seconds later, a soft touch on my lips filled my body with an unprecedented sense of pleasure and the breath of life. I wanted to stay wrapped in that feeling, but I also wanted to breathe.

I stretched my hands out and gripped onto something soft, which registered as clothing in some obscure part of my brain, and then I started to expel salt water, feeling my lungs burn with release.

I could not see anything clearly. My eyes were blurry and stung. As if someone had just interrupted the most beautiful dream, I started to rub my eyes to try to understand where I was.

Two pairs of hands pulled my fists away and a voice told me to stay calm. In my haze, I recognized Stelios' voice, which then became softer, telling me I had given them a fright but that I was now safe.

"My head hurts and I can't see," I stammered.

"You have a cut on your forehead and the blood is pouring into your eyes," said Carlo's voice. As if someone had sharply pulled a curtain to let the light in, I remembered everything. "Did you find the father?" I asked anxiously.

Their silence was enough for me to understand the unhappy outcome.

"The little girl is safe... right?" I asked, hoping nothing had changed while I was underwater.

"She made it. She went with the couple who rescued her," Stelios replied and urged me to get up because we had to get to the Chora immediately.

Still dizzy, I obeyed. Supported by them, I stepped toward the car, stumbling everywhere and slowing them all down. Azim offered to carry me to save time, so without any hesitation I climbed onto his back, wrapping my arms around his neck and my legs around his waist.

I don't know whether it was because of my near blindness, but what I could hear terrified me. The wind growled like a wild, ferocious beast, lunging at us as if it wanted to tear us to pieces.

When we reached the jeep, I stepped down and blindly thanked Azim. Stelios started rinsing my eyes with a bottle of water, which he then handed to me. I continued rinsing while he fetched a bandage for my bleeding forehead from the first aid kit in the trunk.

I could feel my chest burn with salt water. I took a few sips from the bottle in an attempt to assuage that sensation and then emptied the rest into my eyes.

When I was finally able to see, I turned in the direction of the male voices I had been hearing. They had all fallen silent. Stelios, still holding onto the bandage, was standing beside the others. All three were watching the giant waterspout reach the smaller one and slowly swallow it up, like a boa gulping down its prey. The new, swollen water tornado then started to move toward Athora. Our worst fears had just become a reality.

We dashed into the car and once again sprinted off in a race against time. Azim hastily tied the bandage around my forehead, explaining how Gabriel had dived into the sea to save me. I still wondered at my own audacity, at how I had found the courage to jump into the water. Perhaps it was my desperate need to preserve the father for that little girl. Unfortunately, I had failed.

Realizing that they had all saved my life, I leaned forward filled with gratitude. "Thank you, I'll never forget it."

I felt a bit embarrassed looking at Carlo, who had brought me back from the dead with the kiss of life. I could still feel his lips against mine.

Stelios radioed the chief, explaining what had happened. Their conversation was constantly interrupted by static, and we could only hear half of what was being said at the other end, filling the gaps with our own guesses. Over at Pera Mera, they had just learned that the bridge had collapsed and they waited for the storm to hit, cut off from the rest of the island. They had been forced to leave the body on the cliff and would be dealing with it once the storm had eased.

This is complete madness, I thought. *As if a ticking weather bomb is not enough, we have a lunatic on a killing spree.* I was curious about the man's motives, about why he followed such a precise ritual when he killed. He was avenging something; that much was clear. But what?

Lost in my own train of thought, I came back to the present when I saw the now enormous water tornado nearing. Despite myself, I once again felt stunned awe at the majestic power of nature. I recalled some of the most terrible natural disasters brought on by similar weather, leaving thousands of victims in their wake. I hoped that the waterspout was not the forerunner to something similar happening. If it reached that kind of scale, it would wipe us all out.

This time the streets were empty. Everyone was locked up somewhere, and I hoped my parents were down in their cellar. I desperately wished I could be with them, but the nearest safe place was the shelter.

When the car took the turn that led to the Chora, I felt greatly relieved. Soon, we would be safe. Stelios squeezed the jeep through a narrow side street. Moments later, we arrived at the now deserted square by the church and pulled over. We got out of the car, and to my great surprise, I saw my father run toward us, holding his jacket over his head to protect himself from the squall. I fell into his arms. "How did you get here? Mum...?"

"She is inside, Fotini. They passed by and asked us and we decided to come to the shelter." He touched my clothes and the bandage on my head. "You are drenched," he said with a worried frown. "You are hurt! What happened?"

Lightning lit up the square, dispersing the twilight cast by the low storm clouds, a sign that we should hurry. "Not now, I'll tell you later," I replied and we all ran to the shelter. The booming crack of thunder drowned the sound of the heavy door closing behind us.

* * *

The enormous tornadic waterspout was about to make landfall, threatening to swallow up everything in its wake. It was not alone. Other, smaller waterspouts snaked behind it, appearing seemingly out of nowhere. Like a nest of vipers on the loose, they twisted their tails up to the sky and kept their mouths on the surface of the sea, sucking up water and growing larger as they neared the island, ready to unleash their venom on Athora and the seas around it.

The island seemed deserted, as if abandoned by its inhabitants to face nature's wrath alone.

A roar tore through the air like the death throes of an injured animal and the tornado struck land.

If anyone expected the force of the waterspouts to weaken once they hit land, they would have been stunned to see exactly the opposite happen. As if propelled by a strange power, the tornado sucked up everything the gale shook loose as it approached the island's interior.

It hit the dock first, upturning and scattering the small boats like a child throwing its toys in a tantrum. It lifted a speedboat up in the air and spun it, toying with it before sending it crashing down on the main road, where it became a mass of splintered parts.

Like cardboard props on a hastily assembled film set, any loose objects in its path succumbed to the force of the wind, which broke them up and hurled them in every direction. It lifted the soil off the ground, turning the air into an eerie sandstorm filled with debris and salt-water.

Relentless, the tornado pursued its destructive path toward the mountain, hammering the chapel of the Virgin Mary. The bell rang flat in the throes of the wind; an irregular, flat, mournful sound. On the peak across, the large boulder Sophie had carved stayed rooted in the ground like a soldier making a last stand against the approaching enemy hordes.

A little further down, imprisoned and protected, tears run down Sophie's face as she heard her beloved island succumb to the forces of destruction. Glued to the window, she watched the apocalyptic scenes unfolding before her through the crack and the small opening her rescuers had managed to open up before it.

A loud rumble caused her to pull away, fearing another landslide. Like domino pieces, the rocks shifted and started tumbling down one after the other as the ground gave way and started to fall into the sea.

Sophie heard her door creak and suddenly, as if pushed by a ferocious hand, it flung open violently, slamming into the wall and letting the gale invade the cave-like house. Its screams terrified her and she ran to the door, trying to push it shut, desperately fumbling at the latch, but it was impossible. The wind was stronger than any human.

Giving up, she stood in the doorway, gripping the sides of the frame to keep her balance, and looked outside. Through the haze of the storm, she saw that the small plateau that had stood before her house had disappeared down the cliff, as had the large *Anemotafia* that had kept her buried inside it. Only a narrow rocky ledge, barely two meters wide, separated her from the abyss.

Athora *

Chapter II

Entering the shelter, I asked my three companions to refrain from telling my parents what had happened so as not to upset them. We had to organize our stay first. There would be plenty of time to discuss the tragic events of the day later. I felt giddy to be alive. The thought that I had almost drowned filled me with the warmest gratitude for my saviors.

We first helped the refugees settle. They were all here, as they had no other place to hide. As if the trauma they had suffered in their homeland wasn't enough, they now had to go through this. Some of the locals reacted negatively when they heard the refugees would be sharing their shelter, but the majority held sway, protesting that we could not abandon them to the whims of the storm.

Exhausted and emotional, hugging their children tightly, they thanked us for taking them in. Acting as an interpreter, Azim explained the storm alert and then told us they wished for the women and children to go to one of the rooms being laid out with blankets, to lie down.

My parents and some of their neighbors were still stacking shelves with whatever food they had managed to bring from their homes, while Stelios and two coastguards gave directions to people about how the provisions already assembled should be stored and where they should go.

Luckily, the shelter had been recently renovated to become an exhibition space. The islanders had built it at the time of the Ottoman Empire, to hide their stores from the pirates who plagued the region. It was used as a warehouse by the Italians during the Second World War, who extended it by digging out the rocky mountain behind it.

The door opened into a small hallway leading into the main exhibition area, which was surrounded by a tiny kitchen and three or four smaller rooms. Veering off from the hallway, a long corridor led to the tunnels and some other rooms, which we were told were locked and off limits, as they had not been renovated. Some claimed one of the tunnels stretched all the way under the Chora and came out at the top of the mountain. No one had been inside it in recent memory, so the rumor remained unconfirmed.

I had not been inside the shelter in years and was impressed by the changes. Photos from the most recent exhibition still hung on the walls, depicting tranquil seascapes from around the island. *The Lure of the Sea* read the sign by the entrance. *How ironic,* I thought, thinking of the storm raging outside.

The walls of the shelter were so thick that only muffled sounds came from the outside. The wind whistled through the air vents. Dull thuds and screeching could be heard, objects falling on the cobbled area by the front door or being dragged by the wind. It was strange to think that when this was over I would see the sea once again, as calm and inviting as it looked on the photos. I was sure to appreciate it when that happened.

I estimated there were roughly a hundred people gathered at the shelter; a tiny portion of the island's population, which numbered over three thousand. Perhaps ignorant of the dangers involved, most people believed they would be safe in their homes. Those living in the more isolated areas had probably not even heard the warning. It had all happened so fast it was amazing we had managed to reach so many people in the first place.

Without warning, the lights flickered for a few seconds and then died out. The room was plunged into darkness. Worried cries rang out, but were quickly drowned out by Stelios' reassuring voice that the generator would soon kick in. Before he could even finish his sentence, a dim yellowish light filled the room, as the lights trembled feebly because of the low voltage.

I watched an old man fiddle with the dials of an old radio on his lap, trying to find out what was happening in the rest of Greece and felt like I had traveled back in time. The extreme weather was sure to sweep through the country and I dreaded the news that would await us once it was over. At the same time, I fervently hoped it would be over soon.

I wished I could speak to Professor Marcus and find out what was happening first hand, but even on a clear day, it would have been hard to get a signal through the thick walls of the shelter.

A gentle tap on my shoulder made me jump. The doctor was standing behind me, her medical bag in her hand. She asked me to sit down somewhere so she could check the gash on my forehead. With all the preparations going on, I had forgotten all about it.

I immediately thought of my four saviors. I could spot Stelios and Azim nearby. I looked around the room trying to locate Gabriel and Carlo, but they were nowhere to be seen.

I moved to a wooden bench below one of the ceiling lights and sat down. The smell of iodine hit my nostrils as the doctor opened the bag. Standing above me, she cleaned the wound. "It'll need a couple of stitches," she said. I nodded my consent. To my surprise, I hardly felt anything but a sting. She was done in a few minutes, wrapping a clean bandage around my head. "How are you feeling?" she asked.

"Much better, thank you. My chest burns, though, from all the sea water I swallowed."

"I'd recommend you take it easy for a couple of days. Maybe you should take an antibiotic."

"I don't think I need one at this point. Look, never mind me, you really should be tending to the refugee children who came in soaked," I smiled. "Thank you for all the help." She took the hint, smiled, and left me.

I shivered. My own clothes were drenched and the room was humid. I had to change into something dry, urgently.

As if she could read my thoughts, my mother approached holding a small duffel bag. "There's dry clothes in here. Go change, please, you'll catch your death in a minute if you don't dry off."

I stood up, took the bag and gave her a hug and a quick kiss on the cheek. Stelios' voice rang out just then, asking everyone to gather in the exhibition room to discuss some matters in ten minutes. I had to find a more private spot to change quickly.

Walking through the crowd toward the exit, I spotted Gabriel lining up some benches and covering them with blankets. Locals and refugees alike were helping him out. I thought how when things got hard people either joined forces or turned on each other. I was glad to see us try to cope with the difficult circumstances that had befallen us united.

I remembered the corridor that veered off to the right of the entrance, dotted with a couple of small rooms to the left and right. I walked into one of those rooms and stood still at the door, giving my eyes a chance to focus in the semi-darkness. The musty smell was more intense here and the room was as cold as a butcher's walk-in fridge. Trembling with cold, I walked a little bit further in, as far as the dim light coming from the hallway would reach. There I started to take my clothes off, my skin still damp with saltwater even after I had removed them.

The sounds of the raging storm were louder in this part of the building. If the loud cracks and clangs were anything to go by, by tomorrow nothing would be left standing.

I was naked and trying to dry my skin with the small towel my mother had packed in the bag, along with other necessities, when I heard a loud metallic clang coming from the other side of the corridor, maybe from another room. I was surprised. No one was supposed to be here. Maybe there was a loose vent somewhere and the air was gushing in and knocking things about.

I quickly got dressed and placed my discarded clothes inside the duffel bag. It was probably nothing, I thought. Common sense and fatigue could not extinguish my explorer instincts, though, so I decided to see for myself what was happening.

My eyes had grown accustomed to the dark by then, and I started walking toward the repeated clanging sound, which could still be heard despite the strong noise coming from outside. It was definitely coming from inside the shelter.

A shadow shifted against the wall of the room ahead. Someone else was in there. I gasped in surprise and my heart skipped a beat. I scolded myself for being so jumpy— maybe someone else had had the same idea as me, and was trying to change in privacy. Reason dictated that I turn around. Instead, I crept forward. I took a couple of steps inside the room and hid behind a column.

Naked from the waist up, a man was leaning over a table lit by a flashlight. Tiny metal parts of something were lined up before him. He gingerly picked up a part, dried it carefully, and slotted it into a small black rectangle.

I realized with a start that I was looking at a dismantled cell phone. I could not see the man's features from where I was standing. He finished assembling the parts one by one and switched the phone on. The screen glowed, lighting up his face.

It was Carlo. The scene at the top of Sophie's mountain came back to me: Carlo holding the phone up to his ear as if in conversation with someone. Why was he hiding in here trying to get a connection on his phone? He held it up, evidently still at it, and repeatedly touched the screen trying to dial.

The noise outside and the darkness in this part of the shelter were my allies, providing me cover. He had no idea I was here. He put the phone down on the table and put his shoes on. I pulled back to make sure he couldn't see me and my shoes squeaked. He sprung in my direction, flashlight in hand.

"Who's there?" he shouted, moving toward me.

The light blinded me and I raised an arm to shield my eyes. "It's me, Fotini," I said hesitantly.

"What are you doing here?" He turned back to the table and picked up his t-shirt.

"I came to change out of my wet clothes and then I heard a noise...What are you doing here?" I asked, looking at his still moist t-shirt.

"Same as you," he replied, sounding very sincere.

Everything my father had told me about the priest's murder and the witnesses' depositions suddenly flashed through my mind. Carlo was a witness. The chief of police had kept his passport, considering him a suspect because he had arrived on the island just the day before.

The buzzing sound of the cell phone made him jump. He turned the flashlight toward the table and grabbed the glowing phone. He brought it up to his ear without saying a word. He then looked at the dark screen and cursed under his breath, flinging it back onto the table.

Keeping in mind that standing before me was one of the people who only hours ago had saved my life, I said, "What you are doing is none of my business, but if you can somehow get in touch with the outside world, I'd like to know."

"You just saw for yourself. I can't. My phone was soaked when we jumped into the water to help Gabriel. It no longer works and I don't know if I'll manage to fix it. I'm going to ask you to keep this to yourself."

"Why is it a secret?" I asked, genuinely trying to understand, but feeling very guarded at the same time. All my instincts screamed that, despite his easy, calm exterior, Carlo was hiding something.

"I came to change, just like you did. I tried to fix my phone and see if I could talk to my family, who must be worried. It didn't work. That's it, I don't see anything wrong in that." His sounded increasingly offended as he spoke and I thought that maybe he was right, maybe I was being overly suspicious.

"I'm sorry," I said. "I didn't mean to imply anything. We are all highly strung right now and I didn't even get a chance to thank you earlier."

"Forget it, Fotini. It was nothing. You would have done the same thing. As for now, well... never mind," he shrugged. "Never mind."

His last two words sparked a vague memory, but I could only catch a glimpse before it sank back into the depths of my mind. No matter how hard I searched, I could not make it resurface. I stared at him, confused.

"Are you okay?" he asked, touching my hand.

"I'm fine, still a bit dizzy," I muttered, trying to explain my bizarre behavior. "I'm going back to the others; we're having a meeting in five minutes."

"Yes, go ahead. I'll just gather up my stuff and be there in a moment. If I ever manage to get a connection on this thing, I'll let you know."

"Thank you once again. I'm sorry for the sudden intrusion," I apologized.

"Never mind," he said, and before I had even fully turned to walk away, I realized what it was about the way he said those two words. He sounded just like Leonard Cohen singing "Nevermind," as if he was repeating the chorus.

I took a couple of steps and suddenly remembered the man I thought had been following me on my way back to the hotel, after the reception at Berkeley. I'd heard the chorus of that song through his earphones. I hesitated and then turned around. "Carlo, were you in California about a month ago?"

I could not see his face clearly in the dim light, but he replied without missing a beat. "I haven't been to California in years, why do you ask?"

I realized how insane my question must have sounded to him, so I backtracked a little. "I just had a feeling we've met before, that's all. My mistake, obviously," I shrugged.

He was silent for a few moments, as if trying to understand what I was saying. "Well, I'll see you in a bit," he said, pulling on a baseball cap and turning to gather his things.

I stopped at the room where I had left my things, picked up my bag, and started to make my way back to the main room. The hum of voices grew louder as I neared. Everyone had already gathered there waiting for Stelios' briefing.

* * *

Everyone had squeezed into the main room, joining the refugee women and children who were already camped out there, to hear Stelios. He had become our informal leader, the main director of our temporary home.

He began by stressing that no one was to leave the shelter, at least not without previously notifying him. Anyone choosing to leave would be doing so at their own risk. Then he started to explain how the space was to be organized, pausing as he spoke to give Azim a chance to translate for his compatriots. Everything had to proceed calmly, orderly because that was the only hope we had to survive this storm unscathed. At night, the generator would be turned off to save fuel. No one could tell with any certainty how long we would be spending here.

Our only means of communication with the outside world was the radio the elderly man had brought in with him. The only words he had managed to pick up were the distress call of a Russian vessel sailing close to Crete. The captain kept repeating that giant waves were battering his ship, which would not be able to hold much longer. Then there had been silence.

I watched everyone's somber, worried faces as he spoke. Taking a more careful look, I realized the only person missing was Carlo. I decided that, as soon as Stelios was finished, I would inform him of what had happened in that little room. The man was surely hiding something. Maybe it was nothing serious, but his behavior was certainly mysterious.

A little later, the conversation had started to go around in circles. It was becoming obvious that no one could solve all the matters that had arisen because of the storm, and everyone was getting hungry and tired.

My mother and some other local women took over. All the refugee women stood up to help. I would have loved to help too, but cooking was not my strong point.

I beckoned Stelios over and we walked to the entrance, where we would not be overheard. I described what I had seen. Stelios was silent for a minute. "Look, trying to make a call is not necessarily something bad. I mean, it is what we would all be doing right now, if we could. What bothers me is the timing; the murders happened just after he arrived on the island," he whispered.

"I don't think he had anything to do with that," I protested. "His behavior is puzzling, though."

"Fotini, there's not that many of us here. But, I have this feeling the murderer is among us."

I froze. "What makes you say that?" I asked, looking furtively around me.

"It's going to sound crazy, but the chief thinks there may be more than one suspect."

"I don't understand..." I frowned, trying to understand his reasoning.

"All the foreigners who arrived during the past few days coincide with the murders. That's no coincidence."

"Who do you suspect?"

"Carlo, the Arab, and Gabriel," he confidently replied, leaving me speechless.

I smiled awkwardly. "You have a very vivid imagination, Stelios. Gabriel couldn't have... He was on Ikaria and we arrived together yesterday. As for Azim, well, I think you are just being prejudiced. Think about what you are saying. A man risked drowning on a refugee boat just to kill someone?" I said incredulously.

"Gabriel may not have been here when the priest was killed, but he was in Pera Mera yesterday, as was Carlo. Plus, look at how quickly they all got on with each other, three *random strangers*?" His voice dripped with irony as he stressed the last two words.

I was honestly dumbfounded. If his theory were correct, it would mean the three men knew each other beforehand. It all sounded like the script for a thriller, not real life.

I opened my mouth to protest when we heard a different kind of banging against the metal door. It took us a moment to realize it wasn't some object being flung against the door but the pounding of a person's fists. Stelios unlatched the small, metal window in one of the doors. The face of Petros, dripping with water and wide-eyed with shock, stared back at us.

Stelios pulled the latch and opened the door just wide enough for Petros to stumble through, shaking, followed by a sharp gust of wind. As I heaved my shoulder against the door to slam it shut, I caught a glimpse of the collapsed bell tower. Outside, it looked as dark as midnight.

Once we had secured the door, I turned to Petros. He had sunk to the floor, gasping for breath, as if he had just run a marathon. Three or four people came near us, hearing the commotion. Carlo was one of them, his baseball low on his brow, as if he wanted to shield his eyes from us.

"Petros, what's happening? How did you get here?" I asked anxiously, forgetting everything that had happened between us.

He was still struggling to catch his breath. I kneeled down beside him and rubbed his back. He took a couple of deep breaths and spoke in a shaky voice. "It's mayhem outside. We put all the guests in the hotel basement and set off with Kimon to go to my house. The road has split open and it was impossible to get there." He was still trembling and struggling to get the words out. "We decided to come here. We had no other choice. The wind threw the car into a ditch. We got out and continued on foot."

He paused and stared blankly into space, his pupils dilated. It was as if he was watching the nightmare play out before his eyes. I dreaded what was coming next. Kimon's absence could only have a tragic explanation.

"It's hell outside. Hell," he whispered. "We could hardly stand up and walk. Just before we reached the first houses, the wind tried to sweep us away. I was lucky. I managed to grab onto a tree." He raised his bloody palms.

"Kimon?" Stelios asked with a worried expression.

Petros cradled his head in his bloody palms, leaving red streaks on his face. "The wind lifted him up, like a rag doll...Then he was swallowed up by the tornado. Just like that... He disappeared. I screamed out his name, but he was gone."

Tears streamed down his cheeks, mingling with the bloodstains. I rubbed the back of his neck, trying to calm him down. I thought of what Sophie had said about the Harpies and how they snatched the souls of the dead.

Petros' body shook with a silent sob. "I ran from tree to tree between each gust, trying to stay on the ground. I don't know how long it took me to reach the alleys on the outskirts. The Chora looks bombed. The waterspout has rained fish. There's dead fish splattered everywhere, smashed."

The moment he said that I sensed a faint smell, probably coming from fish guts stuck on his shoes.

"The wind dropped for a few minutes, but now it's back. It's alive. It's a howling, starving beast ravaging everything in its path. I escaped, but Kimon..." he broke down in loud sobs.

"It's over now," I said soothingly. "You are safe. Let's go find the doctor; she should look at your hands," I urged.

Petros suddenly sprang up and shouted. "We heard it on the car radio. It's going to get worse tonight, a lot worse! We'll be wiped out!"

I could hear everyone around us gasp in shock. Stelios was quick to react. He shook Petros by the shoulders and spoke in a loud, assured voice. "We are safe here, Petros. Nothing will happen to anyone. Let's go inside. We are safe here."

I saw Carlo turn around and go back down the dark corridor that led to the side rooms. I wondered if the man who had saved my life was also a murderer.

We left Petros with the doctor and I went into the small kitchen. I stood by my mother and mindlessly shredded a lettuce, trying to still the whirlwind of thoughts swirling in my mind. I ordered myself to think like a scientist: methodically, calmly.

We all felt small and insignificant in the face of what was happening. All we could do was wait for the madness to be over; but what if the madness was here, among us?

* * *

Gabriel, Carlo, and I sat around a table, picking at our food. Petros, exhausted, was fast asleep on one of the makeshift beds. I had told my parents what had happened by the bridge. They stopped by to thank the two men and then went to get some rest.

Stelios and one of the coastguards were huddled in another corner of the room trying to get the military radio to work, without much success. Mumbled curses escaped the two men with each unsuccessful attempt to make contact. I asked them to stop; there were children in the room with us. The curses were replaced by muffled, angry grunts of frustration.

Azim wandered around the rooms holding a box of small candles, which he placed on the tables. We would be turning the generator off shortly. He put the last candle down on our table and asked if he could join us. I shifted on the bench and he squeezed in beside me.

The room was quiet. No one felt like talking much. Every now and then, a smattering of scared whispers would break out for a few seconds and then die out just as quickly. One of the refugee children was crying and the soft sound of his mother's lullaby filled the room. Her sweet voice washed over us like a soft, soothing balm. Gently, the tune became softer and softer, dying in a whisper as the child drifted off to sleep.

"What did the song say?" I asked Azim, still transported to the safe cocoon the woman's voice had magically spun around us.

He sighed. "It's about a boy who got lost in the desert. He talked to the stars at night, asking them to show him the way home. They heard his pleas and took him back on one condition: that he look up at the sky every night and smile, saying 'thank you'."

"Beautiful voice..." Gabriel said, still under the lullaby's spell.

"She lost her husband and her son in a bomb strike two months ago. She decided to escape the war, to find a better future for her daughter and herself. If only you knew the stories of everyone who was on that boat with me... They had ordinary lives, just like you and me. They lost everything in a moment and they never did anything wrong."

"War doesn't make distinctions—" Before I could finish my sentence, Stelios and my father came over to our table. My father was holding a book, which he placed before me.

On the open page, I saw a picture of a mutilated male body and a long text beneath it. I looked at them, puzzled.

"Read what it says... out loud, in English, for everyone to hear," Stelios said.

I scanned the text and started translating slowly. "*Maschalismos* is the practice of rendering the dead physically incapable of rising and taking revenge after death. It was meant to punish those who had committed heinous crimes or prevent them from committing any such acts after death."

I cast a sideways glance at Stelios. He was intently watching the other three, checking out their reactions. I took a deep breath and read on. "The most common method was the amputation of fingers, hands, feet, nose and other extremities, which would then be placed under the armpits of the corpse or in its mouth. Sophocles and Aeschylus' tragedies feature acts of *maschalismos*, and there are references in the Odyssey. The custom also appears in different cultures around the world and at various historical periods, with some variations as to the ritual mutilation of the dead to prevent their wrath from affecting the living..."

I scanned the rest of the page. I had gotten the main points across and there was no point in getting into the historical details.

Everyone was staring at me with the exception of Stelios, who still had his gaze fixed on the other three. I had come across signs of human mutilation on our digs, but I did not know the term and its symbolism. It was clear then, that our murderer was taking revenge by committing murder in this manner. "How did you find this?" I asked my father, impressed.

"You may Google everything these days, but nothing can match a good book. I had it buried in my library. I started looking for it after Father George's death, and here it is." He patted my back and walked off, leaving the book on the table.

Like five poker players we all sat sizing each other up. Azim spoke first. "In Syria, the jihadists kill many people like this. Not to punish them for crimes, but—"

"So you are familiar with this method," Stelios interrupted, not caring to hide his evident prejudice.

Outraged, Azim slammed his hand on the table and raised his voice. "Stop that! Ever since you first laid eyes on me, you have been implying that I had something to do with this. You have no evidence. What proof is there that you are not the murderer?"

The two men stared at each other in stony silence. Gabriel let them cool down a bit and then tried to smooth things over. "What matters now is that we all stay united in these difficult circumstances. If we start accusing each other, especially with no evidence, it can only harm us all."

Stelios opened his mouth to say something, but Gabriel continued. "You are the representative of the law here and we must all respect that, otherwise there will be chaos. But it is better to wait for the storm to be over before you resume *all* of your official duties."

"*If* anyone can resume *all* their duties once we are back outside," muttered Carlo.

"What do you mean?" asked Stelios.

"I mean that the murders might not be your top priority. It is not unreasonable, what with the dead and injured and all the damage. No one is going to care about a murder under the circumstances, at least not in the immediate aftermath."

He was right. I shut the book and spoke calmly. "I think we all need to calm down and get through the night. We are tired and not thinking clearly—"

I was interrupted by a loud thud, as if something huge had just landed on the roof over our heads. A thin cloud of dust descended on the candle. Trying to diffuse the tension between us, I ignored it and carried on. "We don't know how long we'll be stuck here. Let's set our differences aside and relax. I think I saw a bottle of wine somewhere. Who wants to join me for a drink before we go to sleep?" I tried to sound enthusiastic and distract them. They looked like a pack of angry wolves, ready to rip out each other's throat.

Stelios drily announced that he did not drink while on duty and angrily walked off. The other three remained at the table and nodded.

I stood up and followed Stelios. When we were out of earshot, he pulled me to one side and whispered, "I want you to be careful, Fotini. You think the danger is just outside, but I worry that danger may be lurking in here too."

"Don't worry, Stelios, I'll be careful. I saw you watch them while I read out from the book," I whispered conspiratorially, trying to show him that I understood his concern.

"The only one to react was Azim. The other two were indifferent." He cast a furtive look around us, then moved closer and took my hand. "Don't trust anyone until we clear this case up. I would not want anything bad to happen, especially to you. I've known you all my life Fotini and... I care," he said tenderly. "Remember when those dogs chased you and you climbed up a tree to escape?"

I felt awkward but smiled at the memory nonetheless. He smiled back in response and gave me a meaningful look. I pulled my hand away and pretended not to notice. "Thank you for saving me then. I owe you dinner when this is over, if any restaurant is left standing," I joked.

"Deal! If anything happens in the meantime, if you need me, just holler." He took my hand again and held it longer this time, gazing into my eyes. I was taken aback. I had never suspected Stelios might have feelings for me. I blushed and felt uneasy at the same time. How could I let him down gently, without wounding his pride? I pulled my hand away and said, with forced cheerfulness. "You need to rest, my friend. Go get some sleep!"

"Goodnight," he replied and turned away, giving me a disappointed look.

I sighed with relief. I still could not believe that Stelios had been flirting with me. He had never shown any sign of seeing me as anything other than a childhood friend. How could he possibly choose this moment, in the midst of all this madness? On the other hand, maybe it was this sense of impending doom that had brought it on. *Strange,* I thought, but was too tired to think about how I would actually handle this situation.

On my way to fetch the wine and some plastic cups, I passed by the corner where my parents slept on a couple of blankets. Seeing them in each other's arms, in the warm candlelight, I felt a familiar warmth spread through me. They still loved each other so much. I decided there and then that I would either ask them to move to Athens or come to the US with me when this was over. I hated the thought of anything like this happening again, them being so cut off and me so far away. *Should we all make it out of here safe and sound...* I shook off that morbid thought and hurried away.

Back at the table, I handed out the cups while Gabriel uncorked the bottle. Azim put his hand over his, saying he did not drink alcohol. Carlo and Gabriel happily filled their paper cups to the brim. We raised them in silent cheers and sipped. Outside, the sounds of the raging storm still filled the air. Trying to start something resembling a normal conversation, I turned to Carlo. "I heard your company is into wind farms. I imagine your company might not be so keen to invest in Athora after all this."

He smiled and took another sip. "Well, it's windy enough to power the whole of Europe at the moment," he joked. "It's a shame we can't harness it."

"We human beings could do wonders if we understood our full potential, whilst realizing how insignificant we are in the face of nature and the universe," Gabriel chimed in. He turned to me as if we were the only two people in the room and added, "If we think that, this very moment, there are other disasters way more terrible than this taking place in a vast universe, we might feel a little bit better. Stars are turning to dust in the space of a few minutes."

"What we call a disaster depends on how it affects us personally," said Azim. "My personal disaster might be insignificant to you because it does not affect the universe but me personally, or the people around me at most. To me though, it's still a total disaster. When the danger we face is common, that is when people forget what is personal and look at how it affects them as a whole. Now, for example, we have set aside all our small problems and differences and have focused on the urgent need to survive, which requires us to work together."

He seemed like an educated, intelligent man, and I felt sorry that whatever had happened in his life had forced him to escape the Turkish regime on a refugee boat.

The wine, its taste, the scent that filled the small space around our table, seemed to make everyone relax a little.

"You are right," Gabriel agreed and pointed to me. "We've just been at a conference on Ikaria. It was about longevity and life spans, but some scientists, like Fotini here, raised other important issues that have nothing to do with the present but with our presence on earth over thousands of years. Our survival instinct and a series of disasters have led us to where we are today. We survived, in part, thanks to the destructive force of the elements, on earth and the Universe as a whole. As we were saying on the boat with Fotini, we are lucky the dinosaurs became extinct. Every disaster has contributed to the rise of our species."

He paused and drained his cup. The bottle was now empty, and looking at their faces, I realized they were up for another round. I fetched another bottle and, as soon as I uncorked it, I was surprised to see Azim hold out his cup. "If it's the end of the world tonight, I might as well be too dizzy to notice," he joked. We all giggled, and then fell silent again, each one of us lost in our own thoughts.

I looked at the three men and still could not convince myself that one of them might be the man who butchered Father George. I pretended to study my cup but cast furtive looks at Gabriel, who was gazing absent-mindedly at the candle flame at the center of our table. I thought about how intimate our conversation had been the previous night and how we both acted as if nothing had happened the following day. The instinct to survive had overwhelmed all other instincts... Well, maybe not in my case, as I watched his lips part to take another sip.

I topped up everyone's cups and raised mine. "To tomorrow! May we once again brave it!" I said and took a large gulp, then reverted to our previous conversation. "Stephen J. Gould, an American scientist, once said that extinction was the natural destiny of all species. In other words, survival is the exception and extinction is the rule."

Gabriel nodded, showing he was familiar with the concept. I glanced at him and continued enthusiastically, feeling a little tipsy and enjoying the lightheadedness. "Seventy-five percent of all water life disappeared during the Permian. Seventy percent of all land life too."

"When did that happen?" Carlo asked, surprised.

"About two hundred and fifty million years ago."

"So could it happen again? At any moment?" he asked.

"Maybe it is happening already and we just don't know it," I replied, thinking of Professor Marcus' theory. "The Permian was the last Paleozoic era. All of the earth's landmass was joined in a single continent. It's still unclear whether the mass extinction was due to a meteorite or a volcanic eruption. The fact is that at the end of that period, the planet was decimated. Very few life forms survived."

Gabriel looked at me as if he wanted to say something. I smiled and took a sip of wine, letting him continue. "The chances of another disaster or even our extinction occurring is a worrying prospect, but only to us," he said. "What I mean is that it's an event on our scale, not the scale of the planet. Earth is not in the same kind of danger as we are, as a species. To an ordinary person, reaching his maximum lifespan on this planet is a momentous achievement. To a scientist like Fotini, however, who knows a bit more, the lifespan of a human on this planet is so small, it can't even be measured."

"If a similar disaster to that happened now, how long would it take for the Earth to recover?" asked Carlo, looking fascinated by what he was hearing.

Gabriel and I exchanged a look and he nodded at me to answer. "Based on what we know, around seven million years. But that doesn't mean life will look anything like the world that preceded the disaster."

"Meaning?" Azim asked.

"Chance would decide which life forms would evolve following a disaster; chance and circumstances. Humankind owes its existence to series of completely random events. It's important to remember that five-sixths of Earth's history took place before even the first life form appeared. That's when, miraculously, the first living organisms appeared—and they had no resemblance to life as we know it today."

"So, if something similar happened now, it's not certain that man would rise again in a few million years," Azim said.

"It's unlikely," I agreed. "The most likely scenario is that other randomly decided life forms will dominate. Like I said, chance and circumstances. In any case, throughout the history of the planet, there have been at least five mass extinctions and life still went on. We are very lucky none of them happened during our era." I paused and gazed at the ceiling, where the clattering continued. "Let's hope it's not happening now."

"Couldn't we foresee such an event?"

Gabriel replied this time. "We don't have the means to predict something like that yet. The history of humanity is the most unpredictable thing you can imagine, not because it lacks reason or is the result of random events, but because it is not governed by any law of nature."

"Knowing all of this, I wonder why people follow dogma and religion that goes against everything science has proven," Carlo said, distributing the last of the wine.

"The world wouldn't be as we know it if it weren't for religion," Gabriel said shaking his head at the proffered bottle. "All religion arises from a fear of death and the afterlife. The notion of resurrection makes many people anticipate that they will find some justice in the afterlife, that they will meet everyone who departed before them or will join them later. It's very soothing to believe you will be resurrected someday... even if you spend a lot of time being dead," he said pulling a funny grimace that made us all smile.

"The fact is that the fear of punishment after death has acted as a deterrent for a lot of people. On the other hand, the thought of an impending end of the world has led many people to acts of insanity. You've all heard of cults and mass suicides just before the new millennium. What happened in the end? Life went on as normal. This insane idea that some kind of catharsis comes through disaster has other dimensions too. Did you know that the Xhosa people in Africa, Nelson Mandela's tribe, did not resist the slavery imposed on them by their occupiers because they were waiting for the arrival of their ancestors, which would lead to a new world order where they would all live on the fertile prairies happily ever after?"

"How can you be sure, though, that it will not happen?" asked Azim intently. "How can you know there is no life after this one? Who can say for certain that the life we live isn't the preparation for another life after death when we will be rewarded with all sorts of happiness?"

Gabriel listened to him with a wry smile. "As a scientist I must rely on proof. Based on the evidence available to me, death is the end. So we should live this life in the best way we can, as nothing proves there is an afterlife."

"So, if there is nothing after death, all sins must be punished in this life," Azim noted, staring at Gabriel intently.

For a moment, I wondered if there was another hidden layer to their conversation, some meaning only the two of them could grasp. I felt as if they were communicating in some kind of secret code.

"We all hide small or large sins. For some of them, yes, we should be punished. The point is who will be the judge of that?" Gabriel said.

Azim leaned forward on the table. "The man killing people here on the island. He is punishing them, right?"

"Maybe he thinks he is or maybe he is mentally unwell and nothing more," Gabriel said with a shrug. "I can't know what his goals are or what has led him to commit these acts."

"That's a nice, cheerful conversation we are having," Carlo teased, interrupting the intense exchange between the other two. "Disasters, death, the afterlife, punishment... I thought we were drinking to cheer up." He seemed a little tipsy, but he wasn't wrong. Things were gloomy enough as they were.

"He's right, you know," I said. "It's getting late; we should all get some rest. It's going to be a hard day tomorrow." I stood up slowly, stretching my stiff limbs. Azim and Gabriel followed suit. Carlo pointed to the nearly empty bottle. "I'll finish this off and find somewhere to crash. Goodnight."

We left him at the table and half-walked, half-felt our way through the dark room toward the couple of smaller rooms at the other end. They had been converted into dormitories. Azim wished us goodnight and disappeared into one of them.

I looked at Gabriel, suddenly at a loss as to what to say. I awkwardly asked, "Did you manage to get through to Lesbos?" I did not want to say "your wife."

He seemed taken aback by my question. "No. No contact since yesterday," he replied. "I guess things are bad there too. I wonder how all those thousands of refugees and poor immigrants are doing." He seemed unwilling to discuss anything of a personal nature.

My body, heavy with exhaustion, screamed at me to go lie down. I could barely stand on my feet. Gabriel seemed to notice. "Go rest, Fotini," he said tenderly. "Tomorrow will be better, you'll see."

"I wish..." I replied. Without thinking about it, I stepped forward and kissed his cheek. "Thank you," I whispered. "I'll never forget what you did for me today."

Our bodies were almost touching, as we stood near each other, neither one of us taking a step back. He took my hand and held it low, between us. "We have a lot to talk about, Fotini," he whispered. "When all this is over..." He turned and walked toward a shelf stacked with blankets. He picked one up and turned to the men's dormitory, smiling before he disappeared into the darkness.

Although I could not be sure what he meant, my heart skipped a bit. I raised my hand to my cheek, still feeling his warm breath on it. I caught Petros, half raised on a bench, staring at me with a jealous look in his eyes. I ignored him and walked to where my parents were already asleep and lay down beside them. I felt relief flood through my limbs as I stretched out on an old quilt beside them. After the day I had had, it felt more welcoming than the most luxurious mattress.

The flickering candlelight, the closeness of my parents, and the peace that had descended over the room lulled me and I felt my eyelids grow heavier. My brain, however, refused to follow suit. I opened my eyes once again and watched the shadows on the ceiling. The events of the previous day danced around my mind. I felt exhausted but too overwrought to sleep. I was curious about what Carlo was doing. Had he returned to the small room I had caught him in earlier that evening?

I got up quietly and looked at the table where we had been sitting before. No one was there. Only Stelios and a couple of the coastguards were huddled at another bench, having a hushed conversation.

I thought about alerting him for a second, but in the end, I decided not to cause an unnecessary commotion. I tiptoed out to the hallway and turned left down the corridor by the front door, creeping toward the room at the end. The further away I walked, the darker it got. Soon, I would not be able to see enough to make my way to the room. I scanned the darkness ahead and listened carefully. All was still. Maybe he had just gone to lie down. Maybe I was so tired I was not thinking straight.

"Are you looking for me?" Carlo's hoarse voice rang out just in front me and I jumped in fright. I had not seen nor heard him walk down the corridor toward me.

I tried to think of something to say and drew up a blank.

"I really can't understand why you're watching my every move, Fotini."

"What are you doing here?" I asked aggressively, ignoring the question.

"I don't think that's any of your business," he replied frostily.

"We were all asked not to leave the designated rooms. Why should we make an exception for you? We can't all start acting as we please. We have to follow the rules or we'll lose any sense of order."

"What are you doing outside the designated rooms, then?" he retorted.

"Looking for you; you disappeared first. What are you doing in here again?"

"Same as before, Fotini—I'm trying to make contact with the outside world."

He put his hand into his pocket and I felt my throat constrict with fear. He pulled out his phone and I tried to hide my relief. "Did you manage to speak to anyone?" I squeaked.

He shook his head no and put his phone back into his pocket.

"Can I see your phone?" I asked suspiciously.

"I'd rather you didn't."

"If you are not hiding anything, why won't you show me?"

"Because it's an unreasonable demand. Don't worry. If I manage to call anyone, you'll be the first to know."

He smiled and turned back down the dark corridor toward the room. I stood there at a loss, not knowing what to think. *It's not unreasonable to be trying to contact your family, to find out what is happening,* I told myself. *I'd be doing the exact same thing. But why be so secretive about it?*

I wondered whether I should let Stelios know. Know what exactly? That I was suspiciously following the man who had saved my life just because he seemed to have a satellite phone and wandered off without telling anybody? I decided to keep it to myself. Stelios had enough on his plate as it was. However, I was sure to keep a watchful eye on Carlo for as long as we remained trapped in here.

Athora *

Chapter 12

The sound of children's voices woke me from a deep, dreamless sleep and filled me with a sense of happy optimism. For a few minutes, caught in the state between sleep and consciousness, I could not recollect where I was.

I lay buried under my blankets, listening to the other sounds that slowly emerged around me—adult voices talking softly, benches scraping the floor, the clatter of cutlery. Everyone was already up and moving about.

My mother saw me raise myself on my elbow and rub my eyes. She pointed to a plate and a mug of coffee on a nearby table. I stretched and sat up, pulling my shoes on. My body felt stiff and I ached all over. A sudden sharp pain on my forehead brought back all the events of the previous day.

I went and kissed my mother good morning. Looking around me, I saw some of the locals and the refugees, but none of my companions from the previous day. I imagined they were milling about in the main exhibition space and I sat down to breakfast.

The warm coffee hit my taste buds and chased away the lingering cobwebs in my brain. "Where are Stelios and the others?" I asked.

My mother smiled. "Do you know what time it is?"

I had lost all sense of time in the windowless room. "It's nearly ten, Fotini," she said. "You were sleeping so heavily you didn't even hear Stelios call you this morning. I scolded him for trying to wake you up, so they went outside without you."

I hastily swallowed and nearly choked. "They did what?" I shouted. "What do you mean outside?"

"Outside, in the Chora. One of the coastguards went outside this morning and said the weather was better. Others have gone outside too, to see what's happening and bring back more food."

I jumped up, picked up the last piece of bread, and headed for the exit. My mother called out for me to wait. I turned and saw her come toward me holding a jacket. "Put this on, Fotini, and be careful. I don't think you should be going. Your father has also gone outside. Tell him to come back, please, I don't understand what's gotten into him."

I grabbed the jacket and nearly ran out. Outside, by the front door, Azim stood looking up at the sky. He smiled the moment he saw me and said, "If you are going out, I'm coming with you. It looks like the weather is getting better."

I remembered Professor Marcus' e-mail about the eye of the storm and shook my head. He'd warned the storm would last for days and that we shouldn't be deceived by any temporary lull.

"I'm going to find the others. Let's go," I said buttoning up my jacket. It was still very windy, although nothing like the previous day.

We didn't have to walk far for the full scale of the damage the storm had wreaked to hit us. The Chora looked like it had just survived a massive airstrike. Leaves were raining down from the sky, like injured birds no longer able to fly. The small cobbled street that led to the square was smashed and littered with debris. Looking at all the shattered pieces, it was impossible to tell what objects they had once belonged too. The roofs of many houses had blown away, defenseless against the violent gusts, and the bell tower had collapsed through the church roof, which gaped like a crater.

Picking my way carefully through mounds of rubble, I saw the corner of an icon peeking out from beneath what looked like broken bricks and plaster. It had all been deposited there by the tornado. I bent down and brushed the rubble away, then picked the icon up. The carved wooden frame looked familiar—it was the icon of the Virgin Mary, which Father George had been holding during the procession to the chapel. I gently wiped the dust off and hugged it to my chest as I carried on walking toward the square, Azim beside me. "This is what my country looks like, with the war," he said sadly, looking around him.

The stench of dead fish was everywhere. I could pick out guts and fish heads and tails among the rubble, a grim reminder that the tornado had wreaked havoc at sea as well as on land.

Darkness still reigned outside, heavy low clouds obscuring the sun's rays. Only occasionally did the darkness lift, when the wind chased the thick clouds away for a few seconds before new clouds raced like crazed horses to take their place.

The square was full of those who had dared step outside. My father saw us and immediately came toward us. "Good morning," he said. "You were sleeping so heavily, we didn't wake you up."

"That's okay, dad. Any news?"

"Not really, sweetheart. The phones still don't work. Thank God, everyone in the Chora seems to be okay—other than poor Kimon, that is. We don't know what's happened in the more remote areas, though. Most of the roads have collapsed." He looked at what I was holding in surprise. "Where did you find that?" he asked.

"In the rubble. Do you want to take it with you, back to mum?" I asked, handing it over.

He did not seem to like my suggestion but agreed nonetheless. "Fine, I'll head back to the shelter. Stelios said that if the weather stays like this until lunchtime and communication lines are restored with the outside world, whoever wants to can return home."

I did not want to scare him by telling him that maybe it wasn't over yet. I urged him to leave and, as soon as he was on his way, I walked toward Azim who had joined the others. I could not see Gabriel or Carlo anywhere. Petros, on the other hand, cast me a look of complete indifference without interrupting his conversation with a couple of other men. This new turn of events had made him lose all interest in me, but that was no concern of mine.

I touched the wound on my head, trying to fix the bandage that had slipped during the night. A wave of dizziness washed over me and I had to grip a wall to stop swaying. Thankfully, it was over in a couple of minutes. Looking up, I saw Stelios standing on the roof of the coffee shop, holding the army radio up to his ear. It looked like he had managed to get through to someone, but the wind scattered his words and I could not hear what he was saying. His expression though spoke volumes and the news would not be good.

He clambered back down and stood on a bench, waiting for the conversations to die down before he spoke. When everyone was quiet, he started talking in a loud, clear voice. "Last night was a nightmare for everyone on this island. As far as we know, there has only been material damage in the Chora, with the exception of poor Kimon. In Pera Mera, things are much worse. Many have been injured. I've just talked to the chief. Neither one of us has had any contact with the outside world. We can only radio each other, on the island. As you already know, the bridge has collapsed and the two sides are now cut off from each other. The storm, or whatever that devil it was, may be over but the winds at sea are still strong, around 10 on the Beaufort scale. So we don't believe any help is on its way."

He sighed deeply, looking out toward Pera Mera. "As we know, the man who was swept away on the bridge is missing." I felt my chest tighten as I thought of the man's self-sacrifice to save his daughter. Stelios continued to list other losses. "A foreign couple who tried to get to Pera Mera were killed when their car was blown off the road by the wind and smashed against the rocks. They are trying to free the bodies from the wreckage as we speak."

A loud murmur rose on the square, as people anxiously voiced their fears. Stelios raised his voice even louder. "We have no idea what the weather holds. We have no idea what has happened outside the island. If by lunchtime the weather keeps improving, you can go home if you want to. The shelter will remain open for—"

"It's not a good idea," I shouted as loudly as I could. Everyone turned toward me. I stepped on the bench and stood beside him. "I'm sorry to interrupt," I said, "but this is important. Before the storm broke out I was informed by a very reliable source that it would last, possibly for days, and I am sure this is a temporary lull."

The voices on the square grew louder but I paid no heed. "It would be better to be cautious and stay in the shelter for a couple more days than risk losing anyone else."

"We have no food," shouted one of the locals angrily, as if we were somehow to blame for everything that was happening. "We can't even wash!"

Stelios stepped in immediately. "Everyone is welcome at the shelter. I think we can manage for a couple of days with even less, to make sure there is enough for everyone. This is an unprecedented situation, so we must all be patient, understanding, and calm."

"I think we need to start preparing for the storm's return now. It can strike at any moment, without warning. There isn't enough time to do much, you must return to safety now." I felt bad undermining Stelios' authority, but there was no time to lose.

The voices on the square grew louder, while Stelios looked up at the sky and seemed to ponder what I had just said, unsure which way to go. The distant sound of thunder tipped the scales on the side of caution. He looked at me and spoke determinedly. "I pray Fotini proves wrong, but it is better to be safe than sorry. I need a few of you to carry whatever you can in one go to the shelter—food, water, blankets. Everyone who's not coming to the shelter, go somewhere safe and take all precautions. However, I repeat. There is still enough room at the shelter—"

He was interrupted by a commotion at the edge of the square, as people parted to let someone through. It was Gabriel, carrying Sophie in his arms, making his way to the shelter. A coastguard walked ahead, asking people to step aside.

She looked terrible but seemed to be conscious. I was about to step down to join them when I heard her shout and point to a side street that had a clear view of the sea. "It's back! Look!"

We all turned and watched with terror as another waterspout formed in the far distance, smaller than the last two, but still a fearsome sight.

Panic spread among the jittery crowd, which started to disperse left and right as Stelios once again repeated everyone was welcome at the shelter.

I stood on the bench, unsure of what to do. Part of me wanted to help and part of me was dying to find out how Sophie had managed to escape from her house and get through the mound of rocks that had buried it.

Stelios pulled me down and leaned close, whispering conspiratorially. "They've probably caught the killer, over at Pera Mera."

I was stunned! "But...how..." I muttered, astonished. He waved at me to hush and said, "We can't let a soul know until we are certain it's him."

"What happened, how did they catch him?" I whispered back, ignoring the people milling around us.

"Chief didn't say much. They found him at dawn, wandering around the cliff, blood on his hands. When he saw them, he ran away and tried to hide."

"That doesn't mean he's the murderer!"

"Also, the corpse is not there anymore, it's disappeared. Someone moved it."

Someone or something, I thought, looking up at the sky. "Who's the suspect?" I asked, burning with curiosity.

"Chief didn't say. Too much going on over there. I'll call him again before we get back inside the shelter."

I wanted to find out more, but someone was persistently calling out his name. He told me once again to keep this to myself and hurried off. I hoped the man they had caught was the murderer. I hoped there would be no more murders. I hoped the weather would spare everyone's life too.

I saw Gabriel and Azim, arms loaded with water bottles, and I ran over to help them. I grabbed as many bottles as I could carry and asked them if they had seen Carlo. They all shook their heads. The three of us set off toward the shelter walking as fast as we could. As we walked, I looked around to see if I could spot him, but he was nowhere to be seen. All around us, people were carrying bags of food and water.

We had reached the far end of the square when we heard the first shouts and screams. We turned around and saw a fight had broken out. Despite the howling of the wind, their voices could be heard clearly, along with the sound of glass being smashed.

People stepped in to try to break up the fight, but it seemed to engulf them too and the brawl spread across the square. I put down the water and was about to walk toward the rioting crowd, but Gabriel held me back. "Not a good idea," he said. I stood and watched people who had known each other all their lives fight and I could not understand why. Azim watched the scene unperturbed, as if it were an ordinary sight. He caught my surprise and said, "I've seen this before. They are fighting over a piece of bread."

He was right. The most intense fighting was at the steps of the coffee shop. I saw Stelios and one of the coastguards shouting at people to stop, trying to restore order, to no avail. The coastguard took out his gun from its holster and fired twice in the air. All went still. People stopped where they were, as if they had turned into statues. Many were holding food and water they had looted in their arms. The wind had smashed most of the shop's windows, but the frenzied crowd had completed the destruction inside the shop.

Most hung their heads in shame and listened to Stelios' telling-off. Some protested. We could not hear what was being said, but when one pointed angrily at us, I realized he was protesting that we were giving the refugees food and shelter.

Azim seemed to sense what was happening and asked me to translate. I could not bring myself to tell him the truth. "They are complaining that we are taking all the food and water to shelter when many people have chosen not to join us there," I said. He did not seem to believe me.

"Let's go back," Gabriel said. He was right.

It was safer for us to leave while Stelios was still there. If this was happening on the first day after the storm, I dreaded to think what might follow.

* * *

We were all back at the shelter, along with another fifteen people who had decided to join us, deeming it to be safer.

The doctor had tended to Sophie, who was now sleeping alone in a tiny room, exhausted. She said she had managed to climb down from her house using ropes after another landslide had swept away the rocks. She had then made her way to the Chora with great difficulty.

I went to the room and stood by her bed. Were it not for the shallow, rhythmic movement of her chest, you would think she was dead. Her face was deadly pale and still. She had injured her leg, probably fractured it. The doctor had bandaged it lightly and she needed a cast, which of course was not an option right then.

I was not in the best shape either. There were times when I thought I would fall asleep standing upright.

I had looked for Carlo as soon as we returned to the shelter. I had not managed to locate him and I was beginning to worry. If he was still outside, he was in great danger. The last couple to arrive at the shelter reported that clusters of great sea tornados were heading toward Athora once again. In my exhausted, dizzy state, I really believed that the island had been cursed.

I sat down on a bench next to Stelios, who looked worried. I touched his arm in sympathy. "You don't look too great," I said. "Maybe you should get some rest."

"I'm fine. Fotini, you saw what happened at the square...I'm afraid things will get worse." He took a deep breath. "I'll get some rest when we've locked the door. Although with all the horrors outside, I don't know if that's possible. And I'm not talking about the storm..."

"No, I know what you mean," I replied. "I don't know if you've noticed but Carlo is missing."

He looked surprised. "Where is he? The weather is getting worse again."

On cue, the long-familiar howl of the wind screamed over the roof of the shelter and slammed the front door loudly against the wall.

"I don't know, I haven't seen him since last night." I looked around and, without thinking too much about it, decided to confide in him. "Stelios, there is something I need to tell you," I whispered. "I couldn't sleep last night and I got up to stretch my legs. I caught Carlo trying to call someone again."

"So?"

"Don't you think he's acting strange? He keeps disappearing... he has a satellite phone...what kind of company gives its employees satellite phones? Plus he arrived at Athora the day before the first murder."

Stelios smiled. "Isn't paleontology keeping you busy enough? Now you want to be a detective too?" he teased. "Fotini, I already told you, the murderer has been arrested. However, let us assume, for argument's sake, that he's not the man we are looking for. Why Carlo and not Azim? Azim also arrived just before the murders began. Or do you believe everything he says, just because he claims to be another poor refugee? Have you considered that you might be a little biased?"

"Maybe you are biased against Azim! What has the man ever done to you other than getting shipwrecked on this island trying to escape certain death?"

We had been raising our voices without even realizing. I thought there was no point in arguing right now. We were both on the verge of exhaustion and overreacting.

Stelios must have had the same thought. He stood up and spoke softly, beseechingly. "Let's not fight, please. I can barely keep my eyes open and you look unwell, Fotini. You are very pale."

"I'm just really tired," I said following him to the large steel front doors.

Stelios took one last look outside, then slammed the door shut and bolted it, locking an extra chain that had been fitted with a large padlock. He put the key in his pocket and said, "This way no one can go in or out without us knowing."

We returned to the main room and saw Gabriel, Azim, and Carlo chatting with my father. Although my father's English was poor, he was managing to hold a conversation with great ease, waving his arms about and mimicking any words he could not remember. He was gesticulating eloquently, explaining something to them.

I stared at Carlo in disbelief. I was dying to ask him how he'd gotten in, but I bit my tongue and casually asked, "What are you guys talking about?"

"I'm telling them about Sophie," my father said.

"What about her?"

"How no one knows exactly when she arrived on the island. She registered with the local council about thirty years ago, with a Canadian passport. I was telling them how I used to work at the registry and that I am the only one to have records of everyone who settled on the island that long ago. The records from back then aren't computerized yet. I told them how all my files are stored in the cellar, so nothing will happen to them there." He looked at the men, then back at us with a worried look. "Maybe I shouldn't have," he mused.

"Why not?" I asked and looked at the men who were watching our Greek conversation perplexed.

I couldn't ignore the burning question any longer, so I turned to Carlo. We'd just locked the front door, so how did he get in? "We thought you were still outside and we were getting worried about you... When did you get back?" I asked him with eager forthrightness.

"Same time as everybody else. Maybe you didn't see me. I was at the back, stacking supplies," he casually replied, then turned to Stelios and changed the subject. "Everything okay at the square in the end? No more trouble? If you need any help I'm at your disposal."

Stelios, who was also giving him a curious look, thanked him. "Everything is under control. I would like to ask all of you though, once again, not to wander off without letting me know."

He turned away, but Carlo stopped him with a question. "Any news about the murders?"

Stelios hesitated and replied over his shoulder, "No, nothing at all." He then walked off, followed by my father. There was no way that Carlo could have walked in with everyone else without me noticing.

Gabriel's voice interrupted my thoughts. "I have studied groups under extreme duress and I'm afraid that if the weather doesn't improve shortly, it will get out of control. Those outside think of us as privileged."

"But they could join us here if they wanted," Azim protested. I was sure he'd understood what some of the locals had been saying about the refugees back at the square.

My head still hurt and I suddenly felt very weak. My knees buckled and I would have collapsed on the floor, were it not for Gabriel's quick reflexes. "You don't look well," he said.

Everything around me was a blur and I grabbed his shirt to stay upright. The other two came near and helped lower me to a chair. "You're burning," Azim said, touching my forehead.

I felt my entire body break out in a cold perspiration and realized that something was wrong. Carlo left and immediately returned with the doctor and my worried parents. The doctor asked them to move me to the room Sophie was in so she could examine me.

Azim and Gabriel put their arms around my waist and half-walked, half-lifted me there. I was struggling to take a few steps. Petros saw what was happening and followed us into the room.

They hurriedly pulled a few benches next to where Sophie was fast asleep and threw a blanket over them. They stretched me out on the makeshift bed and I felt the last of my strength evaporate. I closed my eyes and let myself go. I heard Stelios' voice anxiously ask what was wrong with me. Then, silence.

When I opened my eyes again, they were all gone, as if whisked away by magic; or so it seemed to me. Only the doctor was there, putting a clean bandage on my head. She covered me with a blanket, and then rummaged around her bag. I was shaking and I huddled down under the blanket, trying to warm myself up.

"What is it, doctor?" I asked as she placed a pill in my mouth.

"It's for the fever and to help with the pain," she said, bringing a glass of water to my mouth. I took a sip and swallowed the pill. "Your fever is running high and I think you need antibiotics. The wound doesn't look good. I'm worried it's been infected."

My father walked back in the room accompanied by the others. The doctor told them about my condition and the fact that she had only had time to grab her first aid kit. There were no antibiotics in the shelter. Dizzy as I was, I heard her say that there would be antibiotics at the pharmacy, at the other end of the Chora. They all conferred in a whispered conversation, although I could not make out what they were saying. I saw some of them hurry out of the room and I called out, asking what was happening. I felt disorientated. My father and Stelios came closer to my bed. I saw Petros, who was standing by the doorway, shrug and leave.

"They are going to the pharmacy to bring antibiotics. I would have gone myself, but I'm needed here," Stelios explained, evidently troubled.

"But how will they get there in this weather? You must stop them."

"It's too late now, sweetheart," my father said. Three men who had saved me from drowning were about to risk their lives again to get me the medication I needed.

"It's too dangerous, why did you let them do it?" I shouted at Stelios with all the strength I could muster.

"They didn't give me an option. Carlo volunteered, then the other two. They didn't think twice about it."

My mother came in and handed me a cup of tea. I sat up to take the cup and my eyes met Sophie's gaze. She had woken up and was giving me an appraising look.

* * *

Day had almost turned into night, and the force of the wind stirred up otherworldly sounds, like the howls of animals being slaughtered.

Carlo, Azim, and Gabriel walked with great difficulty through the narrow alleys of the Chora, following the directions they had been given.

They ran the risk of being hit by one of the stray objects, so they were constantly forced to stop and seek shelter. Above them, high up in the sky, the storm seemed to be getting stronger. It would not be long before it unleashed its rage once again.

Azim barely managed to avoid being struck by an iron rod that fell suddenly from the sky. He stayed back and, convinced it was impossible to continue, stood there screaming at the others to turn back, shouting that if they kept going they would surely be killed.

Carlo and Gabriel, however, gestured that they would be continuing. Azim dithered for a moment and then turned around to return to the shelter.

The two remaining men, talking loudly to be heard above the screeching wind, decided to go follow a particularly narrow lane rather than the main road, so as to hold onto the walls of the houses lining the street. That decision proved to be a mistake. In the narrow passage, the force of the wind was even greater.

Lightning cracked the sky, closely followed by the racket of thunder. Seizing a momentary lull in the force of the gusts, they started running in the direction of the pharmacy.

Carlo grabbed Gabriel and pointed to a broken shop window. Inside the shop, all the shelves had collapsed, scattering the boxes of pills and creams all over the floor. Some of the small boxes had flown onto the street and were dancing to the tune of the wind.

Holding onto one another, they climbed over the broken glass that jutted out like sharpened knives and stepped into the shop, its thick stone walls offering a brief respite from the wind. Gabriel started rummaging through the fallen boxes for the medication the doctor had scribbled on a piece of paper, to no avail. The pharmacy had evidently been looted. Even the stacks of drawers at the far end of the shop had been turned upside down onto the floor, something that could only have been the act of human hands.

In desperation, Carlo flung a locked wooden cupboard onto the floor. It broke open, spilling its contents. He picked up one of the boxes, which read "wide spectrum antibiotic" and held it out to Gabriel, but it wasn't what they were looking for. Bereft of any other options, they decided to take some of those boxes with them and stuffed them into their pockets.

Thunder rolled. The place shook once more. They had to hurry, their chances of returning safely diminished with every passing minute. Disappointed at their failure to find what they were looking for, they walked to the front of the shop, only to realize that nature was barring their way.

* * *

Lying down next to Sophie, I tried to talk to her. Lost in her own thoughts, she stared at the ceiling giving no reply, as if she couldn't hear me.

"Thank you for saving Lukas," I said in what I decided was the last time I would make an effort to get through to her.

Sophie raised herself slowly and sat at the edge of her bed, looking in my direction. "The Harpies, they wanted to take him with them that day. But they did not succeed," she whispered, as if she did not want them to hear us. "Have you ever seen those clouds, the ones that take on strange forms and seem to rest on the edge of the horizon?"

The picture she was describing sprang clearly to my mind and I nodded.

"Those are the Harpies," she said. "Woe unto us now that they have awoken."

I was impressed she knew the Ancient Greek myth about those female monsters. I raised myself with great difficulty so I could see her better. My head hurt less. The painkiller had probably kicked in. "How did you manage to get out of the house?" I asked.

Instead of replying, Sophie picked up the branch she used as a walking stick and hobbled around to my bed, examining me intently all the while. Her face and hands were scratched, but her eyes were remarkably focused and clear.

She rested her walking stick against the wall behind my bed and carefully removed my bandage. I held perfectly still, as if hypnotized by her gaze.

"It needs looking after," she said after examining the wound. She fumbled around her neck and pulled a small chain over her head. Like a pendant, a small clay pot hung from it. Without another word, she picked up her walking stick and limped out of the room.

I tried to follow her, but I could not sit up. I sunk back onto my blanket, exhausted.

Time was passing haphazardly for me. Sometimes it felt nauseatingly fast and at other times laboriously slow. I do not know how much time had passed before I saw Sophie return accompanied by my mother, who was carrying a steaming cup carefully in both hands.

They helped me sit up and gave me the drink, a brew so bitter I wanted to spit it out. Sophie realized this and pressed my chin hard to keep my mouth shut, ordering me to swallow. Her hand maintained its vice-like grip and I felt the liquid drip down my throat.

The bitterness was replaced by a burning sensation all over my chest. It was hard not to throw up and I sharply pulled my head back, releasing myself from her grip. My face felt numb and my body was on fire.

My mother was looking at me, a terrified look in her eyes. She cradled my head and soothingly stroked my hair. Sophie asked her to bring dry clothes for me and my mother got up without a word to do so, leaving us alone.

"Your body is trying to get the badness out," Sophie said, passing me a bottle of water. I drank a sip and collapsed onto my pillow. She started to wrap me up tightly in a blanket.

"I'm burning," I croaked and tried to throw it off. She stopped me and tucked it in more tightly. "Be patient. You'll feel better in five minutes."

It was hard to disobey her tone. I surrendered to her and her strange potion. Sweat broke out from every pore of my body and she gently wiped the droplets streaming down my face with a towel, muttering incomprehensible words that sounded like distant spells to me. A small rational part of my brain still protested that this was ridiculous, but I had no strength to resist. All I could do was wait and see what happened next.

My mother walked back in the room, closely followed by Stelios.

"Are they back?" I asked anxiously, thinking of the three men who were outside looking for my antibiotics.

"No, and the weather has worsened again," he replied, desperately shaking his head. "What's wrong with Fotini?" he asked, turning to Sophie.

She ignored him, took the bundle of clothes from my mother and gave him a pointed look that he should step outside so I could change.

"Please let me know as soon as they are back," I cried out.

He smiled yes.

Once Stelios was out of the room, Sophie placed my clothes on a chair and put her hands on my belly, urging me to breathe normally. With every breath I exhaled, she pressed a little harder.

The hum of the voices coming from the main room soothed me. The peals of children's laughter as they chased one another around the tables were the most hopeful, delightful sound I had heard since setting foot in this place.

Sophie asked me to stand up. As soon as I did, she and my mother stripped me naked, throwing my clothes on the floor. They made a dull, wet sound as they landed, as if someone had just dunked them in water. I was already starting to feel a little bit better.

When I was completely naked, she started to pat me dry with a towel. Then, she examined my whole body, scanning me closely, touching and prodding my torso and thighs. Feeling uncomfortable, I looked down and was startled by the bruises that had appeared where I had been pounded by the waves. Luckily, there seemed to be no serious injuries beyond the wound to my head.

The examination was over soon after. She handed me dry clothes to get dressed.

My mother was watching the whole scene, looking awed and dubious at the same time, not understanding what was going on. I could not understand either, but having seen Sophie in action with Lukas, I trustingly submitted to the ministrations of the strange woman.

She handed the bottle of water to me once again and told me to drink it all. The truth is that after all that sweating I was parched. "I feel much better, thank you," I said.

"You are not recovered yet. You need to rest. Your body did what it should; now you must help it. You need to sleep. Then you will be better," she said, for the first time saying so many words in one go.

"I'll go make you something to eat," my mother said and left us alone.

We sat on our beds silently, until I decided to break the awkward silence. "I don't know what you gave me, but it worked immediately," I told her.

She continued to examine her scratched hands and spoke without raising her head to look at me. "Most things that nature causes, nature can heal. For every evil out there, there is an antidote."

Realizing that this was Sophie at her most open, I pressed on, "Even for what is happening now?" I asked, meaning the storm.

"Your job has taught you that whatever happens in nature is born of a need to destroy so something new can be born. Man, on the other hand, only meddles to cause evil."

"How do you know what I do?" I asked, buttoning up the top of my shirt, which I realized was gaping, leaving my naked breasts exposed.

"The wind carries people's words," she said, plaiting her long white hair.

"It's strange how we know so little about you. You've been living on Athora since forever. I remember you roaming these mountains when I was a little girl."

"I remember you as a little girl. I know a lot more about you than you think."

"Like what?"

"Like the man who kidnapped you in America, but the police found him and rescued you," she said, looking straight into my eyes.

"How do you know all that?" I balked.

"I told you, the wind carries the things people say," she replied.

I felt a strange fear grip me and fell silent. I did not want to talk more. I did not want to dig up what I had buried so deep inside me. I rose and slowly started to walk to the main room, to find Stelios and see if the three men had returned.

"Don't get carried away, Fotini, because you feel slightly better. You need to rest," she said and stretched out onto her bed.

I wasn't planning to disobey her. I would find Stelios, grab a bite and return to my bed. I smiled and left the room without a word.

* * *

Carlo was staring through the broken shop window down the alley, which the wind was attacking with renewed force. It carried a number of objects with it, which crashed onto the cobblestones with loud clangs every time the sharp gusts died down for a few seconds.

"We can't leave now," he shouted at Gabriel over his shoulder, trying to make himself heard over the storm's roar. "Help me block the opening."

Pushing the two wooden display panels with all their strength, they brought them forward. Placing the broken cupboard and stacked shelves behind it, they blocked the entrance. Somewhat sheltered, they retreated to the far end of the shop and sat on the floor, anxiously listening to the raging sounds outside.

Carlo took out his cell phone and raised it high, trying to get a signal.

"It's no use," said Gabriel, kicking a pile of boxes away to make room for his legs. "I see you have a satellite phone," he added.

Carlo looked impressed at his observation. He hadn't expected Gabriel to notice such a detail. "Yes, it's my work phone, but it doesn't work." He switched it off and flung it indifferently into an inner pocket of his jacket.

Gabriel raised his eyebrows, but as soon as Carlo turned to face him replaced his doubting expression with a smile.

"Time to rest," said Carlo and stretched out onto the floor. Gabriel did not reply. He leaned his head against the wall and closed his eyes.

* * *

I walked into the main room and was greeted by the intoxicating smell of freshly cut fruit. A woman in a headscarf that accentuated her bright face was making her way around the room, holding a large platter.

As soon as she reached me, I picked a piece of apple and thanked her. I walked toward Stelios, Petros, and my father, who were sitting around a table with a couple of other men.

The piece of apple chased away the lingering bitterness of the brew Sophie had forced down my throat. My legs still felt shaky, but at least the dizziness was now gone.

My father stood up as soon as he saw me and gave me a hug. "Are you feeling better?" he asked and helped me sit down, keeping a protective arm around my shoulders. The others turned to me and smiled.

"Yes, much better. I wanted to know if they're back."

"We were just talking about them," Stelios replied. "I peeked outside and saw that things are really bad. Maybe they found another place to shelter. I hope they did. I've left the door unlocked. If they manage to return, they will be able to get back in. I warned them it was dangerous, but they—"

"Maybe we should go find them," I desperately interrupted. We had to do something to help them.

"Nobody is going outside." Stelios' tone did not leave any room for argument. "Especially you. Don't get carried away with Sophie's hocus-pocus. You need to rest. As soon as the weather permits it, we will go out and find the medication you need. If they don't return with it in the meantime..."

Stelios had a tendency to doubt anything he did not understand. I did not feel up to having a conversation about it though, so I left them, saying I needed to get some food.

Petros acted as if I wasn't even there. He only cared about himself, even though he had just lost his best friend and business partner.

I saw my mother in the kitchen holding a plate with two large sandwiches on it. Behind her, a group of women was busily preparing lunch.

"I'll take it, mum," I said taking the plate from her. "You stay here and help."

"You go lie down," she called out as I left the kitchen. I turned around and gave her my warmest smile. My mother was the personification of kindness and giving. She was the type of woman who would sacrifice herself for her family and others. I wished I could live up to her example.

When I returned to our room, I saw Sophie was missing. I put the plate on her bed and, taking one of the sandwiches, sat down, enjoying every bite.

I had just eaten the last bite when Sophie showed at the door. She was leaning on her walking stick with one hand and holding a cup in the other. As she neared the bed, I shuddered at the thought of drinking the brew. I didn't think my taste buds could withstand a second shock.

"It's not as strong as the last one. I had very little left," she said, bringing the cup close to my lips.

"What's in it exactly?" I asked but received no reply. She gave me a stern look and kept her skeletal hand outstretched.

I couldn't do anything other than take the cup and drink its contents in one go, a funny grimace on my face. A smile escaped Sophie, transforming her features. She looked so sweet when she smiled, almost like a different person. Her impassive mask dropped for once and, before she turned to go to her bed, I caught a look of such tenderness on her face I was stunned.

She picked up her sandwich and started eating, closing herself off once again. Her clothes were torn, but she didn't seem to mind. Her hair was piled up in an intricate web of plaits, which made it look like a tangle of twigs and branches.

As I sat on my bed watching her, I felt my body warm up once again, although this time the burning sensation was bearable. As soon as she finished eating, I drummed up my courage and asked, "How long have you been on Athora?"

"I think I've always been here. But if you're asking when I arrived...many years ago," she said bending down to place the crumb-filled plate on the floor.

I realized talking to her was not going to be easy, but I was curious, so I persevered. "I want to ask you something I can't get out of my head. If you don't mind, that is..." I said and waited for her reaction.

She looked at me without a word, giving me a brief smile. I grabbed my chance. "On the eve of the feast day, when you climbed down the cliff and helped Luka, you looked at the horizon and mentioned the Harpies. Your words have stayed with me."

"Yes, I remember what I said."

"Did you mean this?" I pointed to the ceiling, where the clattering sounds indicated the storm was still raging outside.

"I can't divine the future, Fotini, but after all these years living in nature, I've learned to read the signs. What I saw approaching, came. I didn't expect it to be so violent, of course."

The words bolted out of my mouth before I could stop them. "Do you know when it will leave?"

My question made her laugh aloud. I laughed along, as she replied, "No, I don't know. Nature decides these things. But I think the worst will be over after tonight."

"You seemed well and truly trapped behind those rocks when we left you. How did you manage to get out?"

"Thank you for caring enough to come find me. The mountain paved the way, and I made sure to get out in time. If I had waited, I might not be here now. I might not be anywhere... I'm afraid that by tomorrow not a stone of my house will be left standing."

She made her bed and lay down, slowly raising her leg onto the blankets. Her gaze fixed on the ceiling, she asked, "Have they caught the murderer?"

It was the last thing I expected to hear from her. I did not want to reveal what Stelios had confided, so I dabbed my sweaty forehead with the towel and indifferently replied, "No, not as far as I know."

"What he did to the priest shows a lot of hatred. I heard he did the same to the man they found in Pera Mera. You don't butcher a man unless you have a lot of hatred in your heart."

"Did you know there have been two other murders elsewhere, recently? Just the same?"

She turned to me, startled. "What do you mean recently?"

I was surprised to see her so animated. "I think in the past three months; one in Istanbul and another in a small town in Italy. What's it called again? Somewhere near a lake?" I wondered whether my head injury was affecting my memory.

"Como," she said and sat up.

"That's right, Como" I was surprised she recalled the name so quickly. Then again, there weren't that many famous towns by a lake in Italy.

"And they were all done in the same way, you said?"

"Yes. The methodology is the same. Actually, my dad found a description that fits the mutilations in an old book."

I could tell she was gripped, so I expanded. "It's called Maschalismos, it's an ancient practice." I went on to tell her what the book said.

"So, the man came to Athora to take revenge," she said with an inscrutable expression.

"The police on the island think it may be the work of more than one person. There was a lot of interest in Athens, but it all stopped when the storm broke out. The thought that it might be someone among us scares me. I guess we'll know more when the storm blows over, although there may not be many clues left. Even the church where Father George was murdered has collapsed."

"By your reasoning, the murderer could be you or me," she said fixing me with her gaze.

I suddenly felt as if she was accusing me of something and decided to put a stop to the conversation. "As things stand, no one can be sure about anyone. I think I'll get some sleep, if you don't mind."

"You do that," she said abruptly.

She stood up and pressed the light switch. The flame from a small lantern by the door was the only source of light. The seconds ticked past in heavy silence. "Sophie, I want to reassure you..." I said trying to lighten up the heavy mood.

"Yes?" She was looking at me once again.

"You can sleep easy tonight, I'm not *really* the murderer..." I choked with laughter at that last word and Sophie burst out into a giggling fit.

"Thank goodness you told me!" she joked back.

Not knowing whether I would ever get the chance to break through her defenses again, I decided to ask what everyone had been dying to know. "Can I ask you—"

"I know what you are going to ask," she interrupted. "I heard of Athora at a time when my life changed in the blink of an eye. I left everything behind and followed the pull of my destiny, which led me here. When or why I came does not matter. What matters is that I decided to carry on living."

She paused, distracted by the sound of children playing chase in the next room. As soon as they had trotted past our door, she continued. "Athora kept me alive. I would not have survived in any other part of the world. This place sets you free and, when you are ready, catharsis comes from within. Some part of me, some part of who I am, has been waiting for me here for thousands of years. I just happened to discover it. At least, I think I did."

Her voice dwindled down to a barely audible whisper and I was struggling to keep my eyes open. I wanted to ask her what that metaphorical, metaphysical speech meant but I did not dare. She had spoken as if she expected me to understand her bizarre explanation.

I floated on the sound of her voice as my eyes closed. It guided me to a bright place and suddenly a calm sea of the deepest blue stretched out before me, the sun ready to dip in the waters at the horizon's edge. It was so perfectly peaceful I let it engulf me.

* * *

When I woke up all was quiet inside the shelter. The stillness only made the sounds of the storm outside more terrifying. The wind howled without respite, battering everything in its path. Who knew what the island would look like when we would be free at last.

Sophie was sleeping soundly beside me. The darkness in the next room and the orange glow of a couple of candles showed that everyone must have gone to sleep.

My head no longer ached and I felt feverless. Sophie's herbs seemed to have worked and, though surprised, I felt grateful.

I put on my shoes and tiptoed through the main room. The generator was off and I was surprised at how quickly I had become accustomed to moving around in the dark. The silence was interrupted by the occasional snore and the ruffle of blankets. My parents were asleep in their usual spot, in each other's arms. At a nearby table, the trembling light of an oil lamp flickered before the icon I had rescued from the rubble.

As I tiptoed through the room, I looked out for any sign of the three men, hoping they would have returned while I had been sleeping. I did not see them. I turned toward the icon and fervently prayed that they were safe, sheltering somewhere.

I heard a sound from the far end of the room and moved toward it. Someone cast a long shadow on the wall. Someone was awake. I don't know why, but all my senses were alert. I watched as the shadow shrunk, then moved outside the room.

I picked up a flashlight from a nearby table and stepped out into the hallway. To my right, in the room where the refugees slept, a man stood covering his child with a blanket. We smiled at each other and he stretched out on the floor.

I looked at the front door and wondered what on earth I was doing. I felt as if something or someone was lurking at the end of the corridor to my left. Without wasting any time, I decided to explore further.

When the last of the candlelight had faded, I turned on my flashlight and followed its beam deeper down the corridor. I passed the room where I had changed my clothes, the room where I had caught Carlo trying to fix his phone, and walked on. The corridor widened, then came to a stop. Three doors stood ahead. The middle door was open. I swung the flashlight around looking inside. It was a storeroom piled up with old frames, mops, and buckets. The other two doors were shut.

I remembered that the Italians had dug out many underground tunnels during the war, which were now sealed off. I carefully examined both the other doors, swiping the beam of my flashlight over the bolts and hinges. The bolt of the door to the right was rusty and looked like it had not stirred in years. The other bolt looked similar. Taking a closer look, I saw a long scratch lengthwise, as if someone had at least tried to slide the bolt open.

Carlo was the name that sprung to my mind. He was the one who had disappeared for hours the previous day.

Unable to resist, I decided to try my luck and leaned against the frame, ready to slide the bolt back. To my surprise, the door creaked open. The bolt had become detached from the wooden door over the years and hung from the doorframe. I pushed the door but it only opened partially. The wood had warped over the years and the door jammed on the floor. The gap was just wide enough for a man to squeeze through.

I pondered my next move as a cool breeze stroked my face, carrying with it a strong smell of damp. The voice of reason said, turn back. My explorer's instincts said, push on. I wanted to see the tunnel for myself. I turned sideways and squeezed through the opening.

As soon as I was inside, I could tell not much had changed since the Second World War. The walls were coarse and wet, covered with patches of dark moss. The ceiling hung low and I could just about stand upright without my head touching the roof.

It was cold and I regretted not wearing my jacket. I decided to walk as far as the point where I could see the tunnel make a turn to the left and then return to my bed.

A stone, where the moss had been scraped clean, caught my attention. It was obvious that someone had recently cleared it to try to read an inscription that had been etched onto the stone. I took a closer look but could not make it out.

I kept walking until I reached the bend in the tunnel and turned left. A long straight path stretched out as far as the beam of the flashlight could reach. The air here carried the smell of saltwater and I could hear a sound coming from the end of the tunnel. I hesitated. Maybe I should be turning back.

I knew very well I wasn't going to.

I quickly crossed the tunnel. The farther I walked, the fresher the air became, a sign that I was getting close to some kind of exit.

A couple of minutes later, I stood at what appeared to be the end of a tunnel. I could now clearly hear the sound of waves crashing against the rocks. A rusty, salt-encrusted iron ladder led up to a wooden, half-broken door that obviously led outside. Gusts of winds were making it rattle, blowing in through its cracks.

I carefully climbed the ladder, holding tightly onto my flashlight. If anything happened to it, I would struggle to find my way back in the pitch dark.

I reached the door and carefully pulled it open. The thick darkness swallowed up the beam of my flashlight. I could not make out where the exit led.

With great difficulty, I saw the foam of giant waves flowing below, like shadows. I could only guess that I was high above one end of the channel and that, invisible in the dark, Pera Mera stood across the water. I was probably at the spot where one end of the bridge had once stood.

I was sure this opening could not be seen from the outside. It probably looked like a natural opening in the rocks. All evidence, though, pointed to someone who knew it existed having recently passed through.

Leaning one hand against an indentation in the rock to steady myself before climbing back down, my suspicions were confirmed. I felt a piece of cloth. Someone had dropped a baseball cap. I took a better look and recognized it immediately. What was he doing here and how did he discover the exit?

I carefully leaned over the opening to see if there was any access to the tunnel from the outside. Nothing. Maybe a ladder had once stood there, but time and brine had eroded it.

I turned off the flashlight and tried to get used to the darkness that stretched before me like a blanket, covering everything. I thought I could make something out on the small plateau formed by the rocks below, but I did not dare venture any further. I could sense the force of the winds and the power of the waves, striding through the channel like merciless giants. Eerie sounds filled the air outside, making me shiver.

There was no point in staying here any longer. I switched on my flashlight and started to make my way back to the safety of the shelter. All the way back, I mulled over what had happened, trying to make some sense of it all.

I fell onto my bed exhausted, checking Sophie was still fast asleep in her bed. It would be dawn in a few hours and I wished the new day would bring better weather, so some things could start becoming clearer.

I hid Carlo's baseball cap under my blanket and closed my eyes.

Chapter 13

A small light shone like a red bloodstain against the dark sky where the rising sun struggled to chase the night away. The storm still raged, but with diminished force. The wind carried the torrential rain in all directions, drenching everything in its path.

Carlo stepped out onto the street, closely followed by Gabriel. Looking around them, they decided to return to the shelter while the improvement in the weather still allowed them to do so.

Fallen branches and other debris blocked the streets they crossed and every heavy step was further confirmation of the disaster that had befallen the island. It would take years and lots of money to restore what nature had easily shattered in the space of two days.

Climbing over the mounds of rubble, they managed to reach the square. There, some of the locals had gathered under the ripped awnings of a shop, locked in intense conversation. They fell silent when they saw them and turned toward them.

"Where are do you think you are going?" one of them shouted in Greek.

They shrugged and motioned that they could not understand. Seeing that the two men were foreigners, the man repeated the question in English.

"We are taking medication back to the shelter, they need it. We got trapped in the pharmacy, we are on our way back now,' Carlo replied taking out one of the boxes of pills from his pocket.

The man motioned for them to be on their way and indifferently resumed his conversation with the others. Startled by the encounter, the two men left in a hurry without looking back.

* * *

The shouts I heard coming from the hallway made me jump from my bed and run in that direction. My father and Petros appeared behind me, along with some others who had been alerted by the commotion.

Stelios was giving Carlo and Gabriel a stern telling off. The two men were standing silently before him. Among the small crowd, a couple of children were staring open-mouthed at the unpleasant scene unfolding before them. I asked their parents to take them away, urging Stelios to calm down and tell me what was going on.

He kicked a chair and paced up and down, outraged. "The situation is entirely out of control," he shouted.

Carlo and Gabriel looked at him as if waiting for their sentence. Azim, however, was not with them. "Azim?" I asked them.

Both men looked downcast. "He was struggling to keep up so he decided to return to the shelter. If he is not here…" Carlo said.

Stelios pointed at the two men and shouted, "Azim is missing and these two did not give a damn!"

I asked them to give me the details. Stelios was evidently too upset to speak coherently. They told me everything that happened on the way to the pharmacy, adding that they expected to find Azim back here and that they had no idea where he could be.

I felt awful. By the time they finished their story, I wanted to disappear from the face of the earth. This was all because of me, needlessly so, as I was already feeling much better.

Sophie watched everything from a corner of the hallway without uttering a word.

Stelios asked everyone not immediately involved in the matter to leave. Most of the people reluctantly returned to the main room. Having regained his composure, he turned to the two men. "I'm sorry about the shouting, but how can I keep calm when people go missing? What's the weather like now?"

"It seems to be improving," Gabriel explained. "The damage is worse, though. We didn't have any trouble coming back and I think we can go outside." He turned toward me and started emptying his pockets. "The pharmacy was looted. This is all we could find. I don't know if it's what you need, though."

Paying no attention to the boxes, I approached both of them and took their hands in mine. "Thank you for everything you've done for me. Please, let's go find Azim now."

"Fotini, you shouldn't go outside," Stelios sternly intervened. "It's not a good idea. We'll go. You rest. Remember how sick you were last night."

There was no way I was staying back here. They all protested, but nothing they said could change my mind. In the end, they gave in and we all agreed to meet again in a few minutes.

Stelios informed everyone about our decision, but asked that the children stay behind in the shelter, as we did not know what was waiting for us outside. I saw my father at the back of the room, trying to explain in broken English and miming what was happening to a group of refugees. I felt Azim's absence stronger than ever. I hoped he was well and that we would find him or I would be forever tormented by guilt.

Gabriel and Carlo walked further inside the shelter to change out of their wet clothes and I followed them. Gabriel stepped into the men's dormitory, saying he would meet us out front. I nodded, and then grabbed Carlo by the arm as he made to follow Gabriel into the room. "You, come with me," I ordered.

He followed me into the small room I shared with Sophie, who was absent, luckily. I went straight to my bed and pulled back the blanket, revealing the baseball cap. Looking him straight in the eye, I said, "I believe this is yours."

He picked it up and examined it coolly. "So you found the secret passage, too," he whispered.

"Yes I did, but I can't fathom what you were doing there or how you managed to get in from the outside."

"I didn't get in from the outside," he scoffed. "Why would I do that? *How* could I do that? I'm sure you've seen the cliff below. I told you the truth; I came back in with everyone else. I just made sure you didn't see me and start following me around again."

"What are you two whispering about?" Stelios' voice made me jump. I hadn't heard him creeping into the room.

Calmly, Carlo turned and looked at him. I was impressed by his self-control, his mastery in keeping a poker face at all time. He looked at me and smiled wryly, as if amused by all the attention. "Fotini and I were talking about the secret passage. She found my cap there and now she is interrogating me about it. I don't know why she's so surprised. The place is full of tunnels. Aren't you curious to see where they lead? I wanted to see if it led to a high point or some kind of opening where I could get a signal."

He gestured to Stelios that he was reaching into his pocket, and then slowly pulled out his phone. "This is my satellite phone. Going into the secret passage yesterday, I managed to make a brief call from the top of the ladder at the end. Where you found my hat, Fotini," he said.

Stelios did not look surprised to hear of the tunnel and that we had both been in it. "Hold on," he said. "Let's take this from the beginning. You both went into the tunnel that leads to the cliff opposite Pera Mera?"

I briefly explained what had happened and stressed how I was just being curious about the place, but realized something else had happened once I found Carlo's hat. I did not want to reveal that Carlo's strange behavior was the reason I was snooping around in the first place.

"Fine, we'll talk about what you were doing later," Stelios said and turned to Carlo. "You said you managed to make a call?"

"Yes, briefly, then the battery went dead." Carlo offered the phone to Stelios, who promptly ignored it.

"Shouldn't you have informed us?" he asked angrily. "We've been trying to make contact with the outside world for the last two days and you made a call without telling us anything?"

"I was going to—"

"When?" Stelios roared. I was sure they heard him all the way to the entrance.

"I suggest you calm down," Carlo said coldly.

I felt I had to step in and soothe everyone's ruffled feathers. "Carlo, please understand that we are all anxious to find out what's happening to the rest of the country. Did you find out when the storm will be over?"

"I told you, it was a brief call. I didn't even get a chance to deal with any of my stuff. I only found out the damage has been extensive, especially on the islands."

"That's it?" Stelios insisted, still upset. "Anything else?"

"No, nothing else. The battery went dead."

"And we can't call again?" Stelios asked, looking at the phone Carlo was now twirling in his fingers like a toy.

"All my things are in Pera Mera," Carlo shrugged. "My charger too. I used up all the battery during the last call."

"How did you know about the secret passage?" Stelios asked suspiciously.

"I heard an old man talking about it at my hotel. That there was an exterior ladder once, but that it was hard to spot the opening from the outside as it was no longer there. I thought the signal might work up there. I was right. It worked for about half a minute."

I gave Stelios a meaningful look but he just shrugged. Carlo did not miss the exchange. He indignantly shook his head in disgust and walked out of the room.

"Do you believe him?" I asked Stelios as soon as Carlo was out of sight.

Kostas Krommydas

"I have no reason not to. I'm more troubled by Azim's disappearance."

Gabriel's voice calling our names hushed us. He appeared in the doorway, looking baffled. "Come on, what are you still doing here?" he asked. "Where is Carlo?"

"Who can ever know?" I snapped in frustration. I recovered my composure as soon as I saw Gabriel's questioning look and gave him a tight smile. "I guess he is changing too."

"Let's go then," Gabriel said impatiently, putting an arm around my shoulder and leading me to the exit.

Lost in my thoughts, I let him guide me. A strange web was being spun around me in twists and knots, blurring everything. In vain did I try to shed some light on everyone's intentions. There was something vague, obscure in their words and deeds that made everything seem unreal. I could not tell where hard facts ended and my own feelings began.

Take Azim, for example. Did the sympathy I feel for the man and the emotions his Odysseys had stirred in me prevent me from seeing him clearly, objectively, as Stelios maintained? If he had nothing to do with the murders, why would he run away at the first opportunity? Had he run away or was he missing, injured or dead?

And Carlo? He had resuscitated me. He had risked his life to go find my medication. Why did I still think he was hiding something? Was I being unfair?

I looked at Gabriel. At least I could be sure about him. We had been on Ikaria together; we had made our way to the island together. The confusion I felt was a result of mixed emotions. Not just my emotions, though. His own behavior

- 265 -

was full of contradictions. One moment he was declaring his love for his future wife and the next, he was showing his keen interest in me, just as he was doing now; holding me so tenderly I felt a warm tingle ran down my spine.

I saw Sophie walk toward us and I thought about how hers was the only mystery the storm had solved. The aura of mystical remoteness that surrounded her had collapsed. She certainly had her own secrets and was a quirky, unusual human being, but very human in the end—an excellent herbalist and a kind person, as evidenced both times when someone had been in need.

"You shouldn't go outside," she said staring into my eyes hypnotically.

"I feel much better," I replied. I touched her hand and emotionally added, "Thank you, Sophie, for everything."

"Don't thank me, thank Mother Earth. She saved you." She pointed to the exit and added, "I would love to join you but I doubt I can walk all the way to the square. Please, could you have a look at my mountain? See if anything is left standing."

"I don't know what it's like out there, but yes, I'll do my best," I reassured her. "Especially if we go to my house, I can get a clearer view from there. I'll come back and let you know."

People were heading toward the exit. I said goodbye and followed everyone else. Just before I stepped outside, I wished that was the last time we were leaving the shelter in these circumstances. I wanted everything to be over, to return to America.

As if guessing my thoughts, Gabriel stopped and looked at me questioningly. I felt awkward and lowered my head, trying to hide the maelstrom of feelings rising to the surface now that everything seemed to be over.

He gently raised my chin and looked deep into my eyes. "Are you okay? I worry about you, you know," he whispered softly. I stroked his cheek tenderly. He sighed, took my hand and gently lowered it. "Everything will be fine," he said. Still holding hands, we both stepped outside.

* * *

Like a convoy of refugees, we all slowly walked together through the wreckage of the Chora. Stelios and Gabriel walked beside me, one on either side. My parents walked ahead, holding hands, speechlessly staring at the apocalyptic destruction before them.

Luckily, the old stone houses had withstood the storm and still stood upright, bereft. The wooden roofs, the potted plants, doors, and windows had been smashed or swept away.

We all stopped and stared in awe at a car, upturned on a collapsed roof. It felt surreal to see our island like this. Our eyes took in the sights around us but it would be a while before the scale of what stretched before us sank in. I wished over and over that this was the end. A small spark of hope had taken root inside me, but Professor Marcus' words about a "temporary improvement" stopped the spark from turning into a flame. After all, he had been right in everything he had predicted so far.

The wind was still blowing, strong but bearable. The clouds were now a dark gray, backlit by the rays of the sun still hiding somewhere behind the stormy blanket, waiting for his chance to reappear once again.

Other residents were slowly stepping out from their cellars, taking stock of the damage they had sustained. Looking at all these people milling about, helplessly, timidly, I once again thought how small and insignificant we all were before nature; and how arrogant and destructive at the same time. Our own impact, our own acts were affecting the environment and speeding up climate change, and I hoped that what had happened here was not an indication of a looming change across the globe.

Many of those who had sought refuge in the shelter were leaving to make their way back home. Stelios kept warning everyone to be careful and return to the shelter at the slightest change, stressing that it would remain open for as long as was needed. The rest of us reached the square, where other locals had already gathered.

The church of St Porphyrios had received another battering during the night. Whatever had been left of the bell tower had completely collapsed into the main building, swallowed up by the gaping open mouth of what had once been the roof.

People gathered in small groups trying to tally up the damage. Some held their cell phones high, vainly trying to get a signal. My phone was still in the police jeep. I gave a startled laugh at that thought. The chances of ever finding my phone, the chances of ever finding the jeep, were slim.

Stelios resumed his role as co-coordinator and once again stepped on the same bench, trying to radio the chief over at Pera Mera. Hearing him talk, I absent-mindedly looked to the north, my attention caught by a huddle of white dots against the clouds. I squinted trying to understand what I was seeing. Seagulls, flying toward

Athora! My heart burst with joy. I took their appearance as a sign that the worst was over, that the weather would now improve.

Stelios' words made everyone fall silent and turn in his direction. This time we could hear what the chief was saying clearly. The soldiers stationed there had managed to make contact with Athens and the weather was expected to gradually improve. Eventually, when the winds allowed it, help would arrive from Lesbos. Although that island had also been caught in the storm, the weather had not been as violent, and Lesbos was in a better state than Athora.

As soon as Stelios stepped down, one of the locals shouted out, "The port is completely destroyed. Every boat has been smashed on the rocks or sunk."

People were still tense, teetering on the verge of panic. Stelios sensed it and rose to the occasion. "The only thing we can't bring back are the people we've lost. Everything else we can fix. You heard it yourselves: help will soon be on its way. Stay calm and be patient for a little longer."

"What if it doesn't come? Just because they said they would, doesn't mean they will," the same man shouted back.

Stelios, who evidently knew the man, looked at him and swallowed his rising anger. "Then we will do what must be done, Nikos. Go see what has happened to your homes, your property. Please report any damage and look for those you haven't heard from, so we know if any more people are missing."

Everyone turned to each other and started talking all at once, asking about this and that person. Shouting at the top of my lungs, I asked if anyone had seen Azim. I received no reply, as if no one cared. Disappointed, I returned to my parents, beckoning Gabriel to approach. Carlo, who had stayed back at the shelter, appeared at the other end of the square looking for us.

"Your mother and I are going to the house," my father said. "See what's happened, pick up my pills. If the weather gets worse..."

I did not let him finish. "You are going nowhere yet. I'll go get your pills." Carlo came and joined our little circle, so I gestured toward him and Gabriel. "If Gabriel and Carlo would like to accompany me..."

"Fotini, it's not a good idea. You are still not fully recovered," Gabriel said warmly, with a look of concern. "Tell us where the house is and we'll go get your father's pills." Carlo gave a nod of assent.

"I feel much better," I replied. "I want to see the state of the house myself. It's hard to give you directions with all the street signs and landmarks possibly gone. Plus, I want us to look for Azim."

"If he didn't manage to find shelter, I'm afraid we may never find him," Carlo gloomily said looking at the damaged buildings all around the square.

I didn't want us to waste any more time, so I signaled we should head off and informed Stelios of our plans. He did not seem happy.

A few minutes later, we were climbing up toward the outskirts of the Chora, where my parents' house was. The main road had been badly damaged, so I took them through a narrow pedestrian alley full of steps.

The landslides and flash floods had completely altered the landscape. At a higher point, I paused and turned toward the Chora. I doubled over as if I'd just been punched when I came face to face with a panoramic view of the havoc the storm had wreaked. I heard the men beside me gasp in horror. Although neither of them knew the island as well as I did, they were both aghast at the devastation.

The thick fog that had lingered on the island's edge began to lift and the sea emerged. I had never seen the water look so murky. The white foam of the waves crashing against the rocks could be seen even from this distance. Farther out, masts jutted out from the water, the broken hulls of ships dancing manically around them.

More people were coming up the steps behind us, heading toward their homes. By the time we reached the small neighborhood where my house stood, the wind had dispersed most of the clouds and a cold, gloomy sun shone down. The sharp gusts of wind whipped our face at this altitude, trying to jostle us back down the slope.

Similar scenes of despair greeted us there. I spoke to everyone along the way, exchanged news and sensed everyone's hopelessness. They all wanted to know what the forecast was, their eyes constantly scanning the horizon, anxiously wondering if the storm had truly passed. Carlo had taken his phone out once again and was trying to get a signal. A woman asked us to help her shift a large branch that was blocking her doorway. Both men ran to help her, telling me to keep going as they would catch up later.

As soon as I saw our home, my eyes filled with tears. Our wooden balcony had disappeared, leaving behind a series of jagged beams that jutted out, like a shark's serrated teeth. All the wooden shutters had been ripped from the windows and the front door hung open from a single lonely hinge.

I gently pushed the door and stepped inside. Everything had been turned upside down. The wind and the rain had invaded the house through the gaping windows, soaking everything. Paintings, lampshades, shelves, and ornaments had been ripped from the wall. The house looked like it had been ransacked by a crazed burglar. I reminded myself I should be thankful we were safe and that the house was still here; the rest could be replaced.

I don't know if it was the effect of Sophie's brew, but I was sweating profusely. Perhaps the long walk and the heavy humid atmosphere were to blame.

I walked to the bathroom cupboard and put my father's pills in a backpack. The kitchen was tucked away at the end of the house and had sustained less damage than the front room. Miraculously, my laptop still stood on a bench, fully charged. I put it in my bag, although there was no hope of an internet connection. All the phone lines on the island were down.

I climbed the stone staircase to my bedroom and was surprised to see that it was more or less intact. The wooden shutter had withstood the force of the wind and protected the glass window.

I opened a drawer to find something warm and comfortable to wear and began to discard my wet, sweaty clothes. Naked, I stood before the mirror and examined my body. My back and sides were bruised. Coupled with the bandage on my forehead, I looked like I had been the victim of a serious beating.

As I stood looking in the mirror, the reflection of another figure crept onto the smooth surface. I recoiled and then saw that it was Gabriel. I hadn't heard him climb up the stairs. He stood on the landing, watching me. I did nothing to cover my nakedness. Holding very still, I steadily returned his gaze through the mirror as time slowed down, then stopped.

He moved first, stepping into the bedroom. In the mirror, I watched him approach, like a movie scene unfolding in slow motion. A soft breeze flew into the room and caressed my body, making me shiver. My brain had stopped working, instinct taking over.

He stood close to me and at the thought that he was about to touch me, my body tingled with sweet anticipation, a throbbing numbness spreading through my limbs. The warmth of his body so close made every pore of my skin dilate. His hot breath burned my neck. We stood still a moment longer, our eyes still locked in the mirror.

Unable to resist my own body's impulses any longer, I made to turn toward him but froze on the spot when I heard Carlo calling us. Gabriel touched my neck with his lips, hesitatingly exploring its curve. I closed my eyes to hold on to the last image of us reflected in the mirror.

I only realized he'd left when I heard him call out to Carlo as he went down the stairs. I caught my naked reflection in the mirror; only then did I feel myself blush with embarrassment. I hurriedly dressed and pulled on a pair of comfortable old hiking boots.

I made my way downstairs and found them waiting in the yard. As if nothing had happened, Gabriel said, "Let's go now, if you're done."

His eyes spoke volumes, but I did not want Carlo to suspect anything had happened between us. "Let me check the cellar first," I replied.

I went down the steps by the side of the house that led to the cellar, still shaken by Gabriel's arrival in my room. Except for a pile of rubbish that had collected outside the door, the cellar was intact. The cabinets that housed my father's collection of old records were still there. Sophie's file must have been among them, but although I was dying to peek at it, it would have to wait.

At the far end of the cellar, I spotted two cots made up with blankets and pillows. My mother must have prepared them before they changed their mind and joined us at the shelter. Had they stayed here, they would have still been safe. I closed the door behind me and went back up to the yard. Somehow, the thought made me glad.

"Do you need anything else from here?" Carlo asked, impatient to leave.

"No, I think I have everything I need. Let's go back to the Chora and see what we are going to do."

We walked back down the same way. Soon, the house was far behind us. The clouds had thinned considerably and, for the first time that day, a small opening in the clouds to the west revealed a morsel of blue sky. I took it as a good omen.

I looked toward where the chapel stood and could just about make its shape through the clouds masking the mountaintop, standing as still and imperious as ever. I was glad it had withstood the storm. Sophie's hill on the opposite side had not fared as well. It looked like it had been cut in half by a giant carving knife, and the side that had been sliced off had tumbled down the cliff and into the sea, sweeping the small house with it.

As we walked, we talked about what might have happened to Azim. Carlo said he was probably dead. Perhaps we would find his remains somewhere, someday, he added cynically. I was horrified at the thought, but not for long. The whirlwind of emotion spinning inside me was dominated by feelings that had to do with Gabriel's presence. I felt angry with myself for thinking about my crush like a teenager when all these terrible things were happening around me.

I had thought my feelings for him had been a fleeting infatuation, but the incident at my house said otherwise. The attraction I felt was deep, insurmountable. I couldn't determine whether it was just lust, but was painfully aware that my resistance was ready to crumble.

As we approached the Chora, we saw people trying to clear up the terrible damage caused by the storm as best as they could. Some stood and stared at the horizon, where the sun shone down like a spotlight through a crack in the clouds, setting the surface of the sea on fire. The wind, still blowing strong, soon closed the opening, pressing the clouds together once again. It was clear, nonetheless, that the weather would soon improve.

There were fewer people in the square when we got there. Most of the locals had felt bold enough to return to their homes, even though there was no power or water.

Stelios came over and told us that the latest forecasts predicted a vast improvement in the weather as of the following day. He also said that the only two people missing were Azim and Kimon. Others had sustained light injuries;

a makeshift hospital was being set up in the town hall to treat them.

I told him what the situation was like on the outskirts of the Chora. I could sense something else was troubling him, so I pulled him aside asking the other two to excuse us for a moment.

"The man they caught at Pera Mera had nothing to do with the murders," he announced dryly. I could sense that, despite his wish to catch the murderer, he felt somewhat vindicated.

"What happened?" I asked him, looking at Carlo and Gabriel drift off in opposite directions.

"The way I understand it, the man had some kind of breakdown. The blood on his hands was his own, where he had harmed himself. The chief didn't say much, but was categorical that the man was not our killer."

"So the murderer is still free?" I asked, glancing around me.

"Yes, and the way I understand it, Athens is still very interested in the case."

"Did you find out anything else about the newcomers?"

"No, other people were around so we couldn't talk freely. We'll radio each other in a while and I'll ask him to check out Carlo and the company he says he works for. I will also ask him to investigate Azim. Find out where he really is from. If he can, with everything else that is going on." His face darkened and he lowered his voice. "Although I'm sure who the killer is."

"Who?" I asked, although I knew the answer.

"The missing man." Stelios uttered the phrase slowly, looking at me intently. Before I could respond, he continued. "We'll deal with this later. We have things to attend to, now that the weather seems to be clearing up. If it holds, help will be here tomorrow. You could go help the doctor at the town hall if you want to."

He turned to walk away, but I grabbed his arm and forced him to stop. Startled, he gave me a questioning look. "It's always easy to find a scapegoat," I insisted. "Don't be so sure Azim is in any way involved in this murder business."

"Do you want to bet we'll never find out what happened to him?" he said, freeing his hand from my grasp.

"No, because he could be lying in a ditch, smashed by the wind, or in the water. If he's alive, how could he leave the island?"

He smiled sardonically. "Want to bet on it?" he repeated.

"On what?" I shouted, drawing curious looks in our direction.

"Everything," he mouthed, then waved goodbye and walked away.

I looked around trying to spot Gabriel and Carlo but they were gone. I must have looked strange with my bandaged head because everyone was curiously examining me. I wanted to help at the town hall, but I first returned to the shelter to check on my parents and Sophie.

I told my father about the state of our house. Without wasting any time, he told my mother they were packing up and going home. I pleaded with them to stay one more day, but they would not be swayed. Seeing that they were set on returning, I advised them to go down to the cellar and stay there if the weather worsened.

My father soon reappeared holding the icon I had found in the rubble and their small suitcase, my mother following behind him. I kissed them goodbye and went looking for Sophie.

As I approached our room, I heard children's voices and peals of laughter coming from inside. My curiosity aroused, I walked in and came face to face with a heartwarming sight. Seated in a chair, Sophie was telling them the story of Snow White, speaking slowly so one of the refugee women could translate it into Arabic. Her funny expressions and voices greatly amused the young audience and she pointed a bony finger in my direction as soon as she saw me, making me part of the story. I was cast as the evil stepmother and I laughed so heartily everyone remained unconvinced of my hatred for Snow White.

I waited until she finished and watched how tenderly, how lovingly she spoke to those poor children, whose destiny had pummeled them with so many tragedies. War and nature had already taught them that this was a cruel, harsh world.

They all applauded her at the end. She stood and hobbled in my direction, leaning on her walking stick. I was silent as we walked to the exit, trying to think of how I could break the bad news about her house, her mountain, to her.

"I hear the weather is getting better," she commented lightly, sensing my discomfort.

"Yes, I think it's over now."

"The Harpies took what they came for," she whispered. "I sense the news about my house is not good."

"No, Sophie, I'm sorry. The mountain split in two and the landslide did not just sweep the *Anemotafia* to the sea. It took everything with it."

"Did you see whether the stone with the carved eye survived?"

"No, I couldn't tell from that distance," I replied and saw disappointment and pain distort her features. "I know you carved that stone. Do you want to tell me what the eye symbolizes? Does it have anything to do with the legend of the Harpies? I've heard lots of talk about it, that's why I'm asking. Is it a symbol of some ceremony or..."

"It's all rumors, untruths," she interrupted me and sat down on a bench without another word. I did not press her. I understood that, in Sophie's mind, the Harpies were another word for punishment. I sat down beside her, in case she needed to talk.

"When I first came to Athora, many years ago, I used to camp out away from people," she sighed. "When I discovered that little house, hollowed out of the mountainside, abandoned, I moved in. I fixed it up as best I could and no one ever asked me to move out, in all these thirty years. It's as if that house stood there waiting for me."

"I'll help you find a new house," I said trying to comfort her.

"You won't have to, Fotini."

She asked me to help her get up from the bench, not giving me a chance to ask her what she meant. "I'd like to stay here for a couple of days," she said, "then I'll be on my way."

"I think you can stay for as long as you like until some kind of normality returns. Then we can—"

"The island has shown me what I must do," she said abruptly. "Please, go tend to your own affairs. I'll be fine, don't you worry about me. I like to live under the ground, you know."

Perhaps it wasn't the best time to reason with her. I made sure that her leg did not need further medical attention and got up to leave.

"Did they catch the murderer?" she asked as I was walking off.

"No Sophie." I turned to look at her. "He is still at large, if he is still alive."

We looked at each other for a moment. Her face was an impassive mask. She looked away. I walked out of the shelter.

The fresh breeze on my face now filled me with optimism. The more sunlight broke through the clouds, casting its glow over the island, the surer I felt this nightmare was finally over. As I walked by the church, I remembered the priest's body on the altar and the brief respite was over. Something dark still lurked over the island.

Stelios' suspicions regarding Azim were more bigoted thinking than serious police work, as there was no evidence to support them. I wished Azim had survived, as I was the reason he had left the shelter. Or was I? Could it be that he had used it as an opportunity to leave the shelter and run away? To go where? If he had survived, he would have to reappear at some point.

Lost in my own thoughts I arrived at the town hall. I clambered over a broken table on the pavement and stepped inside. Many people had gathered and the doctor was trying to get volunteers and patients organized. Luckily, no one appeared to have been seriously injured.

The doctor smiled when she saw me and directed me to an elderly woman who had injured her hand. I dressed the wound mechanically, my head filled with alternating images of the murdered priest, the father on the collapsing bridge, the waves closing over my head—and Gabriel standing behind me and kissing my neck.

* * *

Seated on a rock, Gabriel gazed out at the choppy waters outside the Chora. He zipped up his jacket against the cold wind and closed his eyes. He sat like that for a few minutes, letting the breeze stroke his face.

Distant voices made him open his eyes and look for the source of the shouting. A little farther away, outside a shop, some locals were quarreling. Luckily, everybody calmed down quickly and Gabriel's attention returned to the gray, choppy sea. He felt unsettled by the upheaval on the island. He wanted the strange weather conditions to be over so he could leave. For the first time in days, it looked like that might finally be possible.

A small boat was floating rudderless, clumsily dancing to the rhythm of the waves. He looked closely, but no one seemed to be aboard. The wind would sweep it to the shore, to join the ruins of another boat, which had not been so lucky as to survive intact.

Scanning the horizon, he saw the weather was changing for the better. He stood up and decided to return to the Chora.

On the way, he ran into one of the coastguards, who, along with a group of men, were trying to clear a heap of broken branches that blocked the road. He helped them and asked if there was any way to reach Pera Mera across the channel. The coastguard shook his head no. The small dock had collapsed and taking a boat across was too dangerous, as the waves were still high. In any case, it was unlikely any boat had survived the sea tornado. Even the ferry from Ikaria had split in half, inside the port. Once the wind eased, a ship might arrive and drop anchor farther out. Anyone who wished to leave could board it on smaller boats that would transport people from the shore.

All of Gabriel's belongings were over at Pera Mera. He could not even remember where his cell phone was after everything that had happened and his laptop had been left on the small coffee table inside the hotel villa. Though he desperately wanted to get to it, it would have to wait.

He gladly accepted the invitation of a local couple, who saw that he was stranded, to stay with them. Even though he wanted to see Fotini again, he preferred to keep his distance. Meeting her had affected him in ways he had not expected. He certainly hadn't anticipated the turn things would take. He would soon have to leave the island forever, however, and so would she.

* * *

Looking outside the broken town hall windows, I watched the horizon. It was nearly afternoon and the damaged roofs that dotted the skyline were the only reminder of the previous two days. The clouds had lost their ominous heaviness and dispersed, allowing the pale blue sky to appear in ever-increasing patches. A pale pink haze to the west indicated that the sun would soon be setting.

Seated around a table, we snacked on the food the neighbors had brought over. All the injured had returned home and I was about to return to my parent's house, certain that they needed my help.

Carlo would be spending the night at the shelter with Sophie and the refugees. I hadn't seen Gabriel for hours and wondered what had become of him. I soon found out.

One of the coastguards, recognizing Carlo and me as one of Gabriel's friends, informed us that Gabriel would not be spending the night at the shelter but at one of the local houses. I was surprised to hear it. I could not understand why he had not joined us here, but I figured he must have had his reasons. On the other hand, many of the locals from Pera Mera who had been stranded here would be spending the night at various local houses, so maybe his decision was not that unusual. It would certainly be more comfortable than a night in the shelter.

Stelios told us that the weather forecast agency had confirmed the improvement in the weather was permanent. The following day, around lunchtime, a navy frigate was expected to arrive from Lesbos, bringing help. More ships were due to arrive as the weather improved.

All the refugees had been ordered to leave the island on the frigate, he added, leaving us stunned. There had been no sign of Azim and we all feared the worst. If the wind could lift a car as if it were a feather, we could only guess what it could do to a human caught in its path.

* * *

It was dark by the time I returned home. My parents had cleared what they could and were preparing to go to bed, exhausted.

I was about to do the same, although I was desperate for a shower. I would have given anything for running water, even freezing, to wash off the sweat and the dust hammered into my skin by the wind during that long day.

I stood before my bedroom window and gazed up at the dark sky. The stars were out again, glittering and sparkling against the black dome. Even the wind had died down and only a dog barking in the distance disrupted the heavenly, welcome silence that reigned.

I huddled under my blankets and gently touched the wound on my forehead, which was starting to throb once again. I felt better, but intended to check myself into a hospital and have it thoroughly examined first chance I got.

It felt strange to be without electricity and any of the usual lines of communication. For the first time in many years, I felt free of all the constraints the phone, laptop, and technology had imposed on my life. At the same time, I was desperate to call Gabriel, as in the night before everything changed, and let his voice sweep me up again.

* * *

It was past midnight and the entire neighborhood had settled down for the evening, resting before another daunting day ahead. It would be a while before life returned to normal. People had lost their possessions, lives had been lost, and on this first night after the storm, people had hunkered down where they felt most comfortable—at home, with their families. Candles and oil lamps flickered on many of the windows, holding a silent vigil.

In an alley, a lone male figure made its way through the dark. He walked cautiously, sticking close to the walls of the houses that lined the street, despite the cover provided by the absence of street and house lights. A baseball cap hung low over his forehead and he moved as soundlessly as a cat.

As soon as he reached Fotini's house he paused, scanning the street to the left and right. Then he gingerly stepped over the broken garden wall, taking each step carefully, trying to avoid the rubble and branches that might give his presence away.

He crept to the steps leading to the cellar and descended carefully. The door was unlocked. He pushed it open, inch by inch, pausing with every creak. As soon as the opening was wide enough for a man to pass through, he sidled inside.

The darkness was even heavier inside the windowless room. He took out a small penlight and scanned the room with its narrow beam. It did not take long to spot the cabinets that housed folder upon folder. He had not expected them to be so many. He pulled open a drawer and started to peruse them, ignoring anything that bore a more recent date.

A few minutes later, he found what he was looking for. He took out the yellowing folder and pulled out the sparse, handwritten pages. Some were marked with faded official stamps. An old passport photo showed a young woman with long hair. He shone his penlight directly on the faded face and took a closer look. He secured the light on a nearby shelf and started to replace the pages in the folder. The penlight rolled to the floor with a dull thud and died out. He swore and fumbled around in the dark for it, accidentally knocking over a pile of boxes to his right. The loud noise made by the boxes and their spilling contents made his heart stop. He was certain it must have traveled all the way to the sleeping house above. He felt his fingers touch something cold—the flashlight. His heart thumping in his chest, he switched it on and stuffed the folder under his jacket. He walked to the door and flung it open, ignoring the loud creak, and ran up the stairs and over the low garden wall, sprinting down the narrow street until he was swallowed up by the darkness.

* * *

The loud thud made me jump out of bed. The oil lamp in my room had died out and I fumbled my way to the window, in the dim moonlight. I looked outside and saw a figure running down the street.

The sound of my parents' voices drifted up the stairs. I grabbed a pair of jeans and a t-shirt from my closet and pulled them on, then ran out to the landing. My mother stood at the bottom of the stairs holding a candle. "Someone has broken into the cellar," she whispered.

I saw my father come out of the kitchen holding the bread knife. Under any other circumstances, I would have laughed at the bizarre sight. "I think he's gone," I said. "I saw someone ran away."

I went downstairs and stepped outside holding a flashlight, followed by my father who refused to put the knife away. We cautiously walked to the stairs leading to the basement. I turned the flashlight toward the open door and stupidly shouted, "Who's there?" Of course, there was no reply.

My father walked in first and I followed closely behind, scanning the room with the flashlight. A pile of boxes that had spilled on the floor was the only sign of an intrusion.

The sound of footsteps on the stairs made us jump. My mother appeared at the open doorway, brandishing a broomstick. We tried to calm her down and started to check if anything was missing. My father bent down to collect all the papers that had spilled on the floor, muttering between gritted teeth.

As soon as the boxes had been cleared, he asked me to bring the flashlight closer and began to examine the open drawer of the filing cabinet. He carefully went through all the files, one by one. "There's a folder missing," he exclaimed.

"A folder?" I asked incredulously.

"One of the old records," he muttered. He started pulling out more folders. "Help me carry these upstairs and when I've gone through them I'll tell you which one."

I handed the flashlight to my mother and picked up an armful of folders. My father gathered another bunch and we returned to the house, my mother lighting the way. I could not fathom why someone would risk breaking into the house just to steal a set of old records. It made no sense. All my instincts screamed that something very unusual was going on.

We brought every candle and oil lamp in the house to the dining table and left my father there to go through his papers. I returned to the yard and checked that no one was around, just to be safe. I walked down the street, but all was quiet. Whoever the intruder had been, he was now far away. I stood in the doorway, looking up at the night sky. Clusters of stars twinkled, spreading their dim light onto the world below.

My father's voice interrupted the peaceful scene and I quickly returned to the dining room. He sat at the table, looking stunned. "Guess whose records they stole?" he asked.

* * *

The night at the shelter had been peaceful. Only the sound of people slowly waking up, preparing for the day ahead, could be heard. In one of the side rooms, Carlo sat cross-legged in front of an open wall socket. He had removed the cover and was fumbling with the wires, trying to charge his phone.

He had turned on the generator despite the early hour and Stelios' instructions that they do not use it, to save fuel in case it was needed in another emergency. He did not care; he had to find out.

The screen of his phone flashed a pale blue and a small smile of satisfaction spread on his face. He placed his phone on a chair to charge and pushed himself up with the ease of a fit, agile man.

He was startled to see Sophie block his way, leaning on her walking stick.

"Did you turn on the generator?" she asked, looking at the phone beside him.

"Yes, I wanted to charge my phone. Is there a problem?" he replied, trying to understand what her intentions were.

"No, I'm just surprised. Stelios was very specific," she replied, inscrutably.

"I know," Carlo replied and strode to the doorway, showing he did not intend to get into an argument or let anyone stand in his way. Sophie stepped aside. "You are not who you say you are," she whispered.

Carlo paused, and then turned toward her, unperturbed. "Everyone's mask will drop soon, you just wait and see."

They stood, staring at each other for a few seconds. Carlo then turned and walked into the main area where food was once again being laid on the tables. Evidently troubled, Sophie limped back to her room.

* * *

The warm rays of the early morning sun on my face woke me up and filled me with cheer. After the events of the previous night and the anxious feelings they had stirred in me, I needed respite more than ever. I walked to the window and watched the rising sun. A few, scattered clouds, pink and purple in the early dawn, dotted the sky. If only I could stay and look at the clear sky all day, everything would be perfect. Nevertheless, my eyes turned to the back garden and my father's orchard and my heart sunk. The trees my father had planted and tended to all his life lay uprooted or broken, like the tortured souls of the damned.

I stretched and felt my body ache. I moved to the bathroom, where my mother had lined a couple of bottles by the sink, and frugally splashed some on my face. I changed my bandage, got dressed, and joined my parents downstairs.

My mother was making breakfast while my father was in the front yard, trying to shovel all the debris into a far corner. He nodded that he was coming and soon enough the three of us were seated around the table, puzzling over the strange theft. None of us could come up with an explanation as to why anyone would want to steal that woman's records.

I wanted to inform Stelios as soon as I could, so we could put our heads together and see what we should do. Even though other matters seemed to be pressing, an alarm bell inside me kept ringing that this was important.

"Be very careful," my father advised as I pulled on my backpack and stepped out.

The scenes on the way to the Chora were a repetition of the previous day, with people trying to clear up and repair the damage to their houses. In an empty lot on the outskirts of town, a group of children was running around kicking a ball and shouting carefree, as if nothing had happened.

I felt my heart fill with joy. *Life always found a way to go on.* In a year's time, this would seem like a brief nightmare. That was the story of humanity. We had survived worse disasters and would be facing new ones for as long as the world turned. I could only hope that they would be mild; that the cost would be bearable. My knowledge that without natural disasters we would not be here today gave me a different perspective. Metaphorically speaking, they were the sacrifice made to appease Nature's wrath. I knew it was a point of view many of the drawn faces I encountered did not share.

Seeing Gabriel coming up toward me, I wondered whether these constant encounters were random. It was as if an invisible force was pulling us together, throwing us into each other's path.

"Good morning," he smiled.

"Hi," I replied and then felt tongue-tied. A ship horn blaring in the distance broke the awkward moment. We both turned and watched as a large navy vessel approached what remained of the port and dropped anchor.

"Shall we go?" Gabriel asked, stretching out his hand. I took it and we walked to the town, hand in hand, fingers entwined. Trying to cover how flustered I felt by the touch of his warm palm, I recounted the events of the previous night.

"Why would someone want to steal her records?" he asked, looking as puzzled as my parents had been.

Even though I feared he might think I was being paranoid, I decided to tell him what I really thought. "I can't be sure, but I have a feeling this break-in is somehow linked to the murders."

He stopped and looked at me, surprised. "Interesting... what makes you say that?" he said, looking out to the frigate, which slowly spun around in the current.

The blades of a helicopter on the ship's deck began to spin. We watched it slowly rise in the air and make its way toward the island.

"Both murder victims were not local," I said. I paused trying to put my thoughts in order. He waited patiently and I could feel all his attention focused on what I was saying. "Sophie isn't a local either. She registered as a resident around thirty years ago with a Canadian passport. Do you remember what my father said at the shelter about her record not being computerized yet? That folder contained all the information available about her, information no one else knows."

"Not even your father?" he asked.

"He said he'd had a look years ago, and then forgot all about it. Anyway, the end result is that Sophie's life before Athora is a complete mystery."

"I'm impressed no-one tried to find out anything about her in all these years."

"Why would anyone bother? She was peaceful, kept to herself, and helped everyone with her herbs and potions," I replied as we entered the town. It looked like a war-stricken town in Syria.

"Let me get this straight. You're saying that the theft is connected to the murders simply because Sophie and the two victims were not born on Athora?"

"It can't be a coincidence," I replied. "Why would anyone want to steal old records when all of this is happening?" I pointed to the ruins around us to emphasize my point.

The sound of the helicopter interrupted our conversation and we turned our eyes to the sky. It circled the town, then landed on the flat wasteland that used to be the soccer field.

"What are you going to do?" I asked him when the sound died out, wanting to find out what his plans for the coming days were.

"I guess you're asking if I'll stay here or leave."

I nodded and waited while he thought. "As soon as we can make some contact with the outside world, I'll decide. I need to get to Pera Mera. All my things are at the hotel. If it's still standing there..."

I was surprised he did not mention anything about his girlfriend in Lesbos, but I chose not to bring it up. We were nearing the square when he suddenly stopped and turned toward me. "We may not know one another long, Fotini, but I have had the chance to get to know you these last few days and realize what a wonderful person you are. If things were different, I would have liked to get to find out more," he said softly, looking at me earnestly and waiting for my response.

"I... I don't know what to say," I stammered. "Our lives are complicated... well, your life is complicated. I sorted mine out, a little."

He did not add anything and we walked silently the rest of way, our hands still entwined. At the square, all the refugees had gathered and were listening to a coastguard explain that the helicopter would transport them to the ship, which would then carry them to Lesbos. Azim's absence was noticeable and I prayed he would suddenly appear, safe and sound.

A heavily pregnant local woman and her husband stood with the refugees, as did a man with a broken leg who had received first aid at the makeshift hospital the previous day, supported by his son. They would all be boarding the helicopter to be taken to the hospital.

I saw Stelios talking to a group of soldiers who had just arrived, carrying telecommunications equipment. "I need you to help unload things from the helicopter," he hurriedly told us.

I decided the news about the cellar break-in would have to wait. His priorities lay elsewhere at the moment, rightly so, and I did not want to distract him. I wanted to check in on Sophie, though, so I told Gabriel to go to the soccer field and that I would meet him there after checking in on her.

"I'll come with you," he offered. Stelios cast us an angry look, annoyed that we were ignoring his request.

Without wasting any time, we hurried through the ruins to the shelter. We looked everywhere but Sophie had disappeared. I even walked down the corridor that led to the three doors and the tunnel shouting out her name, but received no reply. Carlo was gone too. The place was deserted and the only sound was our voices calling out her name. *Where could they be?* I wondered.

"They must have gone outside," Gabriel replied. "Let's go back to the square and then we can look for them in the town."

I wished time could stand still, the rapid-fire pace of events slow down just enough to give us some time when we could be together, undistracted. It was not to be. The voice of Stelios at the entrance to the shelter called us outside. He had surely noticed my preference for Gabriel's company and did not intend to leave us alone together for long. "Come on," he shouted. "I haven't got enough volunteers!"

"We're coming," I shouted back and wondered how much longer I would be putting duty above everything else.

On the way to the soccer field, I told him about the theft. He looked incredulous. "This makes no sense... why would someone break in to steal a record they could just as easily ask for? Are you sure nothing else was taken, that the file isn't just lying around somewhere?"

"You know how meticulous my father is. Only one folder was taken from the cellar—her records. The question is why did he do it?"

"Let's go unload the supplies and then we'll look into this," he replied picking up the pace. I tried to stifle my growing concern and kept up.

Soldiers were already carrying the first supplies toward the town square, but people had heard the helicopter land and a small crowd had gathered around it. Locals and visitors alike jostled and shouted that they needed to get off the island and should have priority over the refugees.

An army officer was explaining that another ship was on its way with more supplies and that it could carry anyone who wished to leave. However, his orders were to take just the refugees for now and anyone who needed hospital care and their companions. For a tense moment, it looked like we would have a riot on our hands. Luckily, common sense prevailed and the helicopter began to airlift the injured and the refugees to the ship. It would have to make two or three trips to carry everyone.

The army officer was counting heads and checking them against a list on his clipboard. He started to ask if all the refugees were gathered and shout out names. Stelios filled him in on Azim's disappearance in the storm.

The sound of the helicopter returning filled the air and the officer asked for anyone not being airlifted to the frigate to leave. We all turned away.

Behind a rocky outcrop on the edge of the field, a man watched the evacuation process, taking extreme care to go unnoticed. The helicopter picked the last men and took off. When its sound faded, Azim snuck out of his hiding spot and looked around, then crept back behind the rocks like a hunted animal.

* * *

As if we were trapped in a war zone, we followed the soldiers to the square carrying supplies, the blades of the chopper roaring over our heads. I paused and looked up, watching it return to the navy ship anchored at the port.

Others had come to help carry the relief boxes to the square. Soon, a small pile had formed at its center. "They sent powdered milk and biscuits, as if we'll be cut off from civilization forever," Stelios grumbled, opening one of the boxes. Then he headed to the coffee shop where the soldiers were setting up a communications center.

I spotted Petros in the crowd milling around the boxes, grabbing packets of biscuits and stuffing them into a large bag. He sensed my gaze and turned his back to me, walking off with his bag about to burst. I looked away, wanting nothing to do with this man ever again.

Gabriel took two bottles of water and brought them over to the bench where I was sitting with a couple of the locals. Every now and then, a sharp pang would remind me of the wound to my head, but all in all Sophie's potion had worked its magic.

Stelios came and crouched beside me, hungrily biting into an apple. "Can you tell me why the rush to take the refugees away?" I asked him.

He wiped his mouth with the back of his hand and swallowed. "I was surprised, too, but they are not giving me any details. I asked the chief on our radio and he just said he received orders to transfer them to Lesbos, but that was all."

"How are things over at Pera Mera?" Gabriel asked.

"Like here. They have a lot of people injured and some are still missing."

"Is there any way to get across?" Gabriel insisted.

"You can swim or hijack the helicopter. There isn't a single boat left. The helicopter will head there next, pick up the injured and give the others cookies and milk." He shook his head in disgust.

"Stelios," I reasoned with him, "what has happened is unprecedented. Let's not judge them so harshly. Let's be thankful it is all over and that they responded so quickly. What's the situation outside Athora?"

"The other islands were hit too, but nowhere near as bad. I wonder how we'll be able to fix this... we don't even have a port anymore."

"It will take a while, but it will be fine," I said looking up at blue sky.

"Easy for you to say," he said bitterly. "We are the ones who'll stay behind to do it."

I was starting to lose my patience with him. I would surely have snapped back something I would later regret, but the sight of Carlo and Sophie appearing at the end of the square distracted me. We all stood up and watched them approach.

Sophie was picking her way through the rubble, leaning heavily on her stick. Carlo was walking next to her, helping her make her way. I pointed to the empty space on the bench, but she shook her head. "I'm going to the shelter to rest. Thank you, Carlo." She hobbled away.

"Where were you?" I asked Carlo. "We were worried about you."

"Sophie asked me to walk with her to the edge of the town to see what had happened to her mountain."

"Did you manage to make your call?" Stelios asked.

Carlo looked at the two men. "Yes, I did."

We all waited impatiently, desperate for any news from the outside world but he was clearly reticent to share anything. "They had no news," he added nonchalantly.

Gabriel broke the awkward silence that followed. "Well, let's hope it's over and never happens again." He shuffled his feet awkwardly. "I'm going for a walk. I might catch up with you guys later."

"Where are you staying tonight?" I blurted out, not thinking that my vivid interest in Gabriel was now plain for all to see.

"Same place as last night, probably—the house by the ruins of the old mill. They are very friendly; they told me I could keep the room for as long as I wanted. I'll leave you three to catch up."

He walked off. I was sure he sensed Carlo's reticence and maybe thought the three of us were in cahoots or that Carlo did not want to say anything in front of him.

Stelios turned to Carlo and stretched out his palm. "If your phone works, I'd like to call the police in Athens to—"

As if he had been expecting the request, Carlo handed over the phone before Stelios even had a chance to finish his sentence. The man's reflexes and self-control were impressive, I realized once again. Behind his mask of utter indifference, he did not miss a beat. He watched us all and registered our moves and reactions; all the little things no one ever noticed. Maybe that's what made me feel so ill at ease around him; what aroused my suspicions. His behavior did not match the profile of a company employee checking out a potential investment.

Stelios picked up the phone and, with Carlo's help, dialed a number. It did not get through. He tried again and again, different numbers each time, with the same result. "None of them work," he said, disappointed.

Carlo picked up the phone and re-dialed all the numbers—still nothing. "Obviously something to do with the local networks," he said. "The regional cell towers must be damaged."

The hiss of static from Stelios' two-way radio was followed by a man's tinny voice. Stelios replied and the news was grim. Kimon's' body had been found. We fell silent. We could only hear snatches of the transmission through the static. To my shock, the description of the body sounded like that of the murder victims.

We sprang into action and all three hurried to the place indicated by the dispatch. A few minutes later, we had reached a clearing behind the Chora. It did not take long to locate the body. Kimon lay on the ground like a marionette whose strings had snapped.

Had we not known it was Kimon, we would not have recognized him. His clothes were torn and his body was a mass of cuts and bruises. His blood had soaked the ground around him a very dark brown.

Two coastguards stood a little distance away, casually smoking a cigarette, as if they were out on a stroll. The man holding the radio said he had stumbled across the body by chance. Stelios asked them to bring something to wrap around the body so they could carry it back.

"Aren't you going to examine the body before you remove it?" Carlo asked authoritatively.

"You are not going to tell me how to do my job," Stelios shouted annoyed.

I stared at them, startled by both Carlo's unexpected interference and Stelios' overreaction. "It's not difficult to diagnose that Kimon has been flung about by the wind. If you look at how the ground has subsided under the body, it is clear he fell down from a great height," I said, gesturing to the small hollow around the body.

Both men bent down to take a closer look. "The occipital bone has been shattered, corroborating this. There, at the back of his skull," I pointed. "He was clearly snatched by the tornado..." *and the Harpies,* I thought.

The two coastguards returned and covered the body with a blanket. Stelios gave the chief an update and asked the coastguards to stay there until they decided how and where to carry it.

"His parents are dead and his two brothers live in Athens," Stelios said. "We'll have to notify them." He motioned to us that we should leave. "I'll meet you at the square. Can you be there in around half an hour, Fotini? I want to show you something."

I was curious about what he could possibly show me, but I did not ask.

"I hope Kimon is the last victim," I told Carlo on the way back.

"Let's hope so. I'm not as used to death as you are. Maybe you should become a coroner. You're very good."

I looked at him trying to see if he was being sarcastic. Instead, I caught him giving me a look of sympathy and a somewhat shy smile.

"I don't think so. I love my job. I'm just used to looking for small detail." I felt myself blush at the unexpected compliment and felt annoyed with myself.

"And what does the detail tell you?" he asked giving me a sidelong look as we walked through a narrow, winding alley.

"That you're awfully calm for someone who came to close a deal and got caught in a deadly storm," I replied.

He laughed heartily. Encouraged by the response, I decided to seize the moment. "Can I make a call to the US on your phone?" I asked. He seemed taken aback. "Yeah, sure, the problem is local. Here." He handed me the phone.

I did a quick calculation in my head and figured out that Professor Marcus must be fast asleep in California. I remembered his words when he'd given me his phone number in California: the supposed end of the world, without the first zero. It could not be anything other than 1012000.

I dialed the country codes and numbers and waited. When I heard his sleepy, croaky voice at the other end of the line, I apologized for waking him up at this hour and told him who was calling. He exclaimed in surprise and was glad to hear I was well, having heard everything that had happened. We spoke for around five minutes and he brought me up to date with what was happening elsewhere in the world as well as Greece. I handed the phone back to Carlo and explained who it was.

"What did he say?" he asked as we neared the square.

"That the storm is over, at least over the Aegean. Extreme weather phenomena are developing all over the world, though. Milder but equally unprecedented. The entire scientific community is shocked by what happened here. No one had predicted the strength of the storm."

"At least it's over now. Let's hope life will soon return to normal."

I could tell he was only half-listening to what I was saying. He was attentively scanning the streets ahead, as if looking for someone.

We came across Petros on our way to the square, accompanied by a small group of people. He asked us where Kimon's body was. I pointed in the direction we'd come from and briefly explained, and they set off.

We had arrived at the square and I wanted to check-in on Sophie, then return home to help my parents.

"Are you staying at the shelter tonight?" I asked Carlo before we parted.

"No, I don't think so. The generator is out of fuel and Sophie should find somewhere else to stay. I told her so when we were out walking this morning. I've found a room near the square, not too damaged by the storm. I'll stay there until I can get my things from Pera Mera. I think I'll head there now."

He turned to go, then, as if suddenly remembering something, spun around and placed his hand on my shoulder. "You must convince Sophie to come with you. She shouldn't stay alone at the shelter tonight."

I was taken aback by his sudden concern for Sophie, but I was too tired to think straight. "I'll try," I promised.

He still stood there, looking at me. "I don't know what will happen next, but I should tell you that I'm really glad to have met you," he said, in a sweet tone I'd never heard him use before. The man had breathed life into me, helped out when I needed medication, and seemed concerned about an old woman's safety. Maybe I was judging him too harshly, being so suspicious all the time.

"It was nice to meet you too," I replied. "Thank you for everything."

He squeezed my shoulder in response and turned away, raising his hand in a silent goodbye.

"See you later," I said and set off for the shelter. He walked off in the opposite direction.

I found Sophie lying down on a mattress in the hallway. She had lit two candles and was lying down in the small circle of light they cast. Other than that, the room was steeped in darkness.

She reassured me she did not need anything.

I sat down beside her, determined to convince her to accompany me. I told her about the theft of her records. Bizarrely, she did not seem in the least perturbed.

"I don't know why someone would do it, but they must have their reasons," she mumbled. She sat up and stretched out her injured leg. I noticed the bandage was bloodstained.

"Please come spend the night with us. You can stay at our house for as long as you need until you sort something out," I begged her.

"I feel at home here, Fotini. I really don't think I can walk as far as your house, not with my leg in this state."

"Your leg is bleeding. Can I take a look?" I touched the bandage, but she gently took hold of my hand and stopped me.

"Thank you, but I can look after myself. It's nothing serious, it bled a little from all the walking around. I'll change the bandage and I'll be fine."

Still holding my hand, she turned it over so my palm faced up. She brought a candle over it and whispered words I could not make out. I did not dare ask. She raised her eyes toward me and softly whispered, "You are what your name says in Greek, Fotini—a light in the storm."

I shook my head doubtfully. She gripped my hand, as if to press her point. "The sea is reflected in your eyes and you should let that light become your guide at some point."

I smiled awkwardly, feeling her forceful personality permeate me. "How can I do that?" I said in a lighthearted manner, trying to lighten the intense mood.

"You'll just have to trust yourself and everything will fall into place"

"I wish it were that simple," I said and stood up, making one last effort to convince her to leave. "We can find a place for you nearby, since my house is too far away."

"I like it here. I told you, it feels like home. I'll be fine, don't you worry about me. I'll go for a little walk later, stretch my legs, but I'm sleeping here tonight."

"I'll bring you some food later, before I head home," I offered.

"I have everything I need," she said pointing to some fruit and bread on a nearby shelf. I saw that nothing would change her mind, so I returned to the square with a heavy heart.

As soon as Stelios saw me, he beckoned me to approach. "I asked the chief to find out if Carlo is who he says he is. He is waiting for Athens to reply," he told me.

"Good move. Hey, where are you off to now?" I asked, as he turned sharply to walk away.

"Follow me," he said impatiently. "There's someone I want you to meet."

He ignored all my questions, but seemed as excited as a child at Christmas. He led me to the infirmary. A pile of broken flowerpots and the remains of the railing blocked the front door, so we clambered in through a low window. The young doctor, tending to a man lying on a stretcher, stepped forward to greet us. The patient raised his hand in greeting, too.

"Do you recognize him?" Stelios asked.

I approached the man and looked at him closely, trying to jog my memory. I had never met him before. "I don't think so…"

"Remember the father who was swept away the day before yesterday trying to save his little girl?"

I froze when I realized that the man on the stretcher was the man we had all thought had drowned. "How did you survive?" I asked, beaming with joy.

He raised himself on one elbow. "The sea sucked me down and spat me out a bit farther down. Luckily, it's not very deep over there and I managed to grab onto the rocks before the waves crashed on me once again."

He showed me his bandaged hands. "I used all my strength to climb as high as I could and managed to shelter in a small cave just below the secret exit of the shelter. I stayed there until the storm was over and then walked to the town today, barefoot."

That secret exit seemed to be anything but a secret after all!

"I'm so happy to see you," I exclaimed. "You were very lucky. Is your daughter well? Did you manage to speak to her?"

"She's fine," Stelios replied. "I'll radio Pera Mera now and he can talk to his family."

At last, something to celebrate, I thought.

A few minutes later, eyes welling up and choking with emotion, the man was speaking to his family who had been mourning him for dead. When he heard his daughter's voice, he started to sob and was so overwhelmed he could not speak. Our eyes welled up and we fell silent before the grandeur of human nature as embodied by this man, who never stopped fighting for survival against the elements.

"If at first you don't succeed, try, try again," chanted Stelios in a high-pitched voice, trying to lighten the mood.

I grinned. Although I was aware of the extent of the disaster, seeing the man who had shown such self-sacrifice alive made me feel as if the whole world had been saved.

We stepped back outside to give him some privacy. When it was time to go, we returned to say goodbye.

"Get well soon," I said. "I hope you'll rejoin your family shortly."

"I can't wait! I've heard the worst is over now."

"Yes, thankfully. Now we must be strong and rebuild our lives; especially those who stay behind on Athora. You have certainly shown us you will not be defeated. I'm amazed you survived for three days in the cave under the exit."

He nodded. "Without any food or water; I strained my clothes to drink rainwater. The storm ended not a day too soon! As soon as it looked like it was over, I set off. Getting to the Chora wasn't easy."

"And to think that the day before yesterday I walked all the way to that exit. I'd never have thought you were just below me."

"If I could have climbed, I would have come up to join you. I only saw the ropes hanging down today, as I was leaving."

"Ropes?" I exclaimed, surprised. "I never saw any ropes!"

"Some tourists used to rock climb there a while back. Maybe they forgot them there," he said, not giving it any further thought.

I could not let it go, though. Something was wrong with that picture. Rock climbers, I knew from personal experience, never left their ropes behind.

I kept my thoughts to myself as we returned to the square. Stelios asked me to wait a minute and stepped into the coffee shop where the soldiers had set up the communications center. A couple of minutes later he was back outside, holding a spare walkie-talkie. He gave it to me, asking me to keep it on me in case he needed to contact me, followed by a quick lesson in making calls and picking the right frequency so we could talk privately. I felt worn-out at the end. All I wanted to do was to go home.

* * *

Another exhausting day had ended. We had spent the evening tidying up whatever we could, then we ate a light supper and returned to our bedrooms, dragging our feet.

I kept the walkie-talkie on and could hear Stelios, the coastguards, and everyone else over at Pera Mera discussing the following day. The top priority would be to construct a temporary dock so that ships could come in and unload machinery and other supplies. Another ship had dropped anchor earlier in the evening and was still unloading supplies, using smaller boats to carry them to the island. Life on Athora was trying to regain its normal, pre-storm rhythm.

I stretched out on my bed and called Stelios, asking him to talk on the private frequency. He was over at the northern side of the island, which was more secluded, checking up on the residents who had opted to stay in their own homes. Luckily, other than a few light injuries, everyone was fine. He'd had to cover part of the distance on foot and would be spending the night there.

He told me he had checked in on Sophie before leaving and that she was well. She reassured him that she would be locking the door in the evening and asked him not to worry about her.

I wanted to tell him about the ropes hanging from the secret exit, but I did not dare. I, myself, thought I might be exaggerating and that I was being overly suspicious. I asked him discretely if he knew what Gabriel and Carlo had been up to, but he said he had not seen either of them since lunchtime. We both decided to get some rest. I told him to contact me if anything happened during the night and we agreed to speak again in the morning.

Stelios had been on call three days running and had barely had any sleep. I was sure part of the reason he had visited the northern side of the island so late in the day was so that he could spend the night there and get some much-deserved rest.

I closed my eyes, but images of everything that had happened during the week flickered before my eyes like a disjointed movie: Kimon, Father George, Azim, Gabriel, Carlo...Their faces appeared in quick succession, blending, distorting becoming one until they morphed into a single figure spreading wings and claws, a monster flying high above Athora, searching for another soul to snatch. The Harpies.

* * *

In his room, Carlo had just connected his phone to a laptop the owners had loaned him, telling him there was just enough life left in the battery. He entered the various passwords but the connection was slow and his irritation mounted. He tapped his foot nervously, sipped some water, and stared at the screen, absentmindedly whistling Leonard Cohen's "Nevermind."

A few minutes later, a map appeared, red dots blinking like buoys across the world. In Istanbul and Como, the marks were a steady, unwavering red dot. Two red dots over Athora were also still. A third dot, however, still blinked on the island.

He rubbed the stubble on his chin trying to think of a way to make the search go faster. Time was running out; the laptop's battery would soon die out. He picked up his cell phone and dialed a number. At the same time, he typed a few numbers on the keyboard, placed the cell phone on the table beside it and waited for the file to appear. Would it show up before the screen turned black?

A photo began to appear on the screen, so blurry he could not make out whether it was a man or a woman. He cursed the slow connection once again. Teasingly, the photo cleared up just a little, almost pixel by pixel, testing his patience. He was staring at it, his nose inches from the screen, ready to pounce on the face that would appear.

He took a sharp breath. "Unbelievable! How can that be?" he muttered and leaned even closer to the screen. The image appeared sharp and clear for a few seconds, just enough for him to be certain, before the screen went black, taking the photo with it.

* * *

I woke up with a start, my heart thumping, and it took me a few seconds to realize I was no longer caught up in the nightmare. My clothes and sheets were drenched with sweat. I shook my head to chase away the dream—my mother trying to resist the ferocious wind, which lifted her up and flung her away.

I got up, trying to exhale the heavy, oppressive feeling in my chest. The dim light of dawn through the window was not enough to disperse the looming shadows. I fumbled for the lighter and lit the candle that stood on my bedside table.

As I changed my sheets, I wondered why the walkie-talkie had fallen silent when I had made certain to leave it on before I went to bed. Then I remembered I must have left it on the private frequency Stelios and I had used last. I picked it up and switched to the shared frequency, turning the volume down so as not to wake my parents up if anyone radioed.

I lay down determined to get some sleep but, despite my fatigue, my eyes refused to obey. I started counting backward from one hundred, trying to relax, when I heard a man's voice on the walkie-talkie calling in Stelios. The man repeatedly asked Stelios to come in among the static, receiving no reply. After the fourth time, I picked it up and stated my name.

It was the chief of police. I immediately asked him if I could be of any help, and he explained that someone at Pera Mera had reported seeing a light at the shelter's secret exit and he wondered if Stelios knew what was going on.

We radioed out and I waved any chance of sleep goodbye. What was that light?

Fully aware that I was acting impulsively, I got dressed as quietly as I could, picked up a flashlight, and five minutes later was making my way to the shelter. Maybe it was nothing, but my every instinct screamed that I should get to Sophie as fast as I could.

By the time I got there, the sky was a milky shade that indicated it would not be long before the first light of day. I turned off my flashlight and surveyed the town from my high vantage point. I could see most of the houses from up here. All were dark, bar a few windows where candlelight flickered on the windowsills. I looked at the house where Gabriel was staying—no sign of life behind the dark windows.

A furtive movement in the narrow alleys suddenly caught my eye. I looked closely but everything seemed still. I kept my eyes peeled and, sure enough, a few seconds later, the figure moved once again, in the direction of the square.

I followed it as far as the view would allow and saw it disappear behind the church ruins. Seized by a sense of foreboding, I broke into a sprint, convinced that the shadow I had spotted was heading for the shelter.

Panting heavily, I reached the first houses, stumbling and tripping over the fallen debris. Without stopping, I spurred myself on and ran across the square, stopping only when I arrived at the short alley leading to the shelter. I fumbled for the radio and turned it off, worried that the static or a sudden voice might give my presence away. I then crept to the last house, keeping close to the walls, and crouched low behind a pile of stones where the courtyard wall had once stood.

In the dim, powdery white light, I could see a man in a baseball cap bent over the entrance to the shelter. He was holding a penlight in his clenched teeth, using what looked like a set of long pins to pick the lock.

The door clicked softly and he looked up. Carlo! What was he doing here? I had to bite my tongue to stop myself from calling out his name. Instead, I crouched down even lower. He looked around to make sure he was alone, pushed the door, and stepped inside.

I hesitated for a few moments not knowing what to do. *Think, think,* I urged myself. Sophie might be in danger.

I stood up and picked a broken plank that lay on the cobblestones a couple of feet away. I hoped I would not have to use it. Raising it like a sword before me, I entered the shelter.

* * *

A man wearing a thick dark t-shirt and a baseball cap pulled low over his forehead slowly walked through the tunnel leading to the secret exit, pausing frequently to catch his breath.

The woman was heavier than she looked. She hung over his shoulder, unconscious, her head dropping low over his back and swaying back and forth as he moved. Her long white hair swept the floor.

In his left hand, he held a flashlight and pointed its beam straight ahead until he arrived by the ladder leading to the exit, where the tunnel widened. He lowered the woman to the ground. She lay on her back, very still. He removed a length of rope from his pocket, then something wrapped in a white towel. Placing them on the floor beside her, he unfolded the towel to reveal a long, sharp knife.

Sophie groaned and turned her head to one side. He paused and looked at her, panting heavily after the exertion of the long walk. Nervously, he tried to untangle the piece of rope with shaky fingers and dropped it in his haste. Losing patience, he picked up the knife and cut through the knot.

Kneeling over her, he gripped her shirt in his fists and tore it open, exposing her bare chest. She seemed to be regaining consciousness. With great effort, she opened her eyes and looked at him as he raised the knife high above his head, ready to plunge it into her heart.

"You?" Sophie whispered.

"Who did you expect?" he spat through gritted teeth.

"Not you... it doesn't matter," she replied calmly.

Her peaceful expression outraged him. "Shut up!" he snapped. "I'm not here to talk!"

"I don't know who you are trying to avenge, but I'm sorry. I wish I could—"

He placed his left palm over her mouth and gripped the knife in his right hand so tightly his knuckles turned white. As if he could not go on, his hand started to shake, the tremor slowly spreading to the rest of his body. He slowly uncovered her mouth.

Seeing the man hesitate, Sophie shouted at him, "Do it! I know why you are here. Do it!" She repeated the last two words, over and over again, imploring him, but the man still seemed to hesitate.

Sophie slowly reached out and gripped the hand holding the knife. She swung it down with all her force, arching her back to get closer to the sharp blade. The man resisted and tried to pull his hand back.

* * *

I paused just inside the shelter and stood still, ears pricked for the slightest sound. In the empty shelter, any noise was sure to echo, but all was quiet. Carlo was nowhere to be seen.

I regretted not thinking calmly and radioing for backup while I was still outside. It was as if I was becoming addicted to danger, following my gut feeling against all reason.

I gripped the piece of wood in both hands like a bat, ready to swing it, and slowly inched forward. I looked around as I walked but there was no sign of Carlo or Sophie.

The creaking sound of a door farther down the corridor made me stop. Someone had just entered the tunnel leading to the secret exit. The flickering candle flames dimly lit the hallway, but the corridor was pitch-dark.

I hurried in that direction, turning my flashlight on and off to see ahead, and entered the tunnel through the open door.

I could distinguish the shadow of a man walking ahead, holding a penlight. He kept his hands cupped around it so that only the narrowest of beams escaped.

Keeping back at a safe distance to mask my presence, I saw him disappear around the bend and heard a woman's voice, though the words were indistinct. Sophie! Carlo must have brought her here and now returned to... to do what?

I hesitated for a moment, but then Sophie's voice rang out again, this time clearly. "Do it!" she repeatedly beseeched.

I hurried in that direction. Carlo had stopped ahead. He was hiding behind a small protrusion on the tunnel wall and peeking out toward the ladder. Beneath it, two bodies were locked in deadly struggle.

Unsure of what I was witnessing, I saw Sophie on the floor and a man with his fist up in the air. I gasped when I saw the knife, but before I could shout out, a loud bang reverberated through the tunnel, followed by an acrid smell.

As if in slow motion, the man's body jerked and fell to one side. A loud scream escaped my lips.

Carlo turned around sharply, pointing his gun and flashlight at me. In a panic, I dropped the piece of wood and froze.

Without saying a word, Carlo turned back and shone his flashlight on the wounded man who lay on his side, drawing in gasping, ragged breaths.

I tried to see Sophie, but she was no longer on the floor. I ran to the injured man, ignoring Carlo who still held him in his sights while waving the flashlight around the tunnel looking for the old woman.

The man on the floor had managed to turn onto his stomach and, like a wounded animal, was trying to crawl away.

Carlo walked up to him. Bending over, he snatched the baseball cap off his head and rolled him over with his foot. I turned my flashlight on and with a trembling hand shone it on his face. I knew who it was even before I saw his features, but I desperately wanted to make sure, refusing to believe it.

When I met his eyes, I felt as if the world around me collapsed. Blood poured out of Gabriel's mouth as he lay on his back, cradling his stomach, where a dark stain was spreading on his t-shirt.

Carlo hastily patted him down, shaking him this way and that and Gabriel groaned in pain. Carlo took the knife and flung it far away. Having made sure Gabriel was unarmed, he handed me the gun saying, "Don't let him get away. I'll go find Sophie."

He reached the rusty staircase and started climbing, two rungs at a time.

I took a step back, unable to accept what was happening. Gabriel seemed to be growing weaker by the minute. He let his head drop to the ground. Judging by the growing stain on his top, he did not have long to live. I wanted to scream and sob in despair.

As if he sensing my agony, Gabriel fixed his eyes on me. "Time is running out, Fotini," he whispered.

I opened and closed my mouth, but no words would come. Carlo returned just then. "Sophie has disappeared," he wearily announced.

Still shocked, I handed him the gun and took off my jacket. Folding it as I knelt beside Gabriel, I pressed it onto his wound, trying to stem the blood loss. He cried out in pain.

"What were you doing? Why... Who are you?" I asked, tears streaming down my cheeks.

Carlo looked at Gabriel and spoke in a voice filled with certainty. "You killed the men in Istanbul and Como."

Gabriel nodded.

"And the two men on Athora."

"Yes."

I gasped. "How can you have killed Father George?" My voice quavered. "We were together that night on Ikaria."

"That's what you think, Fotini, because that's what I made you believe... You were my alibi..." In a coarse, ragged voice, Gabriel started to recount what had happened that night.

Athora *

Chapter 14

Ikaria, four days earlier

A car pulled up by the front door of the hotel. Gabriel stepped out from the passenger seat. Before he even had a chance to close the door properly, the girl driving the car sped away. She was still angry that he had disappeared at the fair and that his colleague, who was obviously coming on to him, had ruined her dress.

The man raised his hand and waved goodbye, an awkward smile on his face. As soon as the car was a safe distance away, the smile disappeared. He lowered his raised hand and looked at his watch.

He glanced at the hotel, where not a soul stirred at this late hour, and walked off quickly in the opposite direction. As soon as he was at the dock, he untied the ropes of the speedboat he had rented using a fake passport and silently snuck out of the port, its motor muted.

He sailed in this manner for about ten minutes, putting some distance between the boat and the dock, and checked the sat nav. Feeling safer, he powered up the motor; minutes later the speedboat was flying on the surface of the sea.

Setting sail for Athora, he unlocked the small cabinet by the steering wheel and took out a backpack. Unzipping it, he removed a baseball cap and checked that everything he needed was there. He placed the hat on his head and took the steering wheel.

Flashes of lightning in the distance were barely visible, foretelling of the coming weather change. He had already checked the forecast, to be sure that the bad weather would last long enough for him to be able to carry out his plans on Athora. At present, however, the sea was so calm the boat seemed to be sprinting on rail tracks rather than water.

Gabriel's gaze remained fixed ahead and the sea breeze further hardened his features. He knew that everything had to be timed perfectly in the few hours ahead.

* * *

Although I heard him describe how he arrived on Athora that night from Ikaria, I still could not believe that the man I had started to fall in love with was the murderer. A ruthless killer, who had snuck onto the island in the middle of the night, killed the priest and returned to Ikaria, unflappable.

Seeing him struggle for breath, I cried out, "Gabriel, why?"

"Why did I kill them?" He turned to Carlo and spoke with great difficulty, the blood gurgling in his mouth. "You tell her... I suspected you weren't who you said you were and I was certain once I saw your phone... that night at the pharmacy. Did you think I didn't know you were closing in? If I wanted to, you'd never have caught me..." He started choking on the blood and had to stop.

"I don't understand," I desperately said. "Do you two know each other? Why did you try to kill Sophie?"

Gabriel reached out and took my hand in his. I felt his blood stick between our entwined fingers. Every word seemed to sap whatever strength he had left and his face turned pale.

"There's a lot you need to know. I just want you to remember that although I used you as an alibi at the start..." He paused and struggled to breathe. I stroked his forehead to encourage him to go on. "What came after... I felt it... I wish we'd met under different circumstances, Fotini. I feel like I have known you all my life. Everything you need to know... my laptop..."

He removed a crumpled photo from his pocket and handed it to me with a trembling hand. Stained by his blood, the image was unclear. I could just about make out the faces of two children smiling at the camera.

"This is where it all began," he whispered, his hand dropping limply by his side.

In a pained voice, he kept talking, but everything he said was so confusing I could not make any sense of it. I glanced at Carlo to see if he could help me out, but he just stood and watched the dying man indifferently.

"Why did you try to kill Sophie?" I asked, watching his eyes begin to glaze over.

"She was the beginning, but I couldn't... maybe it wasn't her fault... never mind... never mind... I want to stay on Athora forever. Start with the photo..." His whisper was growing fainter with each word and he suddenly stopped.

I froze when I brought my fingers to the side of his neck. His heart had stopped beating and I did not know whether I should try to resuscitate him or not. I desperately moved my palms over his chest, but Carlo bent down and gently pulled them away.

"He's gone, Fotini," he said.

Tears were flowing down my face, dripping onto the bloodstained clothes. Carlo crouched beside me and wrapped his arms around me trying to comfort me. I did not know exactly why I was crying. A river of sadness inside me was washing all my thoughts away.

Athora *

Chapter 15

Sitting on a rock by the port, I gazed out at the calm sea and tried to still my mind and my soul. I could not accept that Gabriel was a murderer, and a maelstrom of "why's" raged inside me, tinged with the bitter taste of betrayal.

I suddenly felt the presence of a man beside me. I looked up and saw Carlo standing above me. I had not even heard him approach. He asked me if he could join me and I shifted to make room for him without saying a word.

"I guess there are many things you'd like to ask, Fotini."

I was taken aback by the tenderness in his voice.

"I didn't want to leave them unanswered. Maybe Stelios has already told you I work for Interpol."

I nodded.

"I've been working on a very strange case for a while. It's about a secret organization that helps criminals disappear."

I stared at him, confused.

"Let's say you've committed a crime and there's a good chance you'll get arrested. If you have the money, lots of money, you can pay that organization to erase your traces forever. We are not sure how contact is made. All we've managed to find out is that the organization has existed for many years. With the help of an informant, we started to put together a world map of the organization's... clients and their current location. The plan was to gather as much information as we could and then make our move.

"We already knew that the victims in Istanbul and Como were a part of it. Even if we hadn't, their tattoos would have given them away."

"Tattoos?" I asked and remembered the inky stain on the priest's body.

"Everyone who assumed a new identity had a tattoo of Achilles' death. You remember the Iliad, how the Trojans killed Achilles, an arrow piercing his heel. As you saw, some had taken care to erase this shared mark.

"After the Como murder, we had information that the possible murderer may have flown to Greece. I didn't know how many of them were hiding here when I arrived, just that there was more than one of them. The Greek islands are a good place to hide. Unfortunately, without being able to identify the prospective victims, I couldn't prevent the first two. If the storm had not died out, I would never have received Sophie's photo in time. The murderer was always one step ahead of us."

"Gabriel," I whispered.

"Yes, Gabriel. He left little hints here and there so we could follow him, but was always a step ahead. He acted as if he wanted us to catch him one day. It was as if he did not care for the consequences; nothing else mattered other than carrying out the murders.

"I don't know what his motives were or how he managed to access classified information. I guess once we examine his laptop we'll have the answers."

He covered my hand with his palm and gave it a compassionate squeeze. "I'm leaving for Athens in a few hours. I hope to see you before you return to the US. I'll have more answers then."

* * *

Three days later

Accompanied by my parents, I walked on the temporary dock where the ship for Piraeus would be arriving any minute now. Two days later, I would be boarding a plane and returning to America. I had been tempted to resign and stay on the island to help my parents, but they refused to even entertain that possibility. They insisted they would be just fine without me.

Carlo had already returned to Athens on a police helicopter and would be meeting me there. The prosecutor, coroner, and a team of detectives and foreign police officers had arrived on the island to investigate every detail of the murder. I had grown tired of repeating the same story to different people. Stelios and his colleagues were busier than ever before.

They fetched Gabriel's things from Pera Mera along with his laptop, which kept all the mysteries that remained. His body, the body of Father George and all other evidence were sent to Athens for further examination.

The early works to repair the damaged infrastructure were underway. The army had set up the temporary dock, reconnecting the island to the outside world, and allowing machinery and equipment to arrive and start dealing with the chaos the storm had left behind.

Greek and foreign news crews were transmitting images of the destruction and volunteers from all over the world had arrived to help mend the island's wounds. It was heartwarming to see so many people stand by the locals in every possible way.

The sea had finally regained its usual shades of blue and I could not get enough of it. The azure sky joined the water in a seamless stretch, not a cloud disrupting their union.

The police had arrested Azim the previous day trying to stow away on one of the boats. Stelios had told me Azim had requested political asylum. He was wanted by the Turkish authorities for his alleged involvement in the coup and would remain in prison until his case was processed. I hoped they would not extradite him because that would mean a bleak future for him.

I visited him briefly but we barely had enough time to talk about what had happened. I will never forget his expression when I told him who the murderer was. Despite his own troubles and the difficulties that lay ahead of him, he showed me great compassion. I promised to help him as best I could. He confided that he had been an Economics lecturer at the University of Damascus, which explained the educated man I had been able to discern.

Sophie had disappeared, as if she had flown out of the tunnel's exit that night. Rumors raged about what had happened to her; some even went so far as to say she had managed to swim away. The air of mystery that had cloaked her presence on the island now cloaked her absence. The police searched everywhere for her, but not a trace could be found.

All the evidence pointed to Gabriel having secured the ropes to the tunnel's exit, so he could climb inside, kill Sophie and escape unseen. At the very last moment, for a reason he took with him to his grave, he changed his mind. Sophie's voice begging him to kill her still rang in my ears. Carlo, not realizing that Gabriel had changed his mind, had shot him to save Sophie.

I found it hard to believe that Sophie was also a criminal who had spent all those years hiding.

"Please be careful," my father said as we reached the ferry that was about to sail to Piraeus.

I said goodbye mechanically and boarded the ship. As if in a trance, I found myself on the deck, waving goodbye to my parents. Athora would have been unrecognizable after all it had been through, were it not for the chapel of the Virgin Mary on one of its peaks and the large stone Sophie had carved on the other. Her guard had withstood the storm and now stood alone, without her, gazing out over the vast expanse of blue.

Athora gradually became a dot on the horizon as the ferry pulled away. I stood looking at it until it disappeared, lost in my own thoughts and everything that had changed my life in the space of a few days.

Athora *

Chapter 16

The island, August 14, one year later

We had almost reached the chapel of the Virgin Mary, when the priest at the head of the procession asked us to stop, turning to look to the east.

Carlo, who had been walking behind me, ran into me as I abruptly stopped. He did not pull away until he felt the priest's disapproving eye on him.

It was a scorching summer day and the cicadas were hammering out their incessant tune. I looked at the calm sea and chased away the memory of what had happened at the chapel exactly one year ago.

It was the eve of the feast day of the Dormition of the Mother of God. Observing the old custom, we were walking to the chapel, where we would spend the evening and hold Mass the following day. As a sign of respect and mourning for those who had lost their lives and the painful events of the previous year, the festivities had been canceled.

The young priest motioned for us to continue, firmly holding the icon I had rescued from the rubble on the town square.

There must have been twenty of us trekking to chapel. Carlo seemed to be enjoying it the most.

We had met in Athens just before my departure for California after the events of ten months ago, and he had filled me in on what Gabriel's laptop had revealed.

A skilled hacker, Gabriel had managed to break into Interpol's map and locate his first two victims in Istanbul and Como. Suspecting that the tattoo was more than a symbol, he had removed a microchip from the heel of his second victim. It contained information on other criminals hiding from justice in various parts of the world, including Athora.

Gabriel was a computer genius and could hack any service he wanted, bypassing all safety measures. He had hacked into my computer and could follow my movements, initially using me as an alibi.

He had never been an anthropologist, but was so intelligent and well-read he managed to fool everyone, including me.

I would have expected someone like that to take steps to make access to his computer difficult, but it could all be unlocked with one simple word: "Anna." It was the name of his twin sister.

Carlo's care to keep me informed, to help me gain some understanding, had moved me. I saw real caring behind his actions and a sensitive human being. He wanted me to start my new life without any baggage, without any lingering questions that would keep me tied to those terrible events.

We kept in touch and, day by day, our relationship deepened as we became closer.

* * *

A few months ago, detectives had concluded that father George was, indeed, one of the men who had assumed a new identity to escape the consequences of a crime he had committed.

New evidence was uncovered, shedding light on a secret organization called *Terra Incognita* which had spread its tentacles all over the globe. Many well-respected citizens were unmasked as its members.

For a significant sum of money, criminals could start a new life, free from the charges brought against them— charges of murder, rape, and a whole host of other horrific acts.

That had been the case of Father George, who had raped and killed a little girl somewhere in northern Greece. Rather than let him rot in jail, his wealthy family had paid for him to disappear. He was supposed to have committed suicide after the charges were brought against him. They even held his funeral, although I did not know whether they had buried someone else or an empty coffin.

That was the organization's usual practice. Plastic surgery to make the criminals unrecognizable and a new life for them, on the condition that they would never try to contact anyone from their old life.

The tragic irony was that Father George had managed to enter the church as a priest and obtain a post as a missionary in Africa, preaching to young children. They were still investigating a series of crimes where he had been stationed before coming to Athora.

Such were the crimes they had committed, which is why Gabriel had killed them in such a horrifying way seeking revenge. One of the men protected by the organization had murdered his parents and his twin sister. He had witnessed their murder and somehow managed to escape.

Although the police had arrested the murderer, they later said he had escaped and he was never seen again. Gabriel's files showed that tracking down the monster that had deprived him of his loved ones had become his sole purpose in life.

The photo Gabriel had handed me before he took his last breath was of him and his sister. That was how investigators had managed to link up the clues.

Gabriel had managed to track his family's killer down, but by the time he reached him, the man was dead. He then discovered *Terra Incognita*. Instead of going to the police with the information, he decided to become an avenger and kill those sheltered by it. That was how he ended up on Athora, where three of them lived, unaware of their common identity.

Everyone had been surprised at how effectively the organization was run. Had it not been for Gabriel, it might have been impossible to track them down. There was a clear hierarchy and no one knew anyone else. Everything happened in absolute secrecy so that even if someone blew the whistle, the damage would be limited. Prospective clients could contact them through companies set up in countries where the rules were lax. High-ranking officials, doctors, and other people of prominence were now facing charges in an unprecedented case, on a global scale. Arrests had already been made.

The only one Gabriel did not have enough information on was Sophie, and that was why he kept such a close eye on me when he realized my father still held the sole paper records that might confirm her identity—information that could not be hacked.

Sophie was a medical researcher. She had run a medical trial which had caused the death of many and left scores handicapped. Facing public disgrace, she discovered she could disappear through *Terra Incognita*. She came to

Athora and sought salvation through helping others with her herbs, keeping a safe distance from everyone.

That was the reason Gabriel had broken into our cellar that night. To make sure Sophie was the third person he was looking for.

There had been no sign of her since the day Gabriel had tried to kill her. We had walked over every inch of the island in the two days we had been here, visited every spot where I thought she might be hiding, with no result.

* * *

The landslides had swept away a large section of the old path, so we circled around and rejoined it farther up the hill.

When we arrived at the chapel, everyone stood silently waiting for us. Lukas stood among them, fully recovered from his fall except for a slight limp. He smiled when he saw me. My parents were smiling too, happy to see me make the journey once again. Stelios came toward me, holding the burning incense. A soft breeze stirred it, spreading the scent everywhere.

I noticed the father and daughter who had narrowly escaped death the day the bridge collapsed. She was perched on his shoulder, enjoying the spectacle and giggling happily.

We followed the priest, who chanted as he placed the icon under the church porch. Though the festivities had been canceled, we would still be lighting the bonfire after sunset.

We spent the evening looking at the fiery tongues almost touch the sky, sharing stories of everything that had happened during the storm and carefully sidestepping any mention of the murders.

We stuck to the old custom of the men sleeping apart from the women, at opposite ends of the churchyard. We all spread sheets and reed mats on the floor and stretched out.

I watched Carlo trying to communicate with the locals and could not help smiling. He seemed to be enjoying the experience and never once complained.

I lay down and tried to think of something else, but Gabriel and Sophie's faces kept appearing before me. I had not known them for long, but both of them had left their mark.

* * *

The priest's melodious chanting woke us up early the following morning. We got up and attended Mass, leaving our belongings as they were. As soon as church was over, we lunched off the trestle tables laid with white sheets and prepared to depart.

I asked Carlo if he wanted to return on foot. He nodded without any hesitation. Everyone else was driving back. We said our goodbyes and started to walk back down the mountain without giving any explanations.

In a week, I would be returning to California. From there, my students and I would be traveling to Patagonia for a dig, due to last for over a month. Carlo had just accepted a post at Interpol's Washington office, so we would now have the chance to meet more often. My life had found its rhythm and I felt complete, possibly for the first time.

I walked ahead and, as I looked at the bright horizon, an imperceptible motion on the hill at the edge of the island caught my attention. Shielding my eyes and squinting heavily, I made out the figure of a woman walking. She turned to look in our direction. I desperately wanted to believe it was Sophie, but, without binoculars, I could not be sure.

Carlo approached me and turned to see what I was looking at. Like a vision, the figure disappeared as suddenly as it had appeared.

"What are you looking at?" he asked me.

In the distance, a few white clouds looked like angels resting on the sea foam.

"Tell me what you saw," he persisted, putting an arm around my shoulders.

I remembered Sophie's words in the shelter and I replied, "The Harpies resting on the horizon."

Carlo took my face in his palms and our lips met. His hands slid down my back, pulling me tightly against him. It would not take much for me to surrender. I put up my hand between our mouths and looked deep into his eyes. "Shall we carry on?"

*Before you embark
on a journey of revenge,
dig two graves.*

Confucius

About the author

When Kostas Krommydas decided to write his first novel, he took the publishing world of his native Greece by storm. A few years later, he is an award-winning author of five bestselling novels, acclaimed actor, teacher and passionate storyteller. His novels have been among the top 10 at the prestigious Public Book Awards (Greece) and his novel "Ouranoessa" has won first place (2017). He has also received the coveted WISH writer's award in 2013. When not working on his next novel at the family beach house in Athens, you will find him acting on the acclaimed ITV series, The Durrels and on various theatre, film, and TV productions. Kostas also enjoys teaching public speaking, interacting with his numerous fans, and writing guest articles for popular Greek newspapers, magazines, and websites. If you want to find out more about Costas, visit his website, http://kostaskrommydas.gr/ or check out his books on Amazon: Author.to/KostasKrommydas

More Books

Cave of Silence

A Love So Strong, It Ripples Through The Ages.

Dimitri, a young actor, is enjoying the lucky break of his life—a part in an international production shot on an idyllic Greek island and a romance with Anita, his beautiful co-star. When his uncle dies, he has one last wish: that Dimitri scatters his ashes on the island of his birthplace. At first, Dimitri welcomes this opportunity to shed some light on his family's history—a history clouded in secrecy. But why does his mother beg him to hide his identity once there?

Dimitri discovers that the past casts long shadows onto the present when his visit sparks a chain of events that gradually reveal the island's dark secrets; secrets kept hidden for far too long. Based on true events, the *Cave Of Silence* moves seamlessly between past and present to spin a tale of love, passion, betrayal, and cruelty. Dimitris and Anita may be done with the past. But is the past done with them?

More Books

Dominion of the Moon

Award Winner, Public Readers' Choice Awards 2017

In the final stages of WWII, archaeologist Andreas Stais follows the signs that could lead him to unearth the face of the goddess who has been haunting his dreams for years, all the while searching for the woman who, over a brief encounter, has come to dominate his waking hours. In present day Greece, another Andreas, an Interpol officer, leaves New York and returns to his grandparents' island to bid farewell to his beloved grandmother.

Once there, he will come face to face with long-buried family secrets and the enigmatic Iro. When gods and demons pull the threads, no one can escape their fate. Pagan rituals under the glare of the full moon and vows of silence tied to a sacred ring, join men and gods in a common path.

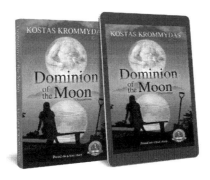

More Books

Lake of Memories

Based on a true story

In Paris, a dying woman is searching for the child that was snatched from her at birth over twenty years ago. In Athens, a brilliant dancer is swirling in ecstasy before an enraptured audience. In the first row, a young photographer is watching her for the first time, mesmerized. He knows she is stealing his heart with every swirl and turn, yet is unable to break the spell. And on the Greek island of the Apocalypse, Patmos, a man is about to receive a priceless manuscript from a mysterious benefactor. Destiny has thrown these people together, spinning their stories into a brilliant tapestry of romance, crime, and timeless love. How many memories can the past hold? Is a mother's love strong enough to find the way? Based on a true story, Krommydas' award-winning book firmly established him as one of the top Greek authors of his generation.

Kostas Krommydas

Very soon more novels from Kostas Krommydas will be available on Kindle. Sign up to receive our <u>newsletter</u> or follow Kostas on <u>facebook</u>, and we will let you know as soon as they are uploaded!

* * *

Want to contact Kostas? Eager for updates? Want an e-book autograph?

Follow him on

<u>https://www.linkedin.com/in/kostas-krommydas</u>
<u>https://www.instagram.com/krommydaskostas/</u>
<u>https://www.facebook.com/Krommydascostas/</u>
<u>https://twitter.com/KostasKrommydas</u>

Amazon author page:
<u>Author.to/KostasKrommydas</u>

Athora *

If you wish to report a typo or have reviewed this book on Amazon please email onioncostas@gmail.com with the word "review" on the subject line, to receive a free 1680x1050 desktop background.

Thank you for taking the time to read *Athora*! If you enjoyed it, please tell your friends or post a short review. Word of mouth is an author's best friend and much appreciated!

Made in the USA
Middletown, DE
19 January 2023

22551329R00203